Praise for *The New*

"*The New Neighbor* is a dizzying descent into a Byzantine maze of psychological suspense. Carter Wilson proves once again why he is one of the best, most inventive thriller writers working today."

—S. A. Cosby, *New York Times* bestselling author
of *Razorblade Tears* and *Blacktop Wasteland*

"I can never resist a book with a well-written, unreliable narrator, and Carter Wilson nails just that in his tautly written thriller, *The New Neighbor*. I couldn't bear to put this page-turner down until I figured out every single detail in Wilson's suspenseful and twist-ridden story of loss, mourning, and new starts that asks if money can ever buy happiness and even if it does—at what cost?"

—Emily Bleeker, *Wall Street Journal* and
Amazon Charts bestselling author

"Damn you. Wilson, I was up all night with this book. The mysteries of Bury are perfectly placed, the tension is thick enough to drown in, and the pages fly by. Brilliant escapism. I can't recommend it highly enough."

—Stuart Turton, international bestselling author of *The 7 1/2 Deaths of Evelyn Hardcastle* and *The Devil and the Dark Water*

"A truly suspenseful and gripping read. I was filled with anxiety and on the edge of my seat throughout. Bravo!"

—Alice Hunter, author of *The Serial Killer's Wife*

Praise for *Mister Tender's Girl*

"This elegantly written, masterful thriller, by turns meditative and shocking, lyrical and violent, will keep you glued to the pages from start to finish."

—A. J. Banner, *USA Today* bestselling author of
The Good Neighbor and *The Twilight Wife*

"Wilson turns the creep factor up to 11, balancing his prose on a knife's edge. A highly satisfying high-tension thriller."

—*Kirkus Reviews*

"The writing is both gorgeous and gritty, and the story so enticing that I gobbled it up in one sitting. I can only humbly request that Carter Wilson hurry up and write some more."

—Sandra Block, author of *The Girl Without
a Name* and *The Secret Room*

"Carter Wilson hits it out of the park with *Mister Tender's Girl*—one of the most suspenseful novels I've read in a long time. This book is a true page-turner, riveting on every level."

—Allen Eskens, bestselling author of *The Life
We Bury* and *The Heavens May Fall*

"Dark, unsettling, and full of surprises, *Mister Tender's Girl* takes the reader on a dangerous journey alongside a woman who must face the past she's been hiding from. A fast-paced, spine-tingling read—and a reminder that imagined dangers are just as worthy of being feared."

—Megan Miranda, *New York Times* bestselling
author of *The Perfect Stranger*

Praise for *The Dead Girl in 2A*

"One of those books you devour in a single sitting. *The Dead Girl in 2A* promises a lot from the start and delivers in spades."

—Alex Marwood, author of *The Wicked Girls*

"Will grip you from the first chapter and never let go. A lightning-paced thriller reminiscent of Dean Koontz. I couldn't turn the pages fast enough!"

—Liv Constantine, international bestselling
author of *The Last Mrs. Parrish*

"Readers will stay up all night with Carter Wilson's latest psychological thriller. With a story as riveting as it is mysterious, Wilson's *The Dead Girl in 2A* is a terrifying plunge into the depths of a childhood trauma rising back into the light. Wilson's characters are as deep as the mystery that surrounds them, and the fast-paced plot doesn't disappoint. This is not to be missed."

—R. H. Herron, international bestselling author of *Stolen Things*

"Carter Wilson's novels slip under your skin with the elegance and devastation of a surgeon's scalpel. In his latest book, Wilson weaves a gripping tale in which the present can die in a single careless moment and the past is as unknowable as the future. *The Dead Girl in 2A* is a high-wire act, exquisitely balanced between shattering suspense and the sudden opening of our hearts. I couldn't put this book down. Bravo!"

—Barbara Nickless, author of the
award-winning Sydney Parnell series

Praise for *The Dead Husband*

"[A] chilling standalone... Psychological thriller fans will be rewarded."
—*Publishers Weekly*

"Carter Wilson's *The Dead Husband* is a perfectly paced and expertly written thriller. The prose is as smooth as glass, and the pages fly by as fast as the reader can turn them. And then the ending provides a shocking jolt. This is a smashing story about families and secrets and all the things you don't want to know about the people closest to you. Read it!"
—David Bell, *USA Today* bestselling author of *The Request*

"How far would you go to protect the ones you love? Rose Yates has come home to a house and a family she'd rather forget. But what waits for her there isn't the closure she's been hoping for. Instead, her past hides in the dark corners and recesses of her mind, ready to spring out at her. Carter Wilson's writing is evocative and tense, his characters deeply flawed yet relatable. In *The Dead Husband,* he weaves a story of a woman running from her past and the detective determined to uncover her secrets."

—Julie Clark, *New York Times* bestselling author of *The Last Flight*

"A rich family with shocking secrets in an affluent small town, Carter Wilson's *The Dead Husband* is *Succession* meets *Big Little Lies,* and I loved every bit of it. This marvelously crafted thriller is the perfect escape, so find a quiet spot and sink in—you'll be glad you did."

—Jennifer Hillier, award-winning author
of *Jar of Hearts* and *Little Secrets*

"Wilson unveils each revelation of some new betrayal with surgical precision en route to a bittersweet finale. A harrowing reminder that you really can't go home again."

—*Kirkus Reviews*

Also by Carter Wilson

THE
NEW
NEIGHBOR

CARTER WILSON

Poisoned Pen
PRESS

Published by Poisoned Pen Press, an imprint of Sourcebooks
P.O. Box 4410, Naperville, Illinois 60567-4410
(630) 961-3900
sourcebooks.com

Library of Congress Cataloging-in-Publication Data

Names: Wilson, Carter (Novelist), author.
Title: The new neighbor / Carter Wilson.
Description: Naperville, Illinois : Poisoned Pen Press, [2022]
Identifiers: LCCN 2021023663 (print) | LCCN 2021023664
(ebook) | (trade paperback) | (epub)
Subjects: GSAFD: Mystery fiction.
Classification: LCC PS3623.I57787 N49 2022 (print) | LCC PS3623.I57787
(ebook) | DDC 813/.6--dc23
LC record available at https://lccn.loc.gov/2021023663
LC ebook record available at https://lccn.loc.gov/2021023664

Printed and bound in Canada.
MBP 10 9 8 7 6 5 4 3 2 1

For Sawyer

orr orr...

"Hush, a body in the lake takes more weight; I'm not looking for revenge, I love this place."

—JAMES, "HUSH"

THE DAY I BROKE

June 2, 2018
Baltimore, Maryland

I THOUGHT I COULDN'T handle another minute in the funeral home, but this church is worse.

My wife doesn't belong here.

Thirty-four years old, and the count stops there. Her biological clock runs backward now, ticking decomposition. I try to push away the thought of her face being anything other than radiant and smooth, but I can't do it anymore. I can only picture it collapsing in on itself, a pumpkin rotting in the sun.

"Daddy, your tie."

I look down. Maggie points at my neck, her fierce blue eyes gift wrapped with streaks of red. Easy to tell when she's been crying.

"What?"

"It's coming off."

I reach up, touch my clip-on, find half of it coming out of my collar. I jam it back in, doubting it'll stay.

I neither own nor know how to fasten a proper tie, so I had to go to a department store to find a clip-on for my wife's funeral. What an experience that was. Holly was two days dead, and I had to stagger into a Macy's and endure the glossy smiles and empty-calorie banter of the staff just so I could look acceptable at the service.

"Thanks," I tell my daughter. I realize she's missing her other half. "Where's your brother?"

"He wanted to stay outside."

"What?"

"Can I go outside, too?" she asks. "I don't wanna be here."

"None of us wants to be here, love. Last place on earth we want to be. But right now, it's where we need to be. Least for a little while." I place my palm on her seven-year-old head. Jesus wept, this is brutal. "Stay here, I'm getting Bo."

It doesn't take more than a dozen steps to get back outside, and I'm both thankful for the bout of fresh air and guilty I made my daughter stay inside.

Bo and Maggie. Twins, but couldn't be less alike. Sun and moon, water and sky. The day Holly and I found out we were having fraternal twins, we'd agreed the girl would have an Irish name, from my ancestry, and the boy would have a Swedish name, from hers. As the years rolled on, we couldn't ignore the huge body of water between them, as if they were truly raised in different lands.

Outside, Bo stares at a tree in the courtyard of the church. A handful of people stroll across the cobblestone, making their way to the service. A coworker from the bar I work at spies me, shoots me a pitied look, and pivots my way. I lower my head. Attention isn't something I crave on my happiest of days. Today, it's poison.

As I reach Bo, I touch his back. His navy-blue blazer is the other thing I had to buy at Macy's, and I guessed a size too big. With his mop of jet-black hair, pale skin, bony frame, and loose wardrobe, he looks like a miniature scarecrow. Shows about as much emotion, too.

"Whatcha doing?" I ask.

He keeps looking at the tree.

"It's an oak," he says.

I look at it, not really caring what kind of tree it is. "Aye. But we have to go inside, buddy."

He doesn't move.

"It's probably older than she was," he says.

I take a breath, bite it in half, spit it out.

"Bo, listen to me, we gotta go inside. I know you don't want to, but we gotta."

Now he turns, fixes his gaze on me. He has her eyes, deep and dark, a thousand lifetimes behind them. "Why?"

"Because you need to say goodbye."

"I did already," he says. "When the ambulance took her."

"You know that's different."

"It's all that counts. I said goodbye. I don't want to see her."

"You won't actually *see* her," I say, knowing exactly how he feels.

"So then I'll stay here."

I feel the muscles tighten in my neck, spread down my arms. I kneel and look into those bottomless eyes.

"Bo. You have to. Right now. I'm sorry, but that's the way it is."

He blinks. Once. Twice. "Tell me why."

I rub his arm, think on it for a second. Logic is a fleeting ghost these days. Then I say, "Because you're her child. And there're folks in there who want to see her again, but they can't. But they can see you. They can see *her* in you. Those folks are grieving, too, and you being there might help relieve a little of that pain for them. Does that make sense?"

He thinks on it. "Not really."

"No, I suspect it doesn't. Well, how about this. *I* need you. You and Maggie. I have to go in there, and I don't know if I can do it without you. You two. My columns. Need you to keep me from crumbling. Just do it for me, Bo. Can you do that?"

He lets this settle with him for a minute, and with no verbal confirmation, he takes my hand and lets me lead him back inside.

Every inch feels like battle, hand-to-hand combat.

The next hour comes and goes in intermittent bursts of clarity, like driving through rolling fog. There's the service, not quite what I want or expect, but how am I to know what to want or expect? I say a few words to the congregation, mumbling them mostly, then do a reading from King James. I choke up, look away from the Bible, and spot Da there in the front pew. My father flew in from Dublin just yesterday. His gaze so hard, willing the strength for both of us, and he gives me this little nod, the slightest thing. But it helps.

Da and I know about death.

I sit down. A few more readings, I don't recall who or what. The priest says words I've heard before at the services of others who were much older than Holly. Hearing these words, my brain comes up with the word *widow*.

No, that's not right. Not widow.

Widower. That's it.

A sudden, irrational flash in my mind. I'm at a cocktail party. A fancy bloke in a slick suit shakes my hand and asks what I do.

I'm a widower, I say.

My name is Aidan Marlowe, and I'm a goddamn thirty-five-year-old widower.

The vision shakes me, the distraction welcome. More words, more fog. Some organ music.

We go outside.

I touch my collar, checking. I'm still wearing the tie.

Holly wears a casket.

Does this make me look fat?

The thought almost makes me laugh. Ends up making me cry.

We carry her: Me, Da, Holly's two brothers, her mother and father. Holly's family all live in Maryland.

I see it ahead. The hole.

More blurring. At one point, dizziness sweeps me, and I think, *I can't bear this weight anymore.*

And yet I do, because I have to. The casket sits beside the open hole. There are more words. Priest's words, flavorless as communion wafers. Bo and Maggie flank me, my arms around them. Maggie sniffles, having run clean out of tears. Bo is as silent and steady as that oak tree, and I don't know how. It worries me a little. Maybe more than a little.

I daze away for a moment and then am aware of a slight murmur from the crowd around me. The priest has a brief conversation with a groundskeeper who's just ghosted onto the scene, his dirty jeans and long-sleeved, green T-shirt in stark contrast to the black donned by the lot of us.

Comforting to see a workingman here. A bloke who'd wear a clip-on tie, I'd wager.

Their conversation ends, the groundskeeper whisks away, and the priest says, "I'm sorry." He follows this up with something about the ground not being quite ready, and I don't know what this means. The ground isn't ready? To swallow up my wife? I might have said this out loud, I don't know.

The priest apologizes a second time and tells us it will be another fifteen minutes or so, that the crew hasn't prepped the site to completion, and suggests we go back inside.

"I'll stay," I say. "I'll stay here."

Others agree, say they want to stay as well, but I tell them no. Even my kids, my family, Holly's family. I tell them to go inside, because I want to be alone with her one last time. That maybe the ground wasn't supposed to be ready, just so I could have this final moment. The priest tells me I won't be totally alone, that the grounds crew will be here.

"Okay," I say. "That's okay."

The crowd trails back to the church like a long, black cat skulking through high grass. Holly's mother holds the hands of my children.

They are gone and, for a moment before the grounds crew comes back to do what they need to do, Holly and I are alone.

So alone.

All my life, I've felt energy. The radiating pulses of others. Good, bad, hot, cold—I could tell a friend their mood before they'd realized it themselves. And Holly…her energy was special. I felt it the first time I saw her, when she strutted into my family's pub in Dublin twelve years ago. She sizzled, an exposed live wire. I thought I might die when I finally touched her but instead came alive for the first time.

Now there's nothing. Not a single crackle or sparkle. Whatever wellspring of energy that's left of my wife has transmitted to some void I'm not allowed to visit, at least not yet.

I've said plenty of things to her, dead and alive, and have an eternity more to say, but what comes to mind is this:

"Shoulda bought a better fucking tie."

I reach up, yank my tie off, jam it into the front pocket of my blazer. "Shoulda spent more money and learned how to tie it. I'm sorry. It's just that…with the funeral. The costs. Everything's so expensive. Your parents are helping out, bless them. But I was in that store, looking for ties, and my brain was swirling, and I just wanted to be out of there, and then I heard your voice. Scolding me, in that playful way you always did. Told me, 'Marlowe, don't spend good money on a tie you'll only wear this once.' You said that. I *swear* you said that. And I ended up spending eight dollars on a stupid clip-on."

And this breaks me in a way I haven't been broken since she died. The simple failure of dressing proper for Holly's funeral, despite the fact she'd see it as an unnecessary expense. I owed that much to her. An extra twenty dollars on a decent tie. I couldn't even do that.

"I'm sorry." I reach over, rest my fingertips on the casket. Honey glaze, cool and smooth. "I can't do this. I canna do this alone."

The bitterest part is she never knew all of me. I never told her everything about my past, and even now, even with her gone, even with only her husk to confess to, I'm still tempted to hold my silence. My unending, poisonous silence.

Tell her, Marlowe. Tell her now, before the ground takes her.

I suck in a deep breath, thinking I'll finally tell her. This thing in me, waiting to come out all these years.

"When I was younger," I start. "Back in Ireland—"

My mobile vibrates. Two short buzzes. A text message.

The only reason I reach for it is the timing. As if Holly can talk to me, but only through text. As I swipe my screen open, I'm 99 percent convinced there'll be a message from her telling me the one thing we always said to each other no matter the time of day, no matter how rushed we were, no matter our moods, no matter how much we even meant it in that very moment. The same thing she last said to me two hours before she died, on her way out the door that morning. The thing we said because it was our one truth, without which everything else would have been a lie.

I love you.

I check my notifications. There *is* a new text, but it's from an old childhood friend in Ireland.

Thinking of you.

I don't reply. Maybe later.

My gaze sweeps over all the older texts, so many unread.

Later.

Then, for no reason other than how my synapses decide to fire in this moment, I look at one of the other unread messages, one I receive twice a week. Every Wednesday night and Saturday night.

The Powerball numbers.

With a Pavlovian lack of thought, I click on the message, hardly aware my other hand still rests on my wife's casket.

These are throwaway texts, discarded in seconds. A few times a year, I might have two numbers match. In years of playing, I've had three numbers match only four times, despite playing twice a week.

I've spent countless dollars playing the same numbers on Powerball for years on end yet buy a shit tie for Holly's final day of rest. Goddamn me.

The text is familiar, with one exception.

Powerball 05/30/18 Winning #s:

01-05-08-10-14 PB 22

ONE Winner

Annuitized $60.4 Mil Cash

Lump sum value: $29.8 Mil

Official results at powerball.com

The numbers.

The fucking numbers.

They're *mine*.

———————

A jolt of electricity bursts through my fingertips, the ones resting on the casket. Travels up my arms, into my chest, up to my brain. It's Holly's energy, I think. One final pulse of it.

Then a sound, like a tree limb snapping clean from a towering oak. I look to my left, to the only tree nearby. An oak, a solid twin for the one Bo fancied in the courtyard, its limbs all intact.

The sound doesn't repeat.

PART I

ONE

A LIGHT SUMMER BREEZE kisses my earlobes as I stand in the driveway, taking in my new home, wondering if it's real.

1734 Rum Hill Road.

Bury, New Hampshire.

I blink, questioning everything.

Is she really dead?

Did we really leave Baltimore and move to some town we've never heard of?

Did I really win thirty million dollars?

Before taxes, the universe answers.

Car doors slam. Fast footsteps.

"It's huge," Maggie says, her voice behind me. "This is ours?"

"Aye."

Bo's voice is less enthusiastic. "We don't even have enough furniture to fill one of the rooms."

I keep staring straight ahead as I answer, "Guess we have some shopping to do, then."

Figure your shit out, Marlowe.

Holly said these words to me once. We were freshly married, living in Baltimore, and I was debating what to do after I got my green card. I wanted to go to school, study the things I never had a chance to. But I also needed to keep working because her salary alone wasn't enough.

We were in bed, and I was running through all the scenarios out loud when she punched me in the arm and, with her signature I'm-only-half-kidding grin, said, *Figure your shit out, Marlowe.*

It's her voice I still hear telling me these same words. And her tone isn't half-joking. It's deathly serious. In those words, I hear:

Don't screw up our kids.

Don't let the money change you for the worse.

Make a difference.

Own who you are.

Figure your shit out, Marlowe.

Let go.

I'm not certain I'm capable of any of these things, but I knew I'd be stuck had the kids and I remained in Baltimore. So I made my best effort at one item on the list. I let go.

I shocked our system. Shocked it thoroughly.

And now, standing here in a hot August breeze, the air of which feels nothing like Baltimore, that shock ripples through me. I can either spend the rest of my life second-guessing all my decisions, or I can move forward and do the best I can to create full lives for myself and my children.

It's easy to say I choose the latter.

But I know me.

I'll always be tempted by the former. The past is your true first love, the one that broke your heart more than all the others, and, despite all your lingering feelings, remains the one you can never get back.

Not ever.

TWO

RUM HILL ROAD.

My gaze sweeps back and forth over our new home. Holly and I scraped by during our years together, paying barely more than the minimum on our credit cards. Now I just bought a mansion in cash, and the world continues to run through my fingers, slippery and surreal.

I found the house online myself, scrolling through listings when this one seemed to jump right off the laptop screen at me, bold and fierce.

A faint hum and the sound of tires creeping over asphalt. I turn and see an ocean-blue Tesla coming to a stop next to my car. The door opens and my Realtor, Christie, pops out. She opens her trunk and unearths a gift basket, which she uses both hands to carry over and offer to me.

"Look at this," I say. "Lovely, thank you." The basket has an assortment of treats that the kids will feast on, including some chocolate bars with the picture of a dog on it. "What's Tuli's?" I ask, reading the name on the wrappers.

"Local grocer," Christie says. "You'll be spending a lot of time there. If you want organic, that's the place." She reaches into the basket, and I catch her scent. I know that smell. Working in bars all my life, I suppose I know every type of human scent in existence. Her perfume is expensive, intoxicating, and just tipping the scales toward desperate.

She pulls a bottle of merlot from the basket.

"Hope you like red," she says. "I wasn't sure."

"Just fine," I answer, suddenly having thoughts of whiskey.

"You have glasses?" she asks. "We could have a toast."

She gives a look, a kind I've seen before, maybe more than a few times. That subtle eagerness, the nuanced flirtation that could easily be denied were it to be called out. Back in Baltimore, I worked at one of the poshest bars in town. I know how to interpret languages, especially those that are unspoken.

"All boxed up, I'm afraid."

Maggie's voice rings out like a sentry spotting an advancing army. "Dad, come on! It's locked and we can't get in."

"Coming, love."

I cradle the gift basket and make my way to the door, Christie and her bottle of wine in tow. I set the basket on the porch and reach for the keys in my pocket, which were just given to me at the closing.

These keys, they shine.

I step up to the front door, a beast of a thing. Properly suited for battle, this oversize slab of wood and iron. I think this door is what first caught my attention. It's the door of a castle, meant to keep the barbarians on the outside.

I insert the key in the lock and turn, feeling the satisfying *clunk* of the bolt. Then, with my kids just behind me, I open the door to eight thousand square feet of our new world.

The door swings open, and I step inside the silent, cavernous foyer for the first time.

Bless me, this energy.

It's not the change in air pressure from the outside to within. No, there's a charge here I'm attuned to, and maybe I'm the only one. It's heavy and heady, a Bordeaux of tingles. The history, the weight of time, it's all here. This house, only built in the 1980s, feels ancient.

I have a sudden desire to know more about its past.

"*Wow*," Mags exclaims, scurrying around me and running through the massive foyer. Bo chases her, letting out a little squeal and cracking a smile that's been all too absent on his face. They beeline for the massive wooden staircase and rush up to the second level. I'm not even sure their feet touched the steps.

Christie's voice floats over my shoulder.

"How does it feel to finally be inside?"

I tell her the truth. "Like it isn't real. Like it isn't ours."

"I saw you sign the papers at the closing." She steps up next to me and folds her arms. "I can assure you it's very much yours."

I turn to her. "You said the last owner just abandoned the place, but I never heard the details."

She shrugs, keeps her gaze forward. "Not a lot of details to give. Logan Yates. Investment banker in his seventies. Just left the house one day and never came back."

"Did they presume him dead? Is that why it went to his son-in-law?"

"Actually, the house was already in his son-in-law's name. The name on the title was changed about five years ago."

Peter Ainsworth. I met him at the closing. Slick and refined, good-looking in an almost supernatural way. Not a lot of smiles or, I intuited, a lot of happiness.

"Maybe the former owner didn't die," I say. "Maybe he was running from something."

"I don't have all the details on the family, I'm sorry." Then Christie changes the subject. "When does the moving truck arrive?"

"There is no truck," I say.

"What?"

"The things that are important to us are in the car. Everything else… we'll buy new."

She turns and smirks at me, a glint in her eyes that might just be the afternoon haze. "You said you were in the restaurant business? Do you own a chain?"

"I'm a bartender."

A small laugh, laced with disbelief. "You must be a hell of a good one."

I haven't told Christie the source of my wealth. I don't tell anybody this if I can avoid it. All Christie knows is I'm a recent widower from Baltimore, looking to start a new life for my family in a safe community with a good school system.

"I'm pretty damn good," I admit.

"Well, if you ever want to make me a drink, I'd be happy to give you my opinion."

A sigh wells up inside me, and I release it louder than I mean to.

Her expression changes. "I guess that's your answer."

"Look, sorry, it's just that—"

She holds her hand up. "No, I'm the one who's sorry. I wasn't thinking." She looks to the ground and shakes her head. "You just strike me as…"

"As what?"

"A puzzle. I guess I wanted to know more about you, Aidan."

I resist telling her again to call me Marlowe. It's not that I hate my first name, but I much prefer my family name. "Trust me, I'm not that interesting," I say, which is the perfect comment to usher in an awkward silence. After a few beats, I add, "But I will need help filling this house up with a few things. Do you have any idea how I do that?"

She smiles. "I can get you in touch with some interior designers. They'd love to decorate this place. A completely blank slate."

Those last two words hit me in a way I didn't see coming. As the shrieks of my kids swirl from upstairs and as I sweep my gaze through my brand-new empty house, I repeat the words in my head.

Blank slate.

That's what I am.

Here, in Bury. A chance to start from scratch.

Blankest damn slate there is.

THREE

THE FIRST TIME I won the lottery was when a girl named Holly walked into my life. She was a million euros wrapped in the smallest package of a girl, her smile bigger than her waistline. I was twenty-three, Holly a year younger.

I hadn't yet gone to university, instead agreeing to help with the family business. The help I gave was pouring drinks at Marlowe's, the Dublin pub my parents poured all their money and souls into.

I grew up on the *lower* side of lower-middle class in the Irish capital's outskirts. Unlike many of our neighbors, our family was small. I only had one sibling: my brother, Christopher.

Christopher was fourteen when he died. I was fifteen.

Ma and Da first owned a music store, selling instruments to the serious-intended and renting them to schoolkids who were forced to try to learn them, either by their school or their parents.

The music store didn't work out. But my folks loved to drink as much as they loved music, so a year after Christopher's death, they managed to put enough funds together with some friends to buy a run-down pub and turn it into our namesake.

As I turned eighteen, my father asked if I'd be willing to work at Marlowe's a couple of years before university, just long enough to help them get profitable. I'd had my mind set on being an English major, having a love of literature that developed unassisted from anyone else in my family. Figuring English wasn't likely changing much in a couple of years, I'd agreed. One more week became one more month, and so on. Five years passed, and I might have stayed forever had Holly not walked through Marlowe's front door.

She was on holiday with her parents and brother, a tour of the UK and Ireland. It was late afternoon in a heavy summer, and Holly came in all alone.

I can't even guess how many people I'd seen walk into the pub over the years, and once in a while, I'd get that stronger tingle of energy from some. Didn't matter man or woman, some people just radiated in a way I could feel, as if they had something extra to offer the world.

Holly, she crackled.

She sat at the bar and ordered a Guinness.

It's my first time in Dublin, so I wanted to have an authentic experience, she'd said. *I thought a Guinness in a local pub would be a good way to start.* Her American accent was gentle and unrecognizable. Definitely not Texas or New York, the ones I could identify the easiest.

I poured her a draught and placed it in front of her, catching her scent along the way. Like flowers, brand new to the world. And her eyes, dark but gleaming. Sounds mad, but she seemed to glow. That little girl, sitting alone on the barstool, was bigger than anyone who'd ever occupied that seat.

What happened to your eye? she asked, pointing to a fresh bruise.

That's the real, authentic Irish experience, I replied. *Sometimes, people need to be told to leave the pub and they don't like that.*

Do you like to fight?

Who likes to fight?

She shrugged. *I think some guys do. Helps them work out issues they can't express through other emotions.*

I didn't reply that she'd just described me, but somehow she knew. From that first moment, Holly wasn't a person I could hide from without serious effort on my part. There's only one thing she never knew about me, the thing I couldn't even tell her while she slept in her casket.

After commenting on my eye, she pointed at the scars on my arms.

You get those fighting, too?

Something like that. Years later, I would confess to her the four white scars on my arms were self-inflicted. That each year until I turned twenty, I'd take out an X-Acto knife on the anniversary of Christopher's death and slice my flesh open. One wound was worthy of stitches, the rest less so. None were as large as the one on my shoulder, the one made by a different X-Acto blade.

You must like trouble, she'd said. Then Holly pointed at the tattoo on my forearm. *That's an ouroboros.*

Aye. You sure like pointing out things on my body.

What does it mean to you? She sipped her Guinness, which painted her with a creamy mustache.

That everything's a circle, I answered. *A circle and a cycle. And behind it all, a reason.* It's a truth I wanted to believe so much, I'd had the circular image of the snake eating its own tail inked on my forearm three years earlier. I'd long cooled to my Catholic upbringing and warmed to the idea we were all meant to be somewhere at the right time for the right reason. That whatever god out there had a beautiful and logical plan that didn't involve shame or guilt or narrow definitions of right and wrong.

The singular ink drawing on my arm represented me, years in the future on my deathbed, nodding and smiling, finally seeing all the logic of the universe at once, and admitting to god, *Well, then, that's quite clever.*

I'm Holly, she'd said.

I'm Aidan. But everyone calls me Marlowe.

Just like the sign on the door.

Exactly so.

She wiped her Guinness mustache and licked the remnants off her hand.

So, Marlowe, what's your reason? What's the reason behind all you do?

I said the first thing that came to my mind. Ridiculous and reasonable, far-fetched and believable, and guided by an instinct foreign to me until that very second.

I'd say to be with you.

If she hadn't spit her next sip of beer out in laughter, it would have surely come through her nose. But spit she did, all over the bar, apologizing through her snorts and giggles.

That's the cheesiest thing I've ever heard.

You'll see, I told her, meaning it. *You'll see.*

I gave her and her family a full Dublin tour the next day and took Holly out to dinner alone that night, an evening that ended with a kiss that made me dizzy in a way I'd never known.

That dizziness ended up lasting eleven years, nine months, and two days.

The day she died, it turned into a free fall.

FOUR

Bury, New Hampshire
Day Three

IT'S HAPPENING AGAIN.

Holes in my mind.

It started not long after Holly's death—maybe within a couple weeks—and I'd be crazy to admit it isn't scaring the hell out of me.

Gaps of lost time.

I'm standing in the kitchen, hands on the cool stone of the counter, when a fresh sense of this lost time washes over me. It's dizzying, like standing up too fast and feeling the rush of blood leave your head.

And so I go through my mental inventory check, following my day from beginning to now. Silly to think I can remember what I did every minute of the day, but I should be able to remember at least every hour.

And yet I don't.

GAP.

There it is, when I reach the period of time after lunch. I clearly remember eating, because I scarfed down some macaroni and cheese remnants I made for the twins. Then, the next thing I recall is going into their room because I heard them arguing, with Mags claiming Bo was picking his nose and trying to wipe it on her (*Was not!* was his watertight defense). That was just after three o'clock. And the two or so hours between those events?

Just a damn hole in my head.

Like waking up from a wicked night of youthful drinking and being told what you did the next day by your mates, only to remember nothing.

But I don't have the excuse of excess alcohol, at least not today.

In a strange way, as frightening as these gaps are, there's also a comfort in them. Like hiding under the covers, convinced that's all it takes to protect yourself from the monsters. Or dipping beneath the water in a bathtub, picturing yourself floating all the way to the ultimate darkness.

Comfort in the silence, comfort in the black.

Maybe I'm going mad.

And maybe, deep down, it's what I want.

FIVE

I SHAKE AWAY MY concern, dispel with the twisted fantasy of losing my mind.

I've got other things to deal with.

Three days into the house, and I'm overwhelmed in a way I could never imagine. Money hasn't caused more problems, but it sure as hell created a lot more paperwork.

Fortunately, my money has also let me hire a superhero.

Her name is Maya. She's my lawyer.

Maya Falk is a partner at Schraeder, Traub, and Falk, a Baltimore law firm specializing in tax and estate planning. They've also dealt with lottery winners.

Maryland is one of only six states where lottery winners don't need to disclose their identity, a fact that turned into a godsend in the spiraling weeks after I'd won. Holly's father had some loose connection to the law firm and made the introduction.

The firm assigned Maya to me. She told me she'd personally worked with lottery winners before and could help me navigate the complexities of my newfound wealth. In fact, she's become my life-support system over the past two months, creating an infrastructure around my life to keep me functioning. Since I hired her, Maya's established an entire estate plan and trust for the kids, and connected me with a wealth management agency that invests my winnings and manages my new and numerous bank accounts. She's provided me a long list of financial dos and don'ts, telling me how managing wealth is a terribly difficult job, one at which most lottery winners fail miserably.

I don't want to fail, and I don't want to spend recklessly. This house will probably be the most expensive thing I buy for myself. Other than that, I just want security, because the things I wish for more than anything else are impossible to acquire.

The doorbell rings, and I know it's her. She's flown in from Baltimore on my request.

I open the front door and find her standing in the soft glow of the afternoon sun. Maya's a pint of a thing, small and delicate, soft features framed by softer skin, and just a smattering of freckles around her nose. She could be Irish by her looks, but her family's originally from Israel. Her father once worked with the Mossad, and Maya told me she inherited his fortitude and determination. She's all of twenty-nine years old and maybe a hundred pounds, but I'd follow her into battle.

"That's a hell of a front door," she says. "Need a battering ram to bust that down."

"Keeps the salesmen away, I suppose."

She flashes a smile of perfectly straight teeth. Could be that my heart leaps a little at the sight of her, though I wish it didn't.

"Come on in," I say.

She hands me a blank, white envelope as she strolls into the foyer.

"What's this?" I ask.

"I don't know. It was on your doorstep. Probably an offer from a salesman who was too scared to knock on that door."

I place the envelope on top of a nearby furniture box, one of many scattered throughout the house. The interior decorator Christie recommended has been fast at work filling the house up.

Maya offers me a hug, which I accept.

"So this is it," she says. "This is the house that lured you away from Baltimore. Your castle." She looks around, hands on hips.

I'd told Maya one evening over cocktails how I'd come to choose Bury as my new town. We met at the Four Seasons in Baltimore a month ago to discuss some remaining items regarding how to structure the kids' trust, and I admitted halfway through my first whiskey sour that I wanted to move. Trip-hop music vibrated in the background as she leaned forward a few inches, her eyes a smidge wider.

Why?

I told her the first phrase that came to my mind. *Because I need to rip the world open, and I can't do it from here.*

What the hell does that mean?

I don't know.

Where would you go?

I polished off that drink in one gulp and told her about the moments after I found out I'd won the lottery. That cracking sound. Then, standing there by Holly's casket, after the groundskeeper resized the hole in the ground, after the others filed back out and stood around me, as I watched them lower her into the ground, how I couldn't get one word out of my head.

bury

It looped there, over and over.

That word ricocheted inside my head in the days and weeks that followed, like a bat trapped inside a house.

bury

On an impulse, I searched the word online, finding thousands of results, none of which resonated with me. Then it occurred to me to try the words *bury town*, and that's when I found it.

Bury, New Hampshire.

Population seven thousand souls.

I fell in love with it immediately.

It checked all the boxes: small, safe, excellent schools, scenic. And, as I soon discovered, very expensive. An hour outside Boston, Bury was a haven for wealthy hedge fund managers and tech gurus. I knew it was within my means to add *lottery winner* to that list.

As I told all this to Maya over drinks that night, she strained under the effort not to roll her eyes.

So you chose Bury because you thought you were destined to be there because of its name?

I was about to hedge my answer but decided I didn't need to be anything but honest with her.

Yes. Exactly that.

She took a moment, composing her thoughts. Finally, she asked, *And even though your kids have their grandparents in Baltimore and their school and their roots, you're just going to up and move?*

No hesitation on my part. *Yes.*

Well, then was her only answer. She clinked my glass in a wordless toast, and we carried on from there.

Now, in my house, Maya's presence holds a sense of relief for me.

"Not quite a castle, but bigger than anything I could have imagined owning," I tell her. "I'm not even sure I've been in each room yet."

She walks through the foyer and to the staircase, where she runs her fingertips along the sleek wood railing. "It even smells rich in here."

"Is that what that is?" I say. "I never had any context for it."

A rustle upstairs and seconds later, Maggie and Bo come tearing down the hardwood steps.

"Take it easy," I say. "Wouldn't be much fun tumbling down those."

"When can we get the TV hooked up?" Bo asks. "You said we'd do it this morning, and now it's already after lunch."

Mags's face hovers over her brother's shoulder, eyes wide and hopeful.

"First things first," I say. "Can you say hello to Maya?"

They turn and give a half-hearted *hi* in unison, not even asking what Maya is doing in Bury. They've never said more than a handful of words to her.

"We'll do the TV in a bit," I tell Bo. "Maya and I have to talk first."

Bo gives me his typical stare. Blank face, expressionless gaze. "There's nothing to do here. I don't think any other kids live in this whole town."

"It's been three days," I say. "And you haven't made much effort, have you? Ride your bikes around, as long as you stay on this street. Maybe you'll find some other kids."

"It's too hot outside," Maggie chimes in.

I feel the familiar rise of frustration and try to push it away. "How about you explore this big house and tell me if you find a room you hadn't already discovered?"

"Not likely," Bo monotones. "I explored everything the first day."

"What's your favorite part of the house?" Maya asks.

Bo barely looks at her. "It *will* be the TV, if we ever get it installed."

"That's enough, Bo," I say. "You can be bored, but you can't be rude."

"I wasn't being—"

"I found blood."

All heads turn to Maggie.

"What?" I say.

"It's not my favorite part of the house," she says. "It's in the room that smells."

"What room?"

"I'll show you."

Maggie scampers; we follow. She leads us down the long corridor branching off the foyer and to the study. I've been in here exactly once before.

It does smell. The faintest lingering scent of cigar smoke, yet unmistakable. The empty room is surely larger than the master bedroom of our Baltimore apartment, with a row of six-foot-high windows looking out onto the front lawn. The wall at the far end of the room is comprised of nothing but floor-to-ceiling empty bookshelves, which is where Maggie now crouches.

"Over here," she says.

I walk up to the shelves, these towering skeletons. Even from several feet away, I can see the wear of time in the white paint where volumes once sat. I wonder what the former owner liked to read. What was he passionate about? Did he sit in here at night, smoking a cigar and reading a thriller? Or was he a man of the classics? Or perhaps the books just sat there to make him appear learned, and actually all he ever read were the daily financial reports.

"Down here." Maggie points at the back of the lowest shelf, and I have to kneel to reach her.

Sure enough, there are some dark droplets and streaks. Not many, so she must have really been playing the investigator while exploring the house. The stains are on the back of the shelf, behind where the books themselves once stood.

"Why do you think it's blood?"

"I dunno," she says. "What else could it be?"

Maya leans down and looks, examining with a squint. "Moths," she says, straightening. "They leave brown marks. I get them in my garage at home. Disgusting."

I look again, this time closer. "No idea," I conclude. "But these shelves need a good going-over with a paintbrush anyway." I stand. "We'll add it to the list."

Maya asks, "What's on the list?"

"Anything and everything." I turn to her. "The list grows by the day. Things that have to be done. Things I *want* to do." I think about the stream of furniture and appliance deliveries coming over the next few days. "It's a bit overwhelming."

"It would have been easier to not move at all," Bo says.

"That's enough." I've had this argument with him before. I've tried to explain how we're meant to do something with our money and how their mother wanted us to be where we are. I've tried, but I've failed to make him understand. Probably because I don't really understand it myself. "Give me an hour, then we'll put the TV up, okay?"

Bo blinks. "Just put me on your list." Then he turns and walks out of the room, his sister trailing.

This kid.

Maya and I spend the next hour sitting at a brand-new, rustic farm table in the kitchen, going over legal agreements. Her presence, her expertise, stabilizes me. At some point in life, everyone dreams of swimming in money. No one realizes, once winning, how easy it is to drown.

She's only staying one day and has arranged accommodations at the Oak Street Inn, a local bed-and-breakfast with all of five rooms. She agrees to come over for dinner tonight, which I tell her will be pizza delivery since I'm still in the process of buying kitchen equipment. It seemed such a romantic notion to only pack what was most essential and what we could fit into our car when moving here, donating the rest of our apartment's contents to charity. In reality, it's a huge pain in the ass. Plastic forks and paper cups occupy a speck of the space in my voluminous kitchen cupboards.

When we're done, I walk Maya out and wave goodbye as she drives away. I glance at my watch and see I came very close to keeping my promised time to the kids, only fifteen minutes later than I'd told them. I'll count that as a victory.

Walking back inside, I spy the unlabeled envelope Maya carried in with her. I pick it up and open it as I make my way up the stairs and to the kids' room.

I pull out a single piece of white paper filled with paragraphs. As I begin reading, I'm expecting a generic ad for lawn service, house painting, or some such.

I stop halfway up the first flight of stairs, realizing there's nothing generic about this letter at all. The piece of paper wasn't generated for the masses.

It was written just for me.

SIX

Mr. Marlowe.

Welcome to Bury! Welcome to Rum Hill Road. Welcome to your new house.

We love your home. We've been watching it a long time.

Question: Did you know that winning the lottery actually INCREASES your chances of suicide? The numbers must really skyrocket when you also take into account a freshly dead wife. It must be a struggle. We can only imagine the effect it all must be having on your little ones.

If you're feeling lonely or stressed, don't expect the people of Bury to be of any help. They're a nasty bunch. Maybe they think you don't deserve to be here in Bury. Or in this beautiful house. Maybe they think you should go back to Baltimore.

But we don't agree. We think you should stay right in this new house of yours.

In fact, we insist upon it. Don't think about leaving— this house needs you. We'll be in touch soon.

With anticipation,
WE WHO WATCH

SEVEN

I RACE BACK DOWN the stairs, cross the foyer, yank open the front door. My hand clutches the letter as I scan the cul-de-sac, peering into the yards of the few neighbors I have. I look for any cars parked on the street. None. I hear nothing, not even the warble of a bird. Silent as grass growing.

I shut the door, lock it. As disturbed as I am by the letter, the emotion I feel isn't fear. It's not even anger. It's *rage*.

I've always had this reservoir of rage, shallow beneath the surface, into which I easily tap. *Triggers*, a psychiatrist told me long ago. *You have more triggers than most people, Aidan. You're angered by a disproportionate amount of things. But, more than anything else, your anger is most likely to be released if you experience or anticipate any kind of loss. That's most likely a result of your brother's death at such a young age. You can't keep it all bottled in. You have to talk, Aidan. You keep it all in a ball inside you, and you could experience PTSD or even a dissociative disorder.*

I don't want to remember those sessions, certainly not right now.

The smug doctor who Da thought would cure everything. I went four times, then told everyone I was fine.

I am not fine.

Not then. Not now.

The kids.

I run back up the stairs, past the second floor and up to the third. There are four bedrooms on this level, of which the twins share one. On our first day in the house, I suggested each claim a bedroom of their own, but Mags was quick to reply they wanted to share. She didn't have to elaborate; the massive, empty house was intimidating, and they'd spent little time apart from each other after Holly's death as it was. I suspect, at every age, the twins will have a degree of insepara-bility about them.

Second door on the right. I slow down, not wanting to seem off. As I turn the corner, I see them each occupying their space in the bunk bed that just got assembled yesterday. Bo's thumbing through a comic book. Maggie, to the best I can tell, is playing with her feet.

"Okay," I say, "who wants to help install a TV?"

They both bolt upright. Maggie is the first to notice something's going on.

"You're sweating," she says.

"Stairs take getting used to," I say.

I walk over to the window and look out. Their room faces the backyard, a sprawling tapestry of mature trees, bushes, hedges, and flowers, the varieties of which I couldn't even hope to name. Hell, I even have a pond.

Movement near the back corner of the fence. I squint to make it out, but then a figure emerges in full view. A man. Jeans, long-sleeved, white

T-shirt, wide-brimmed hat. He carries garden shears, which he uses to start trimming a hedge.

"Hang on," I tell the kids.

"Where are you going?"

I'd answer, but I'm already halfway down the stairs. Through the living room, kitchen, the covered back porch.

Into the backyard, across a lawn groomed to cemetery standards. The air is thick with humidity, heavy enough to stick a straw in.

Suddenly I remember, at the closing, Peter Ainsworth saying something about a gardener. A man who'd worked at the house a long time, and that he could keep doing the grounds work if I wanted.

I slow my pace to a brisk walk as I approach the man, the sweat now threatening my eyes. He stands and holds my gaze, the shears in his right hand. He's dark-toned, his face ashed by stubble, and wears the skin of a man who spends all his life outside. He looks fifty but is probably a decade younger than that.

The name comes to me.

"Carlos?"

"Yes." He nods with vigor.

I stop a few feet short, extend my hand. He moves the shears to his left and shakes my hand with his leather gardening glove. Strong grip, snakelike.

"I'm Marlowe. I just bought the place."

"Yes. I know." The accent is heavy. "Hope is okay I'm here."

"Yes, yes," I say, thinking my own accent must be heavy to him. "Perfectly fine. I'd like you and your team to continue working here."

"No team," he says, then taps his chest. "Only me."

"You do all this work yourself?"

Another nod. "Fifteen years."

"Bless me," I say. "That's a long time." Then I get to the reason I stranded my kids yet again. "Someone left a letter on my front porch today. Did you happen to see who it was?"

"Letter?"

"Yes. A letter. They left it on the front porch. Did you see anyone?"

He shrugs. "No. I don't see anyone. Just got here."

I consider how long he's worked at this place.

"How about ever?"

"Ever?"

"You ever see people around the house?" The words of the letter's signer burn in my mind. *We Who Watch.* "Do you ever see people... watching the house?"

"Watching?"

This is going to be painful if all his answers are one-word questions.

"Yes, watching," I say. "One person, maybe more." The *we* part of the letter is perhaps the most unsettling thing about it.

Carlos squints at me, a subtle way of asking if I'm crazy. I squint back, telling him maybe.

Then he shakes his head and says, "No. I see nothing like that."

"In all your years here, nothing unusual?"

He takes the smallest step backward.

"Some unusual, yes. But no one watching."

I compensate with a forward step of my own. "What kind of unusual?"

"Please," he says. "Mr. Marlowe. I don't want trouble. I just want to take care of the yard. I work hard making it look good, for years."

"No trouble," I say. "I just want some information." I point back to the house. "I just bought this place, you know, and don't know much about it. I just want to know more about its…history."

He shakes his head. "I only know the yard."

"I'm willing to pay for information," I say. These are words I've never spoken in my life. "You said some unusual things happened here. I want to know what things."

Carlos shakes his head. "Not me. I only know yard."

"Not you? Then who?"

He pauses, then lets out the sigh of a defeated man.

"My sister," he says.

"Who's your sister?"

"Abril."

Then Carlos looks left and right before leaning in a few inches and lowering his voice.

"Abril. She was housekeeper for Mr. Yates."

Yates. Logan Yates, the missing man.

"For how long?"

"Like me. Fifteen years."

"And she has information?"

Carlos straightens and shrugs. "Many stories."

"Does she still live in Bury?"

"Yes."

"Can she come over tonight?"

Another shrug. "Depends."

I get it. "Would she tell me her many stories for a thousand dollars?"

He grins, revealing for the first time a missing canine tooth.

"I ask her."

EIGHT

NEARLY 7:00 P.M. AND the summer day continues with only the faintest indication of dusk. Maya arrived an hour ago, and before diving into our pizzas, I took her aside and showed her the letter. It's fair to say my lawyer blanched. She had many questions, all the same ones I do, so I had no answers except to tell her the former owner's housekeeper, Abril, was coming over this evening. That maybe she could fill in some details about the history of this house.

Dinner came and went in chaos. My kitchen, half-filled with boxes of new appliances, glassware, utensils, and dishes. Pizza boxes, paper plates, plastic cups, paper towels for napkins. A six-pack of beer, two-thirds consumed.

A few ticks past eight, the doorbell rings. I open it to find Carlos and Abril. She's also in her forties, I'm guessing, but has weathered time much better than her brother. Her bronze skin is by and large wrinkle-free, her almond eyes bold and striking. Long brown hair pulled back in a ponytail, and an outfit designed for comfort over fashion.

"Hi, Carlos," I say.

He nods. "Mr. Marlowe. My sister, Abril."

I reach out my hand, and she takes it. Soft grip, no smile.

"Nice to meet you, Abril."

"Hello."

I step back and open the door wider. "Please, come in."

Abril hesitates, then takes her first step inside her former place of work. She moves with the uncertainty of a dog walking over a sidewalk grate, and I half expect her to cross herself before making it past the foyer.

She wouldn't be here if not for the money, that's quite obvious.

Carlos follows.

I usher them around the guts of boxes and into the kitchen. No need to ask the kids to leave; they've already bolted back to their new TV and Xbox console.

We sit at the table. I offer beverages. Carlos takes a beer, Abril only water. Maya cracks open another beer for herself and stays quiet. It occurs to me they must think Maya's my wife.

"Thank you for coming," I say. "I know it was short notice. I wanted to ask you a few questions about Logan Yates, your former employer. Is that okay?"

She takes a deep, calming breath and says, "I was told you would pay me to talk to you."

"That's right," I say. "A thousand dollars."

"I would like to have it now, please. Cash."

I realize two things. One, despite her brusque tone, this is a totally reasonable request. She doesn't know me. She *should* ask to be paid first. Second, I don't have a thousand dollars in my possession. I didn't even think about it.

"I can write you a check. It's the best I can do tonight."

"Then I can come back and talk to you tomorrow." Her English is better than her brother's—no room for misunderstanding.

"I assure you my check is good—"

Maya says, "I have it."

I look over at her. "You have that much on you?"

"Yes."

"Why?"

She shrugs. "For when clients foolishly offer to pay a thousand dollars for answers they could probably get for free."

"No," Abril says. "I worked here fifteen years. I know things about Mr. Yates. Not answers you get from others."

Maya walks over to her purse and, sure as her word, pulls out a leather billfold and peels off hundred-dollar bills from a slim stack.

She hands me the cash, the bills crisp.

"You really are Wonder Woman," I say.

She sighs. "Wonder Woman never carried a purse."

I hand the cash to Abril, who in turn gives it to her brother. Then she puts her arms on the table and folds her hands. Gleaming nail polish, raven black.

"I tell you about the disappeared." Her gaze is steady. "No one else."

"The disappeared?" It takes me a second, then I connect the pieces. "Right. Logan Yates."

"No," she says, raising four fingers. "There are four disappeared."

I look at Maya, who gives me the same uncomprehending expression I give her. Turning back to Abril, I say, "Four?"

She nods. "Mr. Yates. Both his daughters. His grandson. All disappeared. *Four*."

My immediate thought: *A thousand dollars is a steal.*

NINE

I'M NOT SURE WHERE to start. I begin with "What can you tell me about Logan Yates?" and it immediately sounds too broad.

"You should google him," Abril says. "He ran a big business in Boston. Finance."

I look over at Maya, who shrugs. "I didn't ever bother," she says. "You wanted this house, you got this house. I never looked into the history of the previous owner. Your real estate agent should have done that."

Back to Abril. "I just gave you a thousand dollars, and there're stories about him all over the internet?"

She shrugs. This family and their shrugs.

"Tell me about the daughters."

"What do you want to know?"

"How old were they?"

"Midthirties."

"Did they live here?"

"One was visiting for a while with her son. A few months."

"That's the grandson who's also missing?"

She nods.

"How old is he?" I don't want to use the past tense. I don't like the thought of any of these people being dead.

"Maybe ten. Eleven."

"And the other daughter?"

"Miss Cora. She married to Mr. Peter," Abril says. "Horrible woman. *Puta.*"

"Wait. Is this the Peter we bought the house from? The son-in-law?"

She nods.

I lean in, elbows on the table. "So you're telling me this wealthy businessman who lived here for decades suddenly just vanished one day. And not just him, but his two adult daughters and his grandson?"

"*Si.* Correct."

I turn again to Maya. "How was this not national news?"

"It was," she says. "I kind of remember it now. There was maybe a *Dateline* on it or something."

"Yes, *Dateline.*" It's the first time Carlos has spoken. "And some other big TV shows, but just for a little bit."

"I hadn't heard anything about it," I say.

"It didn't stay long on TV," Abril says. "But here, in this town, people still talking. People always talking."

"Saying what?"

"Saying lots of things," Abril says. "That they ran away from bad people. Maybe people they owed money. That they were murdered." She says this with such a casual air. "Who knows? Maybe aliens took them."

"No," I say. "I think you know. Or at least know more than others. You said so yourself. So what do *you* think happened to them?"

She takes her time, maybe for dramatic effect. But then, when she speaks, there's an earnestness to her face I hadn't yet seen. She *wants* to talk. To tell me what she thinks, if nothing other than to pass some of that weight onto someone else.

"I was here the night before they were gone," she says. "They were here. Miss Rose. Miss Cora. Mr. Logan. But not the boy. The boy was away. Sleepover."

"Okay."

"I left for the day but came back because I left my phone. Miss Cora wasn't here when I left but was here when I came back."

"Did they know you were here?"

She whisks a finger across open air. "No. They were in the office." That finger now points in the direction of the study, the one with empty bookshelves and lingering cigar smoke. "Miss Cora was yelling."

Maya leans in, now very much interested. "Yelling about what?"

"I didn't go close. But yelling. *You did this. You did that. What we gonna do?* So angry. Miss Rose yelled back. *Not my fault. Your fault.*"

"And the father?"

"He didn't yell. Low voice. I didn't hear the words."

"What did you do?" I ask.

She seems surprised by the question. "I left the house. Didn't want trouble."

"Did you tell this to the police?"

They both recoil in unison.

"No," Carlos says. "No police."

"But why? Surely they would want to know—"

Maya pokes me and not in a gentle way. I look over, and she gives me a don't-be-an-idiot face.

I think on it for a second, then curse myself for taking so long to understand. Carlos and Abril are not U.S. citizens. Not likely even legal residents, and they've been here a very long time. So no police. Not ever.

"I understand," I say.

Carlos puts his beer bottle down. "*No police.*"

I lock in with him. "*I understand.*"

He leans back. "Okay."

"That's all I know," Abril says. "But Miss Cora?" She turns to her brother. "*Más loco que el carajo.*"

He nods and turns to me.

"Crazy as fuck."

Okay.

"How was she crazy?"

Abril's low lip protrudes as she shakes her head. "She gets so angry so quickly. Then real nice. All the time. Back and forth."

I absorb the information, trying to see how it can help me with the real reason I want to know about my home's history. I go straight to the point.

"Abril, I got a letter today. I don't know who sent it, but it said they were watching me. *Us.* My family."

"Watching?"

"Yes."

"What does that mean?"

"I was hoping you had an idea," I tell her. "In all your years working here, have you ever seen…I don't know. I suppose someone literally watching the house?"

"I don't think so. I don't understand."

"Can you think of anyone who would want to…maybe try to scare me?"

"I don't even know you," she says. "You have enemies?"

"Not that I know of." What I don't tell her is whoever wrote that note also knows about the lottery and Holly. Who would even know those things? "But what about anyone who wouldn't want a new owner in this house? Someone here. In Bury."

Now she looks to her brother, and in her brief glance, I can tell she's starting to think I may be *más loco que el carajo*. Turning back to me, she says, "No. I don't know."

A thought then occurs to me.

"If I asked you to come back and work in this house again, would you?" I'm not sure I even want her to, but I'm curious to hear her answer.

Her response comes without delay. "*No*. Bad energy here."

The moment I first stepped foot into this house, I felt its energy. It didn't feel bad to me, but it most certainly felt alive. A hum, a pulse, as if a dozen people had occupied the foyer seconds earlier and left behind detectable traces of their spirits. But maybe I had misread the energy. Maybe what I felt wasn't the pulse of life.

Maybe they were ghosts.

The ghosts of the *disappeared*.

Maya straightens in her seat. "I'm not sure what you were expecting for a thousand dollars," she tells me. "But I'm guessing this wasn't it."

"Maybe not," I say. "But this is getting stranger by the minute."

"You can sell," she says, giving a nod that I interpret with ease. *You've got millions upon millions of dollars. Sure, you just bought this place and would probably sell it at a loss. But such are the luxuries of lottery winners.*

"No," I reply. "I'm not moving."

I say this partly because of what the note said and how it scares me a little.

Don't think about leaving—this house needs you.

But I say it's also because there's truth in that letter. I was meant to be here. I don't know why or for what purpose, but I won't find out by running away.

"How old are the children?" Abril asks, jolting me.

"What?"

"Your little ones. How old?"

The words in the letter flash in my mind.

The effect on your little ones.

"How did you know I have kids?"

She nods toward her brother. "He told me."

I squeeze my right hand into a fist, over and over. "Seven. Twins."

"Okay," she says. "You think of your children. That's all I have to say. Think first of your children."

She's right, of course.

"Abril," I say, "is there any reason *you* don't want us in this house?"

Her brow furrows, and I can't tell if it's exaggerated or natural. "You think I wrote this letter?"

"I have no idea who wrote it," I tell her.

Abril folds her arms across her chest. "I did not write the letter. I'm just telling you this house is bad. You want to live here? That's your business."

Carlos puts a hand on his sister's shoulder. "*Tranquila.*"

She turns to him and spits out a few words in Spanish. I don't know what they mean, but I could guess. *Don't tell me to calm down.*

In the ensuing silence, I say, "Can I contact you if I have any more questions?"

"Maybe," Abril replies. "But not here."

"Why not?"

Her answer is immediate. "I don't come to this house anymore."

TEN

AFTER THEY LEAVE, MAYA speaks first.

"You should take the letter to the police."

She's right, but part of me thinks if I downplay it, then it won't amount to anything. This is the same rationale as the child pulling the bedcovers over her head, reasoning if she can't see the monster, the monster can't see her.

"Maybe this is the first and last of it," I say.

"Let's hope so."

"But I want to know more about the Yates family," I say. "Everything. Can you look into that? Have a…I don't know…paralegal or something look into that?"

"That's not quite what a paralegal does."

"You know what I mean. Someone who doesn't have the same hourly rate as you."

She reaches out, places a hand on my shoulder, then lets it fall after a few seconds. That simple touch grounds me.

"Look," she says, "I know we had this conversation the day you first came to me, but we're going to have it again. I've been the lawyer to more than a few lottery winners, and the only absolute is that life changes completely. I have to say, whoever wrote that letter is right. Winning the lottery makes most people miserable. You lose most of your friendships because people become jealous. You have everyone coming out of the woodwork asking for money. Buying things rarely fills any kind of void. Statistically, you're more likely to be unhappier becoming instantly rich than you were before. It's more likely to break you than make you whole."

"You think I'm breaking?"

"No," she says. "Not yet. But I see a few cracks. You have a lot of stress just from the move alone and starting all over again without your wife. Add on top of it all this creepy-ass letter. And I don't know." She glances me up and down. "You don't look so great, Marlowe. Hate to be so blunt. But you look pale. Tired. So, yeah, I have concerns."

"It's not the money that's breaking me," I tell her. "Don't you get that?"

"I'm just saying don't chase ghosts. Not Holly's. Not the Yateses'. Live in the present, move toward the future."

"Easier said than done."

"Absolutely. But necessary."

I nod, making an effort not to agree with her out loud. There's no way in hell I'm letting this go.

Don't chase ghosts?

It's all I want to do.

ELEVEN

Bury, New Hampshire
Day Ten

IN IRELAND, DA STARTED playing the national lottery when it was introduced in the late eighties. Despite our meager economic status, he figured the cost of a weekly ticket was worth keeping alive a fantastical dream. He played every week. Same numbers.

I asked him once about those numbers. I must have been eight. Asked what meaning they held for him. He told me he chose them at random the first time he ever played, and said random numbers had the same chance at striking as meaningful ones. Probability wasn't a sentimental fool, he'd said. So then I asked why he kept playing the same numbers and not just choose new random ones every time. *Are you crazy, boy?* he'd said. *What if my first numbers finally won and I didn't play them? You have to keep with the same numbers, always.*

Probability apparently has a sense of irony.

I took up the same habit two decades later, after I moved to the States and married Holly. Like my father, I saw it as a minimal investment for a broad swath of hope, infinitesimal as that hope may be. Powerball is two dollars to play one set of numbers, and the drawing is twice a week. Four dollars a week, couple hundred over the course of a year. I figured I'd try it for a few months and stop if any of that foolish hope faded.

But Da was right. Once you play the same set of numbers, you can't ever stop. The idea of quitting and then finding out my numbers hit—even if that were to happen years later—was too much to bear.

Unlike Da, my numbers weren't random. Not at all.

I used my brother Christopher's birthday.

May 10, 1983.

Except with Powerball, you can only go up to sixty-nine, so I only used the month and day.

05, 10

That left me with four numbers remaining. Three more white balls and the Powerball.

Christopher died on August 1.

08, 01

He was fourteen.

14

He'd joined a local football club the year he died. His jersey number was twenty-two.

22

I had my numbers.

01-05-08-10-14 PB 22

What was the likelihood that four of the five white balls would be numbered ten or less? *All the same,* Da would say. *Don't matter if the numbers are one to five, the odds are all the same. And what terrible odds they are.*

I played those numbers as I worked in a string of bars and went to community college in Baltimore, getting an English degree I knew had little chance to spike our income. I played those numbers as Holly worked tirelessly as a social worker for Baltimore's Child Protection Service department, bringing home equal parts tears and smiles each night. I played those numbers even though we were barely making rent. The Powerball drawing became a fixed staple in our budget, nonnegotiable, like food and electricity. Holly, bless her, allowed this, even if I had no good argument in favor.

I played them as our twins were born, as we raised them through beautiful and maddening years. Through the fights and the laughter; the countless family snuggles in bed; the concerns about Bo, that maybe he has autism and how we would help him, that he's just trapped inside his mind more than his sister and that's okay, because we are who we are.

And those numbers. I played them on the day Holly died. I wouldn't have, because who could remember to do such a thing after losing the one person you've ever loved? But I played Powerball ten draws at a crack, so I only had to remember to fill in my ticket every few weeks. So those numbers were in play as she volunteered at the kids' school because it was book fair day, and she took a few hours off work to sit in the school library and be the cashier for all the kids buying copies of books about curious monkeys and moon-faced trains. Those numbers were locked in the moment she stood and screamed, grabbing her head as if a thousand beetles suddenly hatched inside and were eating their way to freedom. In front of her own kids, who had just come in after recess to give their mother a hug, because how cool was it that Mom was at school? In front of twenty-seven little ones and four big ones, Holly fell to the floor. One of the big ones called 911, telling the operator a woman needed help, not knowing there was nothing that could help Holly anymore. Not knowing the blood vessels in her brain were as weak as a water balloon baking all day under a hot summer sun and one of them had finally burst, causing her brain and skull to fill with blood.

She was dead before anyone could take our kids out of the room.

I played the numbers that day.

That was the day they finally hit.

And were I to tell people this story—and how few actually know—they would rightly understand why I know my money has a purpose. Maybe the numbers wouldn't have hit had she not died. Maybe they hit only *because* she died.

All I know is there's meaning.

Meaning in Christopher's death.

Meaning in Holly's.

Meaning in coming to Bury, to this house.

Maybe there's even meaning to this piece of paper in my hands.

I clutch it, knowing it's yet another thread in the mystery of how I'm supposed to move forward in this life.

Another letter.

This one, a week after the first. Found it sitting on my driveway, a rock holding it down.

Might be fear, might be rage, but both hands shake as I read.

TWELVE

Mr. Marlowe.

How has your first week been? We see you've been settling in. Trucks and trucks, unloading so many things. Things brand new and shiny, much different than what you're used to.

    All that money.

    We also know you've been talking to the gardener and his sister. Aren't they interesting? We wonder if you should be trusting them. Probably best not to be trusting anyone, we think.

    What we do know is your family was meant to be in this house, and it gives us great pleasure that you're here. You might get the silly idea of moving away, disappearing in the night on a summer breeze. But we don't want that. We like knowing you're here, desperately trying to figure things out.

Rest assured, Mr. Marlowe, if you moved away, we would find you. And then you wouldn't be so safe anymore.

With heartfelt intentions,

WE WHO WATCH

THIRTEEN

Bury, New Hampshire
Day Eleven

"IT'S HOT."

Bo's voice is nearly indiscernible from his sister's, but the complaining tone is unique to him. I look up to the rearview mirror.

"Aye," I say. "The Subaru's AC is shot. Roll your window down."

He doesn't. "How come we have all this money and not a new car?"

I spy his steel gaze, then return one, forged of titanium. "Haven't had time."

"But you bought a house. Doesn't that take more time than buying a car?"

This kid. A lawyer he'll be.

"We'll be getting a new car soon enough," I say, meaning it but dreading the process. I don't even know where the nearest dealership is.

"I want a Tesla," Maggie says, because of course.

"No," Bo says. "We should get an RV."

"What's that?" his sister asks.

"Those big campers that you can live in. Then we could drive all over and not have to stay in any one place."

Maggie's eyes light up. "Yeah, let's do that!"

I flick my attention to my son. "We've got a beautiful home. No need to live on the road."

"But the house..."

"The house, what?" I ask.

He hesitates, considering. "It's creepy."

I was wondering when it would happen. I think Bo feels energy the same way I do, like a little human Geiger counter. But whereas I feel our house's energy as an affirmation we need to be there, maybe he feels it just the opposite. Maybe rightly. After all, that is why we're driving to our destination right now.

I change the subject.

"How about Dairy Queen when we finish with our errands?"

Bo's tone tells me he acknowledges my misdirection but is not fooled by it. "Is there even a Dairy Queen here?"

"Has to be," I say. "There's one everywhere."

Maggie pipes up. "Where are we going?"

I was vague earlier but may as well be straightforward now. We'll be there soon enough.

"Police station."

"Why?"

I glance at Bo. "Because I want to meet the folks in charge of protecting our town," I tell him. I convince myself he's seven not seventeen and should be buying into my white lie.

He says nothing. Neither do I.

Five minutes later, we arrive. Did I want to bring my kids here? Of course not. But I can't leave them home alone.

I didn't want to call emergency services to report two menacing letters left on my doorstep. I wanted to talk to someone, face-to-face, feel them out, and get their advice.

The police station is a modern facility and larger than I expected. A reception desk sits empty, and the three of us stand next to it for a full minute. Finally, a worn-looking officer carrying a cup of coffee (gleaming, black ceramic mug, *Bury's Finest* emblazoned in silver script) trods by.

"Excuse me," I say.

He stops and turns his head. The man's mustache is bushy enough to be a sleeping animal. Likely a skunk, given the streaks of white and gray. He steals a glance at the empty reception desk before darting his eyes back to me.

"Darlene'll be right back out. Suspect she's in the ladies.'"

I step up to him. "I just wanted to talk to someone."

"'Bout what?"

"To report a…report a…"

I can see the patience leaving his body like heat vapor. "Like I said, Darlene'll be right back."

I lower my voice to a whisper. "I just moved here. And I've received… some threats."

His eyes show the faintest signs of interest, and it's here I notice the stitching on the left pocket of his uniform shirt. *Chief Sike.* It's also here I notice—really notice—the man's radiation. If he's the chief, then he's in charge, but it doesn't feel that way. This man wears defeat like a battered, old piece of armor, protecting him from happiness. At some point, his life didn't turn out the way he expected, I'm guessing, and he's old enough now not to hope for anything different.

"What kind of threats?"

I sense Bo and Maggie only a few paces behind me. "Is there a place they can go?" I whisper. "They don't know."

"This isn't a daycare facility, sir. Though given some of the noobs on staff, sometimes it feels like it. Got a couple chairs over there. If they can sit and keep to themselves, then that'll do."

I usher Maggie and Bo over to the chairs and tell them to stay here for just a bit. When they protest, I ask them to make up a story together, and they have to use Chief Sike as a character. Then, I tell them when I'm done talking to the man—five, ten minutes tops—they have to tell me the story.

This seems to work. Might not buy me more than a minute, but I sense Chief Sike is the man I need to talk to.

I return to him and say, "I received two letters on my property. Anonymous notes, typed. Creepy for sure, and vaguely threatening. Both letters are signed *We Who Watch*."

"Who's 'we'?"

"I don't know. Hence the anonymous part."

He bristles at this.

"Do you have these letters?"

"I do." I take them out of my pocket and unfold them.

As I start to hand them over, he pivots toward Darlene's desk and snakes a couple tissues out of a Kleenex box. He then takes the letters from me while keeping the tissues in his hands, ensuring his prints won't get on the papers. I should've thought of that.

"Where you from, by the way?" he asks. "Noticed the accent."

I get this question all the time, but now there's a sliver of menace to it, real or imagined. Like Chief Sike might not be so approving of foreigners in his little city, regardless of what shade they might be.

Don't expect the people of Bury to be of any help. They're a nasty bunch.

"Ireland," I say.

"You moved to Bury from Ireland?"

"No, Baltimore. I've been in the U.S. over a decade now."

He's already scanning the letters. "Mmmm-hmmm." It takes only a minute for him to read both. "Holy hell, you won the lottery?"

"I did. I don't…I don't want that information spread, if possible."

"Gotta be a damn lucky son of a bitch to win the lottery." He considers the letters again, adds, "Though I suppose not if your wife died."

"I try not to think about luck," I say. "About the letters?"

He looks back down at the pages. "See what you mean. Creepy and vaguely threatening. They sure don't want you moving away. Besides that, no specifics on what it is they want otherwise. Like, what's the point?"

"No idea," I say. "Which is why I'm here. Have you ever seen something like this before?"

"No, can't say I have. You say you just moved here?"

"Just a week or so ago."

"And where do you live?"

"Rum Hill Road."

Based on the twitch of his mustache, this seems to be as interesting as winning the lottery.

"Whereabouts Rum Hill?"

"Do you know all the addresses by heart?"

"The ones that matter."

I hesitate, only because I know my house is one that matters.

"Seventeen thirty-four," I say.

He nods. "So you're the one who bought the Yates house. Thought the name Marlowe sounded familiar. You said you came here from Baltimore?"

"That's right."

"Why?"

"What do you mean?"

"I mean," he says, "why come to Bury?"

"Does it matter?"

He leans in just enough for me to smell the coffee on his breath. "Maybe."

"Chief, I just came here to report these letters."

"Look," he says. "Mr. Marlowe. I don't know you. You don't know me. And, by the way, welcome to Bury. She's a sweet little town, most of the time. We're not nasty people, like the letter says. We get our share of piss storms here but rarely do we get a major shitstorm. The last one we got was nearly a year ago, and it all started at your house."

"When the whole Yates family went missing."

He nods. "So you know. Yes, that's about the sum of it. Didn't just affect the Yateses, either. Good cop in Milwaukee was investigating the matter before there even *was* a matter, and now he's off the force. It was a goddamn fuckin' mess, pardon my *français*. Lots of questions, no answers. I'm standing here with my thumb up my ass, far as anyone thinks. We investigated—we're still investigating—but everything's gone cold. No trace, dick squat, *nada*. But what the hell do I know? And here you are, freshly rich in Baltimore, and you decided to come here. To that house."

"Someone had to buy the house," I say.

"Ayuh, suppose that's true. Just like someone needs to win the lottery."

"I needed to leave Baltimore," I say. "Holly…my wife. She'd just passed. It was too painful to stay, and the kids…they needed a quiet place. A safe home. A new space. Or maybe I needed it more than them, but that's why I came to Bury."

Bo's voice behind me. I turn and he's telling his sister, *No, that's not how it goes.* The sand in my timer is down to the last few grains.

"Look, Chief," I say. "What do I do about these letters?"

"Not much to do right now. I'll log your complaint, and if you get another one, come on in. Also, if you want to leave the letters with me, I can have them dusted for fingerprints. Of course, yours are already all over them. Anyone else's?"

"My lawyer's."

"Okay. I can run any fingerprints through the IAFIS, see if any gets a hit with someone you don't know. Though I doubt it. Most likely the perp wore gloves."

"Fine, fine, please. Keep them. Anything you can do is helpful."

"And feel free to call me anytime."

"What about any other precautions?" I ask. "I'm a single dad with two kids to worry about."

"Worry is a cancer, eat you from the inside out. But I can't argue your point. You have a security system?"

"I do. I haven't…it's not activated."

Sike takes the letters and the tissues, and places them on the reception desk, then pulls his mobile out of his front pocket, scrolls as he talks. "Activate it. Upgrade it. You've got money. Get cameras out front. Motion detection, the works. What's your cell number?"

I tell him.

"Okay, I'm texting you a contact." He scrolls a few more seconds, then looks back up at me. "This guy, he's a buddy of mine, used to be on the force in Manchester. He has his own security company and can help you out with your system setup."

"Can't I just call a security system company?"

"Sure you can. And most of the time, that's exactly what I'd recommend." Sike shifts his weight to his back leg, slips his mobile back in his pocket, then sticks a thumb in his front pocket. "See here, Mr. Marlowe, I'd normally not suggest this, but given your financial means and your justified worry for your kiddos, my buddy—Owen Brace is his name, by the way—can help you out with other security concerns. You know, like a consultant."

"Help out how?"

The chief takes a sip of his coffee, grimaces at the result. "Well, I don't know how much you won in that lottery, but some folks with millions to their name hire a security detail for their kids, worried about kidnapping and such. And these are folks who didn't receive creepy letters."

"You think I should have my kids followed by a security detail?"

"I think you should call Brace and ask his advice."

My initial instinct is to object, to insist I can protect my kids better than anyone else. But it takes only seconds for the foolishness of the thought to fade.

"I'll call him," I say. "Good idea."

"I'm full of 'em. It's how you get to be chief." He extends his hand, his squeeze a touch harder than necessary. "Nice to meet you, Mr. Marlowe. Stay in touch."

I find Bo and Maggie at their chairs in the lobby.

"Are you done?" Maggie asks.

"Aye."

"Was he nice?"

I open the door and a rush of thick, moist heat hits me. "Nice enough." The kids scamper to the sidewalk, and I follow. "You think of a story about him?"

"We couldn't agree on one," Bo says. "So we each came up with our own."

Maggie crosses her arms and huffs. "I didn't like Bo's story."

I turn to my daughter, whose bottom lip protrudes in an exaggerated pout. "What was yours?" I ask.

"That the man has a police dog named Ralph and they solve crimes together. And at night, they snuggle in the same bed, but Ralph is so big, he takes up most of it."

I give her some silence in case she wants to fill in more details, but nope.

"Very sweet, Mags." I turn to Bo. "And yours?"

Unlike his sister, Bo's face is free of nuance. It's like trying to read the emotional intelligence of a statue.

"In my story, the man is only pretending to be a policeman. He puts on the uniform every day and goes around taking things he wants, because everyone just trusts him. They think he's protecting them, but he's not. Sometimes he doesn't just steal. Sometimes he hurts them."

His darkness can be unsettling.

"It's too sad of a story," Maggie says. "Everything always has to be sad with you."

"C'mon now, let's go," I tell them, leading them back to the car. With one child attached to each hand, I feel like the scales of justice, trying to balance out these two very different pieces of me.

FOURTEEN

Bury, New Hampshire
Day Thirteen

OWEN BRACE IS THE third person to whom I show the letters, after Maya and Chief Sike. Well, not the actual letters, since Sike is having them checked for fingerprints, but photos of the letters I took with my mobile. The security consultant is standing in my living room as his small team buzzes around my house, installing the new surveillance system.

He finishes reading and looks up at me. "Well, yeah, these are pretty creepy, all right."

Pretty creepy isn't exactly the professional assessment I was hoping for.

"Chief Sike recommended you," I say. "I'm hoping you can help."

"Walter's a good guy," Brace says. "Always easy to work with when I was on the job and our departments needed to share resources." Brace is not dissimilar to Chief Sike in either age or the permanently etched look of concern on his face. Seems in a lot better shape, though. "Tough son of a bitch. Haven't talked to him in a while. I should stop by the station to catch up."

"Look," I say, "maybe I'm overreacting and maybe you see stuff like this all the time..."

"No, not really. Truth be told, Mr. Marlowe, this is pretty concerning."

He swipes through the letters again, the hazy afternoon sunlight streaming through the window and washing over his gray stubble. "Ninety-nine percent of written, anonymous threats are nothing more than that. Threats. Just meant to scare the recipient and give a sense of satisfaction to the writer. Email and the internet have made writing those messages a lot easier, but some creeps are old-school, putting ink to paper." He hands me back my mobile.

"I'm not sure that makes me feel better. I mean, what the hell do you think they want? And what's the 'we' all about? There's more than one?"

He shakes his head. "Well, Mr. Marlowe, I'm not an FBI profiler, though I've worked with a few before. Can't say if this is really one person or more, but you got to look to the obvious. You say you don't have any enemies and are new to the area, so you hardly know anyone. You won a lot of money recently, which makes you an attractive target."

I cross my arms over my chest. "But that isn't public information."

Brace laughs. "Everything is public information for a price. And you'd be surprised how low that price can be."

"So you think someone knows about the lottery and is after my money?"

"Can't say for sure," Brace says, "but that's the most obvious explanation. Kidnapping for ransom is a real thing. Less so in this country than in, say, Colombia or Mexico, but it exists."

The singular word *kidnapping* brings immediate bile to my throat. "I mean, is that what you really think? That there's a chance they'd go after my kids?"

He shrugs as if I asked him if he thought it would rain tomorrow. "Always a chance," he says. "And if that's their intention, I can tell you people who are willing to kidnap children usually are the same people with enough conviction to mail out body parts until they get what they want."

There's no greater struggle than trying to shut down images your brain insists on conjuring. Right now, I'm picturing a parcel on my doorstep with a small stain where the blood has soaked through the packaging.

"Have you changed the locks since you bought the house?" he asks.

"Aye," I say. "Was done before I moved in. I mean, I know I paid for them to be changed."

"Then I assume they were. That's good." Brace obviously reads the concern on my face. "You need to understand, the possibilities of what I'm talking about are very, very slim," he says.

I lock into him. "But they *are* possibilities, right?"

"Sure," Brace answers. "Sure they are."

I can't believe this conversation is taking place. Just a few months ago, I was creating beautifully crafted cocktails for Baltimore's elite. Now I'm the elite one, only I've been sucking down straight whiskey and fretting about my kids being FedExed to me.

"So do I need to put…I don't know, like, security people with them? I can't imagine that."

Brace scratches his neck, considers the question. "Well, that's really up to you. But if I'm being honest, I'd say a true security detail is perhaps premature, given what we know about the threat. Kids would hate it, in addition to being freaked out by having strangers follow them around. But I can work with you to create a security plan that'll help make you and the family more aware of your surroundings and able to identify potential danger cues. I've done this with several other clients, and then I can check in every few days, and we can discuss how things are going and make adjustments as necessary."

I am nodding halfway through his comments. "That sounds good."

"Okay, fine. I'll email you what I had in mind, and once you sign off on it, we can get started. Now, I'm going to need to collect some personal information from each family member, things like birth dates, Social Security numbers, personal habits, routines."

"What? Is that all necessary?"

"More than you can imagine," he says. "The more someone knows about you, the more predictable you become to them. A predictable person makes an easy target. With your information, I can suggest ways to become less predictable."

The logic leads me to one very fast conclusion. "But then my family becomes very vulnerable to you."

He gives me a look that tells me he's heard this many times before. "Well, Mr. Marlowe, that's absolutely true, and again, that's going to be your family's decision to make. But I'll say I haven't been in business the past eleven years because I've betrayed the trust of my clients."

"I…I need to think about it. Do I need to make a decision now?"

"No, sir, not at all. You have my information. I'm here to help if and when you're ready. In the meantime, I'd suggest you still allow your kiddos their freedom, but maybe not too much. Best for you and your wife to keep them in eyesight, if you can."

How the word *wife* slips between my ribs so easily, nicking my heart.

I don't want to say *I don't have a wife*, because in my soul, I do. And I don't want to say *I'm not married*, because that suggests our love withered and died.

"She's dead," I tell him, not thinking further about it. It's the first time I see him struggle just a bit to react.

"Oh, clearly didn't realize that. I'm sorry."

"It's fine." How I hate when I say that. "I mean, you not knowing is fine. Her being dead is not fine at all."

Brace turns his head, scans the room. "If I can ask, do you have any other adults in the household? Anyone else who can help…keep an eye out?"

"No."

"Hmmm. Another family member maybe? Anyone who might want to come stay in your beautiful house for a few weeks? Looks like you have plenty of space."

And I think of one name that I should've thought of the moment I read the first letter.

Da.

Da might come.

"Maybe," I tell Brace. "Maybe my father."

"Okay," he nods. "Good, good."

Then the frenetic sound of little feet slapping down stair treads. Bo and Maggie scurry into view, nearly colliding into me as they race into the room.

"We're going out front to explore," Mags says.

Brace and I exchange looks. "Tell you what," I say to them, "I'll join."

Maggie smiles. Bo shrugs.

"This is Mr. Brace," I say to my kids. "He's…his team is installing the security system and might be…" Hell, now I don't know what to say, and I realize I could have said nothing and been perfectly fine. "Might be helping out with some other stuff."

"Okay," Bo says, clearly not caring. "Are we going or what?"

I tussle his hair, trying to ease the edge he carries. "Sure, let's go explore. Go get on shoes."

They run off, and I turn back and offer my hand to Brace, which he takes. The grip is a bit harder than I expect.

"I assume you have all you need if we go wander for a bit?"

"Of course. We'll be all done here in…oh, I don't know, maybe thirty minutes or so. You want us to wait so we don't leave an unlocked house?"

My instinct is to say no, not wanting to be a bother. But I fight it off. "That'd be great. I don't think we'll be much longer than that."

He smiles. "Happy to."

"Thanks for everything."

"My pleasure. And…just so you know…" He searches for words.

"Yes?" I ask.

"These things…these threats. Like I said earlier, don't worry too much about them. I mean, really, the odds of anything happening are low. I'm clearly not advising you to ignore the letters, I'm just trying to get you to understand the odds."

I suppress a pained smile. "If there's one thing in this world I know about," I tell him, "it's odds."

FIFTEEN

OUTSIDE, THE MID-AUGUST HEAT swallows us like Jonah's whale. The kids and I go exploring, as promised, though we don't discover anything new except a dead crow in a drainage ditch at the entrance to the neighborhood.

Mags capitulates to the heat after thirty minutes, and we head back. As we round the last street and make our way onto Rum Hill Road, Bo stops and points.

"Who's that?" he asks.

"Who's who?"

"There." He points straight ahead We're three mansions away from home, and sure enough, there's someone at the end of our driveway. A girl on a bicycle.

"I don't know," I say.

She's not moving. She's straddling her bike, facing our house, just staring—*watching*—straight ahead, as if waiting for something to happen. As we get closer, I don't make any effort to mask the sound of our footsteps but neither do I announce our approach. I want to see who this girl is. Ask her what she's doing.

We get within thirty feet when she hears us and turns her head. Long blond hair, unobstructed by any helmet, swishes over her left shoulder. I'm struck by the duality of how both frail and beautiful she is. Eggshell skin, fierce green eyes, and enough makeup to look much older than she probably is. She could be fourteen. Could be twenty. A runway model who would crumble to dust should you hug her too hard.

I expect her to bolt away, as if we caught her in the middle of a crime. But she holds a hawklike gaze as we approach.

Mags is the first to say anything. "Hi."

"Hi, yourself."

"I'm Maggie."

"Okay."

The girl's expression remains flat, and I can't get a read on her. I'm about to ask the girl what she's doing, but Bo chimes in first.

"Why are you staring at our house?"

"You guys live here?" she asks, rather than answering him.

"Just moved in," I say. "I'm Marlowe." I think about going up and offering a handshake but decide against it.

"What kind of name is Marlowe?"

"A last name."

"What's your first name?"

If this girl were younger, I'd have more patience for her attitude.

"What's yours?" I ask.

"Willow."

"What?" Maggie says.

The girl glares at her. "Willow. Like the tree."

I take a step closer, and she places one foot on her bike pedal.

"Well, Willow. I'm Aidan Marlowe. This is Maggie and Bo. Do you live on this street?"

"No. I live a few miles away."

"So what are you doing here?" Bo asks. His tone is more rude than curious, but I don't chastise him.

Willow looks back at me, and now her expressions softens, just enough for me to see a trace of…something. Hard to say for certain, but I'd place my bet on sadness.

"My grandfather used to live in your house," she says.

My stomach tightens. The Yates family has started to take over an inordinate space in my mind, and here is a blood relative, right in front of me.

"You're Peter Ainsworth's daughter," I say.

She nods. "That's right."

That means Willow's mother, Cora, was one of the four who went missing from my house. Cora, her sister, Rose, Rose's son, and the patriarch, Logan Yates.

I don't know how to react. I can't imagine what it must be like to have your mother vanish and not even know what happened to her. Would it make you go crazy enough to start writing creepy letters to the new owner of 1734 Rum Hill Road?

"I'm sorry about…" I let the words trail but then realize it's too late. Maggie instantly picks up where I left off.

"Sorry about what?" she asks.

Willow gives her another look. "Don't you know what happened in your house?"

"What do you mean?"

"Okay, that's enough for now," I say to Willow, then place my hand on top of Maggie's head. "Nothing happened in our house, sweetie."

Willow rolls her eyes so much, I can almost hear it. "Where's your mom?" she asks Maggie.

"She died," Bo answers.

"Damn, how?"

"Okay, that's enough," I say. "We don't need to get into our family history here."

"An *an...your...ism*." Bo enunciates like he's been practicing for this very question. "Her head filled with blood."

My instinct is to tell Bo again *that's enough*, but I stop myself. Just because it's too much for me to handle doesn't mean it's not exactly what he needs.

Willow absorbs this information with more curiosity than empathy. "Well, at least you know what happened to her. My mom just disappeared."

This, however, is definitely a conversation I don't want happening in front of my kids.

"Willow," I say, "is there something I can help you with?"

"No, I just wanted to see the house," she says. "Sometimes I ride my bike over just to look."

"Does that help?" Mags asks.

She blinks a couple times. "No. Not really."

Bo takes a step forward, which is downright assertive for him. "Do you want to come inside?"

"Definitely not," Willow says. "I'm not going inside there again."

"Why not?" Maggie asks.

She rolls her bike forward a few inches in Bo's direction. He stands his ground, less than a foot away, peering up at her. I can't help but think of that iconic image of the Chinese student protester facing down the tank at Tiananmen Square.

"Kid," she says. "I had a cousin. Older than you. Back then, he was eleven, I was thirteen."

I swear I feel the first breath of cold outside air since we moved here. A short huff, proper frost, spot on the back of my neck.

"He lived in that house for a little while," Willow says. "Then he disappeared, too."

"What does that have to do—"

"Bo, quiet," I say. And bless me, he silences.

Willow flashes me a look, as if she knows that *I* know. Then she breaks into a smile, and there's syrup on it that's on the edge of disturbing.

"Guess we both know what it's like to lose ones we love," she says, her gaze boring into me.

Then the smile fades, and Willow mounts her bike. With no further words, she rides away until the distance swallows her.

SIXTEEN

I STEP UP TO the heavy bag, which had been delivered and installed in the garage yesterday. This is the first time I've slipped on my boxing gloves since moving here, and I'm ravenous to hit something.

My right hook connects with the leather surface, a delicious release of pent-up anger.

BAM.

Not that I'm visualizing hitting the teenage girl. But damn it, how dare that kid say those things in front of the twins? Moreover, why did I let her? Because of that five-minute interaction, I had to spend the afternoon assuring Bo and Mags the house isn't haunted, even if I don't fully believe that myself.

Don't you know what happened in your house?

Finally, the twins are in bed and I just want to unravel.

BAM BAM BAM. A steady series of fists: jab, jab, cross. Over and over and over and over, a rhythm of calculated ferocity, pouring out through sweat and pain, impact and resistance. The hitting...it's my meditation. When the combination count reaches fourteen, I suddenly freeze.

Fourteen. That's how old Christopher was when he died.

I smear the sweat on my brow with my forearm. Some of it paints my eyeballs, bringing a sting.

"I'm sorry," I say, resuming, changing my routine to alternating hooks, hitting the sides of the bag. "I'm sorry."

I repeat these two words dozens of times, because when the image of Christopher plants firmly in my head, nothing I can do but let the sorrow take over. The sorrow, the guilt, the shame.

For four consecutive years after he drowned, I made a singular cut into the flesh of my arms on the anniversary of my brother's death, convincing myself it was a twisted kind of tribute to the day he died. But it wasn't a tribute at all. It was me needing to feel pain, to absorb punishment, to self-sabotage because it was what I deserved. Now I hit this bag, over and over, wishing it would hit back so I could taste that necessary pain once again.

No one else knows the truth of that day.

Only Christopher and me, and now I can't keep his voice out of my head. His fourteen-year-old voice, still a squeak in it.

Shoulda been you.

Shoulda been you.

I keep attacking the bag, punching harder and harder, trying to drown out my brother's voice.

BAM BAM BAM BAM BAM BAM BAM BAM BAM BAM BAM BAM BAM BAM BAM BAM BAM BAM BAM BAM BAM BAM BAM BAM BAM BAM BAM BAM BAM BAM BAM BAM BAM BAM BAM BAM BAM BAM BAM BAM BAM BAM BAM BAM BAM BAM BAM BAM BAM BAM BAM BAM BAM BAM

WHOOSH.

The final swing doesn't connect. Blinded by sweat and tears, my haymaker misses the bag by a mile, sending me in a full arc before I lose my footing and fall to the concrete garage floor. Left hip hit first, then shoulder.

Then my head.

The sound is terrible, like someone dropped a melon on the ground.

Time passes. Things grow dark. Life heavy.

Beautiful pain. And then comes the irony of my hoping the bag would hit back.

That's funny. Is that funny?

I'm tired. Heavy drunken tired.

Before the darkness, one thought:

Please don't let the kids find me dead.

SEVENTEEN

I COME TO, ROARING head, cold, damp skin on smooth concrete floor. I remember what happened, a good sign. But I also know I lost consciousness, not so good of a sign. I prop myself on my elbows and see blood on the floor. Not a lot, not a little. I struggle into a seated position and fumble my gloves off. As I do, a telltale trickle of warmth slithers down my face. One drop of blood falls from my chin to my bare leg. Two. Three.

Need to put pressure on that wound.

I stagger to my feet, steeling myself against a surge of nausea.

Please don't let this be bad.

As I turn and make my way toward the door leading to the house, I catch my ghostly, translucent reflection in one of the garage door windows. A semitransparent image of my head, set on the black background of night. I squint, as if that could somehow sharpen the dull image, reveal the extent of my wound. The squint itself brings more pain, so I close my eyes, and when I open them, my reflection has been replaced by the face of a man.

Not me.

Maybe me?

Or someone else, staring at me through my garage door. He's hazy, but he's there.

Another blink.

Then.

He's gone.

Back to my reflection. But it was real.

Was it?

I rush to the window—more of a labored scramble—press my face to the small pane of glass, peer out, see nothing in my driveway. Blood slides into my eyes, streaking my world. I shake my head, and splatter hits the inside of my garage door.

I sense a threatening of unconsciousness again. I have to get inside.

I do, make it to the kitchen sink, throw up.

Concussion. At the very least.

Grab a dish towel, wet it, hold it against my head. Press hard. I'm expecting a rush of pain, but it's more of a dull ache.

I collapse into a chair at the kitchen table, keep the pressure on for a full minute, then chance removing the white towel and looking at it. It's bloody, but not as much as I expected. I dab a clean part against my wound and bring it back down. The blood flow is slowing. I press it again and keep it there as my mind races.

Did you really see someone looking at you through your garage window? It's after ten at night. Why would they be here?

Because they might be the ones leaving the notes.

Isn't it possible it was your imagination? You just cracked your skull on the ground, after all.

It's possible.

Now that you have security cameras, it should be easy enough to check.

That's true. I forgot about that.

I rise to get my mobile and dizziness overwhelms me, nearly collapsing me a second time. I breathe through it, grab the device from the kitchen counter, crumple back down.

Owen Brace's company installed brand-new security cameras inside and outside the house, a total of ten, and he taught me how to check the video feeds. I launch the app on my mobile and scroll through the motion-sensing feeds for the camera mounted above the garage door. The one with a fish-eye view of my entire driveway.

There are three screenshots posted in the last thirty minutes, and none of them show a person. I click on the first video, from twenty minutes ago. The first three seconds of the clip show nothing but my driveway, washed in the greenish hue of night vision. In the fourth second, a bug flies by. Moth, from the looks of it.

The second video is the same thing.

The third video, one taken less than five minutes ago, coincides closest to the time I thought I saw someone.

Again, a moth. The same goddamn moth.

I press the towel harder against my wound, as if losing my mind means it's actually seeping out the top of my head.

I need to see a doctor. I don't know if I can drive, but I don't want to call emergency services. Bo and Maggie would be properly terrified if screaming sirens arrived on the scene to treat Daddy's head wound. After watching Holly die the way she did, I can only imagine their terror at seeing me with a bloody skull.

I don't know what to do. And I don't mean in just this moment. I mean in life. I was so convinced this was the right place to come, following some indefinable urge I convinced myself was Holly's soul, and now I feel in over my head. My bloody, scrambled head.

I don't know how to live in this house, but I refuse to leave.

I don't know how to handle my instant wealth. I must have won for a reason. What am I really supposed to do with all this money? I figure I'll get a job eventually, most likely start my own company or even open up my own bar. A new and improved Marlowe's, carrying on the family tradition of injecting a beautiful numb to those craving a wee bit of deadening.

But mostly, I don't know how to fill the Holly-shaped space that exists everywhere I go. Every room I'm in—the left side of the bed, the kitchen chair across from Bo and to the right of Mags—there's this space where Holly should be. But she's not. There's only an emptiness. A nasty, soul-stinging emptiness.

I look down and see I've brought up Maya's number, which I don't remember doing. I dial. She answers on the second ring.

"You okay?" she asks.

I mumble back. "You think something's wrong?"

"You've never called me this late in the evening."

"Well, then, I suppose something's wrong," I say.

"You been drinking, Marlowe?"

"No, not that."

"Tell me what's going on."

My head volleys a fresh throb. "I fell and hit my head on the ground. Think I might have a concussion. It's bleeding…but not too bad. Can't drive."

"Call nine-one-one" is her immediate response. "Hang up and do it now."

"No, no. I don't want all the sirens and lights. Kids'll freak out."

"Have someone take you to the hospital. Have someone else stay with the kids."

This makes me chuckle.

"I don't know anyone here. Haven't even met the neighbors."

"Marlowe, I don't know what you want me to—"

"I might have seen someone outside. Outside looking into the garage. Coulda been my imagination. And there's this girl. God, this creepy girl. Granddaughter of Logan Yates."

"You're slurring your words and not making a lot of sense. Call nine-one-one."

I didn't call her for sympathy…at least I don't think I did. But her tone is worried and caring. There's a blanket of warmth in that tone. A comfort I haven't felt in some time.

"You're a good lawyer," I mumble. "And a good person. You're good to me."

"Marlowe, hang up and call. If you don't, I will."

The air takes on a weight I hadn't noticed before, pressing down. Somehow, it dulls the pain, takes the edge off. Starts to make me sleepy. Thick blanket on a cold winter night.

"I'm so lost," I say, not sure if I'm saying it to her or me. I remove the towel, stretch my arms out on the table, and lower my face to its surface. It's cool and wondrous. Why hadn't I done this earlier? The mobile balances on my ceiling-facing ear, and after a thousand years, I hear Maya's voice.

"Are you there? Marlowe, you there?"

I have a vague sense of saying, "I need help." Though, when I take the energy I have left to focus a second time, I think what I said was, "I need you, Holly."

And then I fall asleep. Or maybe pass out. Perhaps, I die.

Whatever.

It's lovely.

EIGHTEEN

Bury, New Hampshire
Day Fifteen

TWO DAYS LATER, MAYA walks up and sits next to me on a park bench. We're at a playground next to the Chester Woodall trailhead, which, in the limited research I've done about my new town, is one of the best hiking spots in Bury. The trail begins at the edge of town and quickly snakes into dense woods populated by trees. Could be maple, maybe birch. I don't know. Trees.

We're not here to hike. We're here to give my kids a chance to run around and play, to be children, which is what they're doing. The playground is small but complete with anything a kid could want. Slides, swings, things that spin, others that bounce, and a towering plastic fort in the center. Much nicer than our neighborhood playground back in Baltimore. It even has one of those rubbery ground covers—no sharp wood chips here.

Mags spins Bo on a little merry-go-round. He laughs and smiles, causing me to do the same.

Maya just got into town. She came on her own volition, but I didn't object. Said she had some concerns about me.

The late afternoon sighs, breathing a heady heat on my skin.

"How's the skull?"

"Fair enough," I say. "Concussion, but nothing worse than that. Got a couple staples they're taking out in a week or so."

"That was pretty scary," she says.

"Aye. Though I can't say my memories are too clear, obviously."

Maya called 911 that night, and what I didn't want to happen, happened. Both an ambulance and a fire truck came, lights flashing. Apparently, I was lucid enough to answer the door, which I don't recall. Nor do I have any sharp memory of being taken to the hospital while a member of the fire department stayed with the kids. I was released after a few hours, dropped back home, and spent the morning sleeping and cuddling with the twins, trying to assure them I was just fine.

"So you really don't remember calling me?"

"Not really."

"You were pretty upset."

I tilt my head in her direction but avoid direct eye contact. "Listen, Maya, I really appreciate you flying out here. You didn't have to do that."

"I don't even have a cat," she says. "It's easy for me to work remotely. And it's my job to make sure my clients are okay."

"I doubt you do this for your other clients."

"I would for those I'm truly concerned about."

A breeze kicks up, and I catch a fresh wave of her perfume. It's very subtle, and the fleeting scent makes me think of the ocean. I wonder if it's supposed to do that.

"I think you've started to like Bury," I say. "It's your second visit."

"This place? Not my style." Her nose twitches, as if catching a vaguely unpleasant scent.

"It was just a bump on the head, Maya."

"It's more than that." She pauses for a beat, seeming to search for the right words. "When we spoke yesterday and I asked you how it happened, you said you were boxing with a heavy bag and you missed a punch. The momentum made you lose your balance."

"That's right."

"Okay, I don't mean any disrespect by this, but who the hell misses a heavy bag? I mean, it's right there and it's huge."

"I must've lost my focus."

"Has that ever happened before? When you just missed hitting it?"

I pretend to search my memory, though there's no need. I know the answer.

"No, I guess I haven't. But I don't know what point you're trying to make."

Maya leans forward just a touch, enough to throw some extra gravy on her words. "It's the money. I've seen it happen before. You can certainly research it to no end."

I lean back against the park bench. "Yeah, I *know*, Maya. Money changes a person. Lotto winner's remorse and all that. That's not what's happening with me."

"Isn't it? And I'm not talking about the stress of the money. I'm talking about the worth of it."

"I know what I'm worth."

"I don't think you do," she says. "You know how much is spread across all your bank and investment accounts, your insurance policies, your real estate. But that has nothing to do with how much you value yourself." Twenty feet away, Maggie screams in glee, but I hardly register it. "It's not uncommon that lottery winners feel they didn't deserve to win," Maya says.

I don't want to be psychoanalyzed, though I probably need such a thing desperately. "Why the hell would I play if I didn't think I deserved to win?"

"Because you don't know what it actually means to win until it happens," she replies. "You win, then maybe you feel like you're not worthy of it. That can cause different behaviors. Some people just give all the money away."

"And others?" I ask.

"Most engage in self-destructive behavior. Self-harm. Very occasionally, suicide."

I move half a foot away on the bench. "You think I *wanted* to hurt myself?"

"I don't think on a conscious level you did."

"With two kids sleeping upstairs? You think that's what I wanted? Let them wake up to another dead parent?"

"Marlowe, I'm not trying to upset you. I'm just telling you it happens. I've *seen* it happen. I was a psych major before I went to law school. It's no coincidence I take on clients who are under tremendous psychological pressure. I don't know why I like it, but maybe because I always wanted to be a therapist. The partners in my firm are happy to assign me to—"

"To who? Lunatics?"

"I'm not saying that at all." She exhales with practiced effort, trying to reset the conversation. "This is what I'm saying: I came here because I care about you. Not just you as a client, but you as a person. I'm here for a week and entirely dedicated to you. Use me as a resource as much as you want or not at all." She allows the faintest of smiles. "Either way, you're being billed for it."

"You're here for a *week?*"

"Well, a workweek. Five days. I took a liking to the Oak Street Inn I stayed in last time. And their morning biscuits…best thing about Bury."

I multiply her hourly rate by forty hours. Just shy of twenty thousand dollars. "What if I don't need you here?"

"Then send me home," she says, pulling a strand of hair out of her face. "I won't be offended. But I know you're too proud to ask for help, and God knows you haven't met anyone here anyway, so you have to ask me to leave if you really want me to go."

I don't want her to go. But she's right; asking for help isn't my strong suit.

"What kind of help are you talking about here?" I ask.

Maya stares toward the kids, and the sun hits her face in a way that makes me feel incredibly alone.

"Whatever you want," she says. "We have some business items to go over as it is, namely finalizing your trust for the kids. Aside from that…" She shrugs. "Use me as a friend. A companion. An adult to talk to. I could even get you socializing with other adults in Bury." The look of an idea lights her face brighter than the sun. "I could help you throw a housewarming party. All the neighbors. You could make friends."

Friends?

"I can't think of anything I want less than that."

"C'mon, it would be great. I'd take care of everything."

"No," I say.

Her exhale is just shy of a huff. "So are you asking me to leave?"

"I didn't say that."

"Then do you have better ideas on how to spend four hundred and fifty dollars an hour? Plus travel costs?"

I rub my face, not because I need to but because it feels good to hide behind my hands. Then, I think, maybe *she* could research the Yates family. Surely she could do that better than me. But isn't there a better role to justify the cost of her time? "I don't know, Maya. I just—"

She leans over and puts a hand on my shoulder. "Marlowe, I'm sorry. I'm not trying to be cute here. I just want to let you know the firm is here for you."

I remove my hands and look at her. "I think that's the first time you've mentioned the firm."

Mags and Bo come rushing, out of breath. There's another boy in tow, smaller than my kids, shaggy brown hair, and the wondrous expression of a golden retriever pup. The kid's mom walks up behind him.

"This is Ethan," Bo says. "Can he come over for a playdate?"

Of course not, my mind screams. But politeness finds a better way to answer. "Hi, Ethan, nice to meet you." The mom arrives, introduces herself as Monica, and apologizes for the forwardness of her son. We give her our names, cordial nods all around.

"He wasn't being forward," I tell Monica. "He actually hasn't said a word. But the truth is, we have plans tonight. Perhaps a rain check?"

"What plans?" Bo asks. Though it's not a question. He's calling me out.

I stare daggers. He bats them aside and sends back flaming spears.

"No, of course, that's fine," Monica says. "I wasn't meaning to... we need to go anyway." She looks down at Bo. "I'll get in touch with your mom and dad, and maybe we'll plan a time for you all to get together."

Bo upgrades his expression weaponry, pulling out the flamethrower. But it's Maggie who says what Bo is thinking.

"She's *not* our mom."

Those four words. The backbreaking weight of the world in those four words.

"Oh, I'm sorry," Monica says, "I didn't mean to—"

I hold up a hand. "Quite all right." I stand, retrieve my mobile from my front pocket, and we exchange numbers. "We just moved here, so it's great for the kids to make some friends. I'll be in touch."

That might be true.

Monica and Ethan walk away, and the four of us walk to the trailhead parking lot, where Maya's rental car is parked next to my Subaru.

"Come over for dinner tonight?" I ask.

"Sure, I'd like that."

"I have furniture and everything."

She smiles. "Good to hear."

"C'mon, Dad," Bo says, even though his sister is off chasing a butterfly.

I tell Maya to come over at six, round up my daughter, and the kids and I load up into the car.

As I pull out, I glance in the rearview mirror. First to Mags, who looks distantly out the window. Then to Bo, who makes eye contact just long enough for me to see something's bothering him. It could be one of a thousand things, but I know it's Maya. Any new woman in his life— even if she's just my lawyer—is a threat on some level.

The last thing I notice before pulling forward is the space between my kids, the glow of the rear window in the afternoon sun and the trail in the distance. It looks like an escape, a path to somewhere simple and pure, unbound by memories or bitter nostalgia. I make a mental note to get outside more, travel unknown paths, exist only in the moment for as long as the moment will have me.

I'll come back here.

For all I know, that trail might be the nicest bit in all of Bury.

NINETEEN

DETERMINING THE NICEST PART of Bury is hard to do, because the town itself has a pristine, Disneyesque quality to it. There's a reason Bury is ranked in the top twenty best small towns to live in by all the websites that do such things, and I'm reminded of this on our drive home. The main street leading through downtown is flanked to the west by small but perfectly maintained houses, equal counts brick and wood frame, probably built a hundred plus years ago. That's a blink of an eye for an Irish house, but these don't have the desperate clutch-to-life feel of a Dublin home, at least not the one I grew up in. No, these houses are so crisp, it feels like we're driving through a movie set. Even the lawns appear the same exact height from yard to yard.

The homes give way to a commercial area on the east side, quaint and lively. I couldn't name every business lining each side of the street as we drive by, but they include a coffee shop, insurance agency, antique store, hair salon, at least two restaurants, and a sundries store. Big brands appear anathema to Bury; each place boasts a name unknown to me. I imagine Buryites prefer nuclear holocaust to Walmart.

Live free or die, and such.

A quick stop at Tuli's, the boutique grocer my Realtor recommended. Flank steaks tonight, maybe a side of asparagus and potatoes.

On the drive home, downtown disappears and Bury turns into a mostly residential affair. Though I would classify the whole of Bury within the realm of upper-middle class, the real money is most apparent in my neighborhood. I doubt there's a home here with less than six thousand square feet of living area or a yard smaller than two acres.

We walk inside, groceries in arms and kids scrambling around either side of me. As I enter from the garage, the energy of the house washes over me again, as it has each and every time, starting with day one. Its power doesn't lessen with repeated exposure.

I like to think this power affirms that we belong here. But the words from the notes quickly shift that power in a malevolent direction.

Don't even think about leaving.

We have about two hours before Maya comes over, and I tell the kids to go play out front. They should enjoy the last bits of a sunny day, and the cul-de-sac provides a quiet area to ride their bikes. I resist the urge to keep them at my side at all times.

Just the cul-de-sac, I tell them. Go no farther. Stay where I can see you.

Groceries put away, I pour myself a glass of wine and head into the office, which affords a view of the kids on their bikes. Soon enough, though, my eyes begin to lose focus, and when that happens, my mind slows.

After a few minutes of this calm, I replay the last twenty-four hours in my head, searching for gaps.

The holes in my mind.

They're back.

TWENTY

LAST NIGHT. SPOKE TO Maya briefly. Put the kids to bed. Read in bed and was asleep no later than eleven.

This morning, kids were up before me. They got me up, we made breakfast. We started painting their bathroom, Mags spilled paint into the grout of the floor tile. Owen Brace and the crew from his security company came over to finish the installation of the backyard cameras.

Lunchtime…GAP.

This afternoon, got the kids to finally take baths, did more painting. Took Advil for a stubborn headache. Went to the park and met Maya. Left the park, went to the grocery store, came home.

One gap. Lunchtime. I don't remember eating lunch. I don't remember making lunch for the kids, though I'm sure I did.

I think on this. Really concentrate. But…nothing.

I sip my wine. Breathe in, breathe out. Try to relax, to remain calm, to convince myself I'm not on the cusp of early-onset Alzheimer's. I search for commonalities around the moments of lost time, and as I do, I find one.

Maya.

I seem to have gaps around times I've talked to or been with Maya. I guess that's not too groundbreaking, considering how often I *do* speak with her. Still, that realization bubbles up first, leaving me nothing sensible to do with it.

I'm jolted by my mobile, which rings in my front pocket. I fish it out and see Owen Brace's name.

"Hi, Owen."

"Marlowe, just checking in. Are the cameras working out for you so far?"

I don't tell him about the phantom face in the garage window, my date with a concrete floor, or the cameras revealing nothing to me but a moth. "I assume so," I say.

"Good, good. That's good. Say, did you get my proposal for security consulting? I shot it over to you last night."

I remember, a fact for which I'm thankful. "Saw it this morning. Didn't go through it too thoroughly. I'll need to look at it again."

"Sure, sure," he says. "The thing is, you probably want to move on this pretty fast. I've got some solid ideas about how you can better secure your family without upending everyone's life. As I stated in the proposal, I just need a signed agreement, the retainer, and the answers in the questionnaire I included. That was a separate attachment, don't know if you saw that or not."

I did, and that's what gives me pause about all this. That questionnaire, asking for very specific things.

Birth dates.

Social Security numbers.

Known aliases, if any.

Medications, if any.

Daily habits, including predictable driving routes.

List of phobias, if any.

I mean, *phobias?*

"I saw the questionnaire. I have to say, it creeped me out a little. Maybe more than a little."

"It's all very routine," he says, a line which I'm sure is routine for him. "I know to you it seems strange, but in my industry, that kind of questionnaire is as common as dirt."

I'm about to answer, about to tell him I'm sure he's right but I'm a bit wary about handing over such information, even though I trust him—or I think I trust him (*do* I trust him?)—but before I can reply, I hear one word being shouted, not shouted but screamed, and that one word in that singular panicked tone is enough for me to disconnect the call without a goodbye.

The word comes from Bo, screaming from the kitchen.

"*Dad!*"

I race from the office to find him.

"What?"

I half expect to see him bloodied, maybe having fallen off his bike. But he's intact, though his eyes are wide and he's breathing heavily. Behind him, Mags stands still, as if too scared to move.

Bo lifts his right hand, and now I see the piece of paper. White computer paper, creased in thirds, no envelope.

"This was outside," he says, his voice cracking.

I put my wine down, nearly dropping it.

Another letter.

TWENTY-ONE

Mr. Marlowe.

Mine has a hood, and I lie in bed,
And pull the hood right over my head,
And I shut my eyes, and I curl up small,
And nobody knows that I'm there at all.

So much death surrounding you. We wonder who will be next? You can rely on us to be watching and waiting. We're so happy you're here.

With heartfelt intentions,
WE WHO WATCH

TWENTY-TWO

"WHAT DOES IT MEAN?" Bo's voice isn't its normal monotone. It's peppered with fear.

I read the letter two more times before answering.

"It's nothing," I say. I'm a fool for hoping to get away with such an easy answer. And I don't.

"It's not nothing," Bo says. "It has your name on it. And it talks about death."

"I'm scared," Maggie says.

I fold the letter, jam it into my front pocket, then walk over and put my arm around her. "Nothing to be scared of, sweetie."

"People are *watching* us?" Bo asks. "Is that why we went to the police station? And why all those people were here installing cameras?"

The situation is fast spiraling from my control. Hell, who am I kidding? I was never even in control.

"And that girl," Maggie says. "Willow. Saying something happened in our house."

I realize it's time for some truth. Just a little.

"Someone is playing a joke on me," I tell them. "They might think it's funny, but it's not and I'm sorry it's scaring you. Yes, their pranks are why I went to go talk to the police. But they're nothing more than pranks, okay?"

Bo fights back tears, almost succeeds. "Why would they do this?"

"I don't know."

"We haven't done anything to anyone."

"I know. Some folks are just mean for mean's sake."

Mags releases from my embrace. "I wanna go back home."

"This is our home," I tell her.

"No, no, it's not!" Her shout is followed by a forceful foot stomp.

"Mags, calm down."

Now she leans forward, angles her arms back, and unleashes into me with all her soul.

"I WANT TO GO HOME!"

This sets my blood to boil in a half second, even though my brain knows her reaction is perfectly appropriate. But still I heat because she's triggered me, and it's all I can do not to yell back. God, I hate my temper.

I take a breath, take my own advice, and calm myself. But before I can reply to Maggie, she tears up the stairs, out of eyesight in seconds.

"I want to go home, too," Bo says, standing his ground.

I kneel in front of him, reach for his shoulders with my hands. We're locked into each other, no room for anything else. Just my boy and me, each of us uncertain about everything. It's my job to give him certainty, because he's already had enough absolutes evaporated to nothingness.

"I'm not gonna let anything happen to you or your sister," I tell him.

"But how can—"

"Shhh." I keep my voice calm but tone firm. "Don't question it. Just trust what I'm telling you. Can you do that?"

He doesn't answer. No head movement. No words. I take the lack of answer as an affirmation.

"Good," I say. "And part of your job is to make sure your sister understands that, too."

He moves his gaze from my own and sweeps it along my arm, staring for a moment at my tattoo of the ouroboros, the snake eating itself. "Okay."

I squeeze his shoulders just a bit. "We're not moving away because of some silly pranks, Bo. We're safe here, and despite how much you and your sister want to leave, I want to stay." I let go, drop my arms, then lower myself to a seated position on the floor. "I don't know how I know this, but I think we're meant to be in this house. There's a reason we won that money and a reason for being here. You and I come from a long line of superstitious Irish folks, folks who believe there's no such thing as happenstance. That all things happen for a reason."

"That means Mom died for a reason."

This stabs me, and I let it. I don't run away from his comment, because the same thought keeps crawling around my mind.

"Maybe she did," I say, "and we just don't understand it. Not yet, anyway. But I think…I think she wanted us here." I think back to how the word *bury* burrowed in my brain after her death, leading me here. Did she put that word there? "I don't think she likes the idea of us running away from here. I think she wants us to stay. Protect what's ours. Grow and flourish."

I don't tell Bo about the other letters, the ones telling us specifically not to leave.

Bo doesn't say anything for a spell, and when he does, it's short and to the point.

"I miss her. Sometimes so much, it hurts."

I look into his eyes, picture her back there, swimming in his soul, desperate for the surface. "Me too."

I stand, fight a momentary head rush, steady myself.

"You want to help me make dinner?" I ask.

"No," Bo says. "I'm going to check on Maggie."

"Good idea."

He turns and walks away. I stare at his back, ready to give him one last assurance, one last bit of wisdom in which he can find comfort.

But I say nothing.

There's nothing to say.

TWENTY-THREE

IN THE KITCHEN, MY mind reverts to the letter, which I read again. There's a familiarity to the words, and I know there'll be nothing else to focus on until I figure it out.

I stare at the words, knowing the rhyme is the familiar part. It takes only seconds to thumb the first two lines into Google on my mobile, and the result stops my breathing.

Christopher Robin Is Saying His Prayers

Seeing the title, it all comes rushing back to me. The silly little song I used to tease my brother about. Every time it came on the radio, all I did was look over to him and say, *Where's your Pooh, Christopher Robin?*

How he hated that.

That was our relationship, Christopher and me. We fought often, as brothers do, constantly searching for new ways to needle each other. Once in a while, that needling turned into shoving, and sometimes that shoving turned into fists flying. He was quick to anger, but I was faster to rage.

But how would anyone in Bury know about my brother? And this song's meaning in my past?

I bring the letter to my face, inhale it. Smells like regular paper. When I run my fingertips along the words, I feel nothing other than the smooth surface of the letters. When I examine the print itself, it's nothing out of the ordinary. Typical font, maybe Times New Roman. Whoever did this simply typed it on a computer and printed it out.

No misspelled words. The stanza from the song in italics. Nothing about this letter or the two prior ones indicate haphazard writing. There's a certain…maturity to the writing, leading me to believe they didn't come from that Willow girl, but who knows?

I down the rest of my drink and pour another. One sip in, I dial Maya.

"Be there in an hour," she answers. "Need me to bring anything?"

"I'm good," I tell her. "Well, not actually good." I tell her about the letter, read it to her, explain its meaning.

She reacts as I would expect. Shock. Concern. A suggestion to go back to the police.

But I have another idea.

"I'm rethinking your recommendation from earlier," I say.

"Which one was that?"

"About the housewarming party. I think maybe it's a good idea."

She doesn't miss a beat. "But not with the intention of making friends, I'm sensing."

"No," I concede. "That's not my intention at all."

PART II

TWENTY-FOUR

Bury, New Hampshire
Day Twenty-One

MY FATHER STANDS IN the doorway of my house, a small suitcase in one hand and a wooden cane in the other. He's only sixty-two, but a recent hip surgery has necessitated temporary use of the cane. To tell the truth, I think he enjoys the image it projects. I always imagined he fancied himself Gandalf.

Timothy Marlowe stands at five-ten, and his once-dark, long, and shaggy hair now contains varying degrees of gray and white. Similar in tone and upkeep are his beard and mustache, and together with his very pale Irish skin, he transmits the appearance of static on an old analog TV screen. The only color he projects comes from his eyes, a deep blue that seems singularly purposed to project fierce judgment.

I last saw Da at the funeral, nearly three months ago. I asked him here because Owen Brace said another adult in the house would be a good thing. It's Brace's only advice I've acted upon; I still haven't signed any contract, despite the man's repeated calls. Maybe I'm feeling safer, more distanced from the threat of the letters.

Or perhaps I'm just fooling myself.

A silver Prius backs out of my driveway and continues down the street. My father's Lyft driver.

"She's a beast," Da says, looking up at the house. "Surprised it didn't come with a moat."

"I know. It's a bit much."

He cranes his neck to peer inside the foyer. "Aye, a bit much."

I open the door and he shuffles in, the late-afternoon sun beating on my face. There are no hugs or handshakes. We are willingly in the same room at the same time, and that constitutes the extent of our shown affection. I love him, and I think he loves me, but a stranger would never place us as family.

"I could've picked you up from the airport," I say.

He releases the handle of his suitcase and waves me off. "No trouble. Got to meet a nice young man. Studies at Harvard." He breathes that last word out like it's attached to an incantation. "Imagine such a thing."

"Hard to."

"Then again," he says, "no need for proper education when you can guess the lucky numbers."

The barb doesn't hit with surprise, but it still carries sting. He knows full well I delayed my college education to help out with the family pub, and only when I moved to the States did I finally get my associate's degree. Were it up to him, I'd still be pouring pints back in Dublin.

"Actually, the money gives me the free time to pursue more education," I say. "I think I'm going to go back to school. Get an advanced degree."

He looks surprised. "Aye? From the looks of this little town, no university could fit."

It's taken me years of living in the States to appreciate how thick his accent is. Mine has been smoothed over time, river water on rocks.

"Online schools," I say.

He squints. "How's that then?"

"I can take classes online. Get a degree."

This appears to delight him. "Feck, son, I can order a piece of paper on Amazon, too."

"It's not like that," I start, then stop myself. He's in a mood to joust. Me, not so much.

Four days ago, I called him. On that day, it was nine at night my time, two in the morning his, and I was several drinks into the evening. I barely gave him time to shake off the sleep before I launched into all that was happening here in Bury. The letters. My mysterious house. Even told him how I nearly killed myself trying to hit a hundred-pound heavy bag.

"That's a right mess, there," he'd said after a heavy sigh.

"I was wondering," I'd told him, "if you maybe wanted to come out for a bit. Couple weeks, maybe. I could use the help."

"Aye, of course," he'd said. "But need ya to buy me the plane ticket. Some of us are not millionaires."

And now he's here, and as he scuffles along the foyer, he does so with a caution and reverence that he'd use entering a cathedral. A bit of awe and a bit of fear of being struck down at any moment.

"Feel like Edward Smith, being here," he says.

"Who's that?"

He shoots me a look, always content to know something I don't.

"Cap'n of the *Titanic*."

I almost don't want to ask, but he wants me to. "And why's that?"

Shrugs. "Surrounded by luxury. Doom impending."

"Da, for god's sake, I didn't ask you here to tell me my house is cursed."

"You don' need me to tell you the house is cursed. You can feel it straightaway, a heat. Like a rabid dog, breath beating on your face 'fore it bites."

"That's a bit dramatic."

"You know me," he says. "Always had a thing with words." He turns his head, scanning the house. "And the littles?"

"Upstairs." I call up to Maggie and Bo, telling them their grandfather is here. It takes a second shouting before I hear the footsteps.

How little my own children know my family. My mother died ten years ago, before they were born. They know I had a brother who died as a teenager. They've met my father a total of four times before now, and I've only taken them to Ireland once, when they were too young to remember.

The twins race down the stairs but slow when they reach the landing.

"Here you go now," Da says. "Hugs all around." Maggie and Bo oblige, and Maggie even smiles as her grandfather puts his arms around her. When it's Bo's turn for a hug, he looks only slightly less uncomfortable than if getting a tetanus shot.

"How long are you staying?" Mags asks.

"Long as you'll have me," he says. "You live in a mansion now. How could I leave?"

Bo gives me a frantic look.

"A couple of weeks," I tell them. "He's got a pub to run, after all."

Da shoos me. "Libby can run it jus' fine without me. Doesn't take more than a blind monkey ta pull on those taps."

"I'm sure she appreciates the comparison." To Bo, I repeat, "A couple of weeks."

Relief creeps over Bo's face.

I turn back to my father. "You must be exhausted after that flight. Do you want to go lie down a bit?"

He waves my comment off. "Nah. That'll only promise me a sleepless night. Best to see this day straight through to the end. What time is it?"

I check my mobile. "Four thirty."

"Well, then, that's nine thirty in Dublin. I believe I'll have a gargle. Join me?"

I look over at Bo, and I'm not sure why I do. Maybe because I think he doesn't like it when I drink, and I need his permission. Then again, he doesn't know the expression *gargle* to mean having a drink.

"Sure, I'll join you," I tell my father.

"We're going back upstairs," Bo says. He turns and runs out of the room, and Mags follows, no questions asked.

"Right then, where's the bar?"

"Go into the study, and I'll bring us some drinks," I say.

He leans in. "And which room might the study be?"

I point behind him. "Down the hall, on the right. You can't miss it. It's the one with the big bookshelves."

"Aye. And the jacks?"

"Next door down."

He nods, turns halfway, then turns back.

"And bring along those suspect notes with the drinks," he says. "I want to see them for myself."

TWENTY-FIVE

I KNOW I WON'T go wrong pouring Da two fingers of Jameson, so it's the same beverage for each of us. I carry them into the study, where he's well collapsed into a week-old leather chair, one of two in the room. He's stroking his beard. Not in a thoughtful way—more like he's looking for crumbs from his lunch.

"Here we are," I say, walking up to him.

"Right." He turns and takes the crystal glass from me. "Cheers."

"Sláinte," I say.

"Sláinte." He sips, leans back, purrs like an old cat in an afternoon sunbeam. "Smooth as caramel, that."

I drink, say nothing, and take the seat opposite him. The leather is stiff, as, I think, is everything else in this room. All new. Nothing broken in. Chairs, table, area rug, small desk with a brass banker's lamp, artwork. All chosen by others with minimal input from me.

The only things unequivocally mine are the books, which fill up a quarter of the shelves. My interior designer told me she could round out the shelves with a wondrous variety of old and modern classics, but

I told her no. I don't care if an area rug is something I might not have chosen, but I'm certainly not populating my bookshelves with volumes I've never read nor intend to.

And those little brown marks. The ones at the lower part of the shelves. The little spots Mags deemed blood. They're still there.

"So what is it like, exactly?" my father asks. "Been playing the lottery for years, never had even a nibble."

"I know. Where do you think I developed the habit?"

"Aye." He takes a larger sip, and I realize I should have just brought the bottle with me. "I always wondered what it would be like. Most times, you forget. Numb to the idea of winning. But once in 'while, especially hard times, you take those five minutes outta your day and dream it up. The moment. The exact moment you found out. Have to think you'd scarcely believe it t'all."

"I told you about the moment," I say. "It was at Holly's funeral."

He nods. "The universe fucking with you, I suspect."

He gets me.

"So what was it like, then?" he asks. "Really like, in that exact moment?"

I think back, just as I have a thousand times in the past few months, and I reach the same conclusion yet again.

"I remember looking at my mobile because I thought she was texting me from the grave."

"As the dead do," he says.

This forces a smile. "And I saw the lottery text, dated a couple days earlier. Don't know why I clicked on it at that moment. I saw the numbers…it took a few seconds for them to hit me. And then I heard a large crack, and I thought a tree branch fell somewhere.

I looked around. Saw nothing out of the ordinary. Looked at the mobile again, then back to her casket. And I just felt...like nothing was real. Then I got excited at the idea that I hadn't actually won the lottery, because maybe that meant Holly wasn't dead. But then all of you came back to the grave, and I saw the twins. When I saw them, I knew everything was real. So what was it like? You want to know what winning the lottery was like?" I take a swallow, take a pause. "It was devastating."

He soaks this in, scrunches his face so the wrinkles around his eyes double up on each other. "Suppose that makes sense."

"And I've been trying to find purpose since then."

He grunts. "Listen, Aidan, I know your brain because there's a good amount of me in you." He rests his glass on his thigh. "After your brother died, I nearly lost my mind looking for purpose in it. Fact is, I did lose it, for a little while. Lost my mind, lost my faith. Nearly lost my marriage. And then, when enough time had passed, I could step back just enough to see I was being tested."

Da's as Catholic as they come. My relationship with god is tenuous enough, I don't bother to capitalize the name.

"And did you pass the test?" I ask.

He leans back. "There's no passing. There's only struggle."

"That's a bleak picture."

"So it goes." He takes another swallow, finishing his drink. It's my cue to go back to the kitchen and retrieve the bottle. I return and pour him some more.

"How many relatives have been scratching at your door these days?" he asks.

I top off my drink. "Not too many that I know of. My lawyers set up a point person for any money requests. Besides, I haven't made a habit of telling anyone."

His woolly eyebrows arch. "You surprised I haven't asked for anything?"

I sit back down. "Everything these days is a surprise, because I've never gone through this before. You know I'm happy to give you whatever you want."

"Well, that's the thing, I suppose. Don't much want for anything. Pub's paid off, I've got enough staff where I don't need to be there much. My bills get paid."

"Do you still play the lottery?"

"Every week."

"So you must have an idea of what you would do if you won?"

"Not quite," he says. "I just like the fantasy of winning. That moment. Not sure much about actually having all that money. Seeing how you won. The circumstances. That *moment*. More of a heartbreak." He shakes his head, his way of shifting the conversation. "Show me these letters, then."

"Right." The chief still has my original letters, but I have printouts of photos I took of them. I keep them here in the study, folded inside a Stephen King hardcover on the shelves. Figured the kids wouldn't find them there. I retrieve them and hand them over, and it takes Da less than a minute to go through all three a couple of times.

"Aye," he nods. "Creepy, all right. You say you went to the police?"

"After the second one. Not really much they can do. Told me to come back if there was another."

"Well, this makes number three. So are you going back?"

"Maybe. But like I said, what can they do? The last one was left at the top of the driveway, just out of distance from the security cameras."

He looks back down at the pages. "This one, with the song. You know it, right?"

"'Course I do," I say. "That's the letter the kids found. I didn't tell them it was a reference to Christopher, but they still got plenty scared."

"Who would do something like this?"

"I haven't a clue," I reply. "I don't know anyone in this town, hardly. And no one here knows about my past, that's for sure. But whoever's doing this, they say they've been watching the house for a long time, so I'd naturally want to talk to the previous owner, but he's not to be found."

"You don't know where he moved to?"

"I don't even know if he exists anymore." I tell my father what I know about Logan Yates, explaining he was a wealthy man who ran his own investment firm in Boston and, from what I can gather, was ruthless in his business dealings. I uncovered several magazine articles on him going all the way back to the eighties, and more than one referred to him as a shark. Logan had two daughters, Cora and Rose. Cora lived nearby in Bury with her husband, Peter, and daughter, Willow. Rose lived in Milwaukee but returned with her son, Max, to stay with her father after her husband suddenly died. A few months after Rose came back to live in this house, they all disappeared. Logan, his two daughters, his grandson. All of them, gone.

"Good Christ," Da says. "Maybe they're running from something?"

"Maybe. Or someone wanted them gone. The only other thing I know is the housekeeper who used to work here said both daughters were here the night before they disappeared. Said there was lots of shouting."

Da shakes his head. "And the part in the first letter telling you not to move away...that's the most threatening bit. What do you think that's all about?"

"Don't know," I say. "But I'm not planning on leaving. What if doing that would be the one thing that brought harm to my family? If anything ever happened to the twins, I'd never be able to live with myself."

He nods, lets out a soft rumble from his throat. "You're right, you wouldn't. But of course, maybe the real danger is in staying. Or maybe it's all bullshit and there's no danger at all."

"Exactly," I say. "There's not enough information to make a real decision."

"Well, I'm glad I'm here then," he says. "If we're hunkering down in this castle, best you have me around. I know how to crack a skull or two, if the need arises." Da takes another sip, looks up at the bookshelves with a sweep of his gaze, then settles his attention back on me. "So what's your next move? Just going to wait and see what happens?"

I reach up, place my hands over my eyes, and push onto my lids like I'm just waking up. It's not that I'm tired. Sometimes I just like to hide in plain sight, even if for just a few seconds.

"No," I say, lowering my hands. "My lawyer, Maya. She has a plan."

"Oh, glorious. Let's get the lawyers involved. And what's her plan?"

I exhale, still not sold on the idea.

"I'm going to invite Bury into my home."

TWENTY-SIX

Bury, New Hampshire
Day Twenty-Two

I FEEL LIKE JAY Gatsby, only in New Hampshire rather than New York and with loads less confidence. Saturday night, late August, and I'm throwing a party.

I, Aidan Marlowe, career bartender, am hosting some of Bury's crustiest for a housewarming party. Maya's suggestion created a ripple effect of ideas in my mind, culminating in the thought that one of the guests could be the person writing the notes. Maybe I'll pick up on their energy. See the twinge of guilt in their eyes, hear the slightest hesitation in their voice. Or maybe someone at least *knows* something.

Maya orchestrated everything, and I'm convinced she owns a wand full of pixie dust; otherwise, I have no idea how she got so much done in just a few days.

It's just before seven, and the guests will be arriving any moment. I already feel the clamminess under my armpits, and I'm hoping not to sweat through my royal-blue, button-down shirt. No tie or jacket for me; the idea of it felt too formal. I'm out of place enough wearing slacks instead of jeans.

Caterers buzz around my kitchen, white coats and black pants. Bo and Mags zip around them, sneaking any appetizers already plated.

"'Nuff of that," my father tells them. "For the guests, those." He'd grumbled at having to go buy nicer clothes than he'd packed, but I think he secretly enjoys the chance to play host with me. He even went to the barber for a haircut and beard trim. If he could manage a smile, he'd look a decade younger.

"I'm not mingling tonight," he says. "Don't want to get trapped with some rich bore yapping about their investment funds."

"I don't think it'll be like that." It could be exactly like that.

"I'll do what I do best. Work the bar."

"Da, we hired someone for that."

"Have 'em do something else. I've been pouring drinks since the middle ages...suspect I have more qualifications. That way I can still be chatty but not get stuck."

Maya walks into the kitchen and our conversation. "I'll tell the caterer," she says. "Won't be a problem."

My father turns and beams at her, unleashing the smile that melts his years away. "Well, thanks, love." He met Maya for the first time last night and seems rather fetched with her today. I almost expect him to say something like *were I a younger man*, but thankfully he doesn't.

She pulls me aside and I follow. "So what exactly is your plan for tonight?"

"You think I have a plan?"

Unlike my father, I don't think Maya had to go shopping for clothes for the party. She looks like a lawyer. An expensive one. "I hope so," she says. "We invited the who's who of Bury tonight. You going to pull them aside one at a time and launch into an interrogation?"

"I don't really know," I say. "Suppose all I can do is play it by ear."

"Is there anything you want me to do?"

"Just have fun," I tell her.

"And you want me to tell people I'm your lawyer? They're going to ask."

"Tell them what you want."

"Marlowe." She gives my shirtsleeve the tiniest tug. "I just don't want to give people the wrong impression."

I meet her gaze and understand the look she's giving me. Folks will know I'm a recent widower, that I have money and what appears to be a new girlfriend.

"Just tell people the truth," I say. "The truth works ninety-five percent of the time."

"That so?"

"Well, the numbers could differ for lawyers."

This gets a laugh, which feels comforting.

Then, another sound, which elicits anxiety instead of comfort.

The doorbell.

The first guests are here.

TWENTY-SEVEN

I REMAIN NEAR THE front door, opening it each time the bell rings. I greet my guests as they arrive, make light conversation in the foyer, then ask them to make their way into the living room and kitchen. Without fail, each person gives a surreptitious glance at their surroundings, their expressions a mixture of curiosity and hesitation. They all know. Of course they do. They all know about *the disappeared*.

Most of the faces I've seen before because I've spent hours on social media, scouring for anything I can on the people I've invited to my party.

Next-door neighbors. Anderson, Lana, and Pete. Gilly, Harold, and Lori.

Other neighbors on Rum Hill Road, ten in total who show.

Chief Sike and his wife, Sylvia. The chief looks like he was dragged here or is otherwise a bit on the miserable side.

Christie, my real estate agent, who comes alone.

The town's mayor, Martha Newberry. She also arrives alone and, from the look of it, unhappy. Tells me the arthritis in her hands won't leave her alone but feigns gladness to be here.

Many others, all of whom Maya invited because they are well-known local business owners. When I'd told her I was looking for suspects and not pillars of the community, she'd replied by asking me how she was supposed to know who the hell was the suspicious type. She said she'd focused instead on people it might be good to know.

The last person to arrive is one of the few I asked Maya to make sure to invite.

Peter Ainsworth. Son-in-law of the mighty and missing Logan Yates.

I answer the door, and Peter stands there alone. Unlike me, he doesn't have a lawyer at his side to replace his wife.

He's dressed as if he's just come from a boardroom, crisp and cool, not a wrinkle in sight. He offers a smile that looks more practiced than genuine, then hands me a bottle of wine.

I usher him inside, and his first steps are cautious ones.

"It's a bit unnerving to be back inside here," he says.

"Yes, I guess it must be," I say.

"To be honest, I'm still not sure why you invited me tonight." His mouth doesn't move much when he speaks. He is the perfect Aryan mannequin from a Scandinavian department store.

"I'm just trying to get to know the people of my new town," I tell him. "It's mostly neighbors tonight, but since we met at the closing, I thought I'd extend the invitation to you as well."

"That's very kind," Peter says, without a trace of happiness in his eyes. He walks a few more feet into the house, turns, and sweeps his gaze in an arc, like a prison spotlight. "I've spent a lot of time in this house. Can't say they were mostly good times. Logan Yates was—*is*—a tough personality to be around."

Peter knows I know about the house's history.

"You think he's still alive?"

"I have no idea," he answers. "But if he is, he's no longer the Logan Yates I worked for."

"You worked for him?"

A nod. "Still do, technically. At least for his firm. Over ten years now. He taught me everything I know about corporate finance and fund management. I don't know how to leave. Not sure I want to." He takes a beat, turns his head, says casually, "Sorry about your wife."

"And yours," I reply.

The awkwardness of the ensuing silence is outmatched by the sheer sadness of it, and Peter puts us both out of our misery by saying, "I'm going to go mingle a bit."

"Of course," I say. "But...I'd love to have time to talk some more."

"I'm not sure how long I'm staying, but sure. After you get a chance to spend time with your other guests, if I'm here, grab me and we'll chat." He reaches out and touches the nearest wall, patting it like a dog. "I'd like to hear about what plans you have for this place."

Peter walks away, disappearing into the kitchen.

Before joining the others, I quickly run upstairs and check on Bo and Maggie. The light from the TV dances on the walls, and the two of them are splayed out on the floor, a massive bowl of popcorn between them. Each has a hand in the bowl when I walk in.

"You two doing okay?"

They don't even turn around.

"Uh-huh," they say in unison.

"Do you want me to bring you up some proper food?"

I'd told them I wanted them to stay in their room while the guests were here. If one of my guests is the person writing the notes, I don't want them eyeballing my kids.

"Maybe in a bit," Bo says.

"Okay, but I want you eating more for dinner than just popcorn. I'll be back in an hour, how's that sound?"

"Good."

"And keep your door closed."

"Okay."

"I love you," I tell them.

They each mumble *love you*, and I leave without ever having seen their faces.

Back down the steps, anticipating the one that squeaks. Third step from the ground floor, like I'm stepping on a mouse every time. All the others are silent.

I count thirty-three guests, along with four or five caterers buzzing about. I've never been one for commanding attention, making speeches. But there're quite many things in the past few months I've never been one for.

Giving a toast to strangers feels oddly perfect right now.

I lift a butter knife from a nearby tray and tap it against my wineglass. It chimes louder than I expect.

Sounds like the opening bell of a prizefight.

TWENTY-EIGHT

HEADS TURN, EYES ON me. There's a thickness in this room.

"I just wanted to welcome you all to my home," I say. My voice cracks a bit, my nervousness apparent. It's more than public speaking that has me on edge. "We have a custom in Ireland to invite only those into our homes who we know we can be friends with." This is a total fabrication, of course. "And though I don't really know any of you, I already know we'll be friends." Also bullshit, but still.

Smiles and nods all around. A gentle murmur, like a waking cat.

"I've met all of you briefly tonight, but just to make it official, my name is Aidan Marlowe, and I moved to Bury a few weeks ago with my two kids. Twins. Seven-year-olds Bo and Maggie. We moved here after the unexpected and sudden passing of my wife, Holly."

I scan faces. I see surprise in some, narrowing eyes of others. Some expressions remain unchanged, as if I simply announced the time.

"We moved here sight unseen," I continue. "Came from Baltimore, though I'm originally from Ireland, as you can maybe tell. After Holly... well, we just needed a fresh start. And I'd heard such wonderful things about Bury. So we found this lovely house and moved here, and the twins will be starting up school soon. We hope to make this place our home for a long time, and I just wanted to say thank you all for coming out tonight." I raise my glass in the air. "To future friendships."

Everyone reciprocates the gesture, and a few clink glasses. I sip and let the wine sit in my mouth for a moment, coating my tongue. When I swallow, it feels like I'm coming up for air.

"I heard you won the lottery. Is that true?"

The voice comes from a woman standing only a few feet away. White slacks and blouse, wrists of dazzling gold bangles. She's a neighbor, not next door but one of the other houses on Rum Hill. Elaine? Helen? I can't remember.

"Where'd you hear that?" I ask.

She smirks, as if I'm being coy. Like I actually want this information to be public knowledge.

"Don't you know?" she says. "You can find out just about anything on the internet."

This surprises me. I've googled myself many times after winning just to make sure the news wasn't leaked. From what I'd seen, I was still a complete nobody.

"So you *heard*, or you *researched* me?"

The silence grows louder, ears actively attuned. Her smirk smudges.

"I was just asking."

I glance over at Maya. She gives a soft shake of her head. *Don't blow up at your guest*, I imagine her saying, as a good lawyer would. Still, the anger wells, as it always does, as it always has. An unrelenting assailant.

Everything freezes. This moment, suspended. I think, *If she knows, then everyone knows.* In that case, no use denying it. Own the moment.

I take a sip, the liquid-courage content level of the wine way too low. Should have gone for the whiskey.

"Actually, yes," I say, trying hard to take the edge off my voice while raising it so others can hear. "I did win the lottery. Powerball, to be specific. Won it in May. The day my numbers were drawn was the day my wife died. But I didn't know it at the time. I was preoccupied. I found out I won at her funeral. How's that for irony?"

Another look to Maya. She's gone from therapist to audience member, her look as anticipatory as the others.

"After that," I say, "we moved to Bury. To this house." I look around, wall to wall. "This beautiful, imposing, spectacular, mysterious house. And I'll tell you, I've questioned the decision to come here a few times since we've moved in. Maybe more than a few times. But the place is growing on me, so I expect we're here for the long haul."

Out of the silence, Da's voice.

"Hear, hear!"

A beat passes, then others raise their glasses to me, some with enthusiasm, others just following suit.

I could have said more. A lot more. But the things I left unsaid to the group would be better served in one-on-one conversations.

And so, after refilling my wineglass, I shark my way through the room.

It's time to get to know these people.

TWENTY-NINE

MINUTES FLURRY BY, STACCATO conversations. Pete Anderson is a patent attorney with a voice incapable of varying tone. Lori Gilly is the president of the homeowner's association and tells me to not park on the street overnight, because they fine for such things. I tell her I have a four-car garage and a single Subaru, so that won't be a problem. Mayor Newberry seems bored, and when I introduce her to my father, she struggles to muster a half smile, then orders Canadian Club on the rocks from him. Dustin Taylor owns Rust, an unfortunate-sounding tapas bar and restaurant. I ask him how he chose the name, and he says he paid a branding consultant five figures to develop the name and logo. The logo is just the name in all caps, orange. Jesus wept.

Christie walks up to me, smiling above the glass of red wine she's holding.

"Now I know how you afforded this house, Mr. Bartender."

"Aye."

She cocks her head at me. "Hell of a story about the lottery. And that you called this a *mysterious* house." She swipes a finger once around the ring of her glass. "So what's the mystery?"

I walk right up to the edge of absolute truth. "Something compelled me to this house from the day I found it listed online. That was only reinforced when I arrived and walked into the foyer for the first time. There's a haunting energy here, and I think I'm probably one of a very few who can feel it."

She looks down and away, and I can tell she's a little tipsy.

"Oh, I don't know," she says. "I feel an energy here." She lets that sit for a second and I do nothing with it, so she follows it with, "Weren't you supposed to make me a fancy drink with all your bartending skills?"

She looks up and I smile, slight and tight. Then I jab a thumb over at Da working the bar. "That's my father there. He's been serving the best drinks since I was a teen. In fact, he runs his own pub in Dublin. He can make you a much fancier drink than I can, guaranteed."

She slowly nods, smiles. "Okay, I can take a hint. But don't be surprised if I keep trying."

Before I can answer, she walks away. As she does, one heel slides on the floor, causing the slightest stumble. But she's good. She knows how to catch herself.

I dip in and out of conversations like a hummingbird among flowers, speaking to nearly everyone. I make a point to talk to the woman who found me on the internet. Her name is Evelyn, turns out. She apologizes and there's sincerity in her voice. I don't ask how she found me online, though I know I'll be searching later.

I remind myself to go check on the kids when a voice rumbles behind me.

"Guess your secret is out now."

I turn and find Chief Sike.

"Wasn't planning on being outed about the lottery," I say.

"No, can't imagine you were."

I peer over his shoulder. Sylvia, the chief's wife, is in conversation with Lana Anderson next to the bar.

"I almost wondered if you'd said something. You're the only one in this town I've told."

That mustache of his twitches again. "Mr. Marlowe, I know a lot juicier secrets about folks in Bury than you winning the lottery. And I've kept them all."

"Good to know," I say.

The chief reaches into his back pocket, hands me sheets of folded paper. "Not sure you even want these back, but they're yours."

I reach and take what I know are the letters I'd left with him.

"And to answer the question you're about to ask," he adds, "sorry to say the pages were clean. Well, not clean, lots of prints that I'm guessing are yours and your lawyer's. We can certainly take your prints to corroborate, but it doesn't really matter. Nothing came through in the IAFIS database search."

"I figured as much."

"Even the stupid criminals know to wear gloves," he says, then leans in just a touch. "And how's the house situation? Got those cameras installed?"

"I did."

"You worked with Owen?"

"Yup. He was great."

He asks, "Did he just do the cameras, or is he helping you in any other capacity?"

"Just the cameras for now."

He nods, chewing this over. "Any other letters?"

"Yes, actually, one more."

Eyebrows rise. "Was it like the others?"

"Yes and no." The lyrics from the third letter materialize in my mind. "Short like the others. A bit more…personal."

"You get anything on video?"

"No. It was left at the top of my driveway, just out of camera view. My son found it."

"And his reaction?"

"Not good. I was meaning to tell you all this before, but I'm not sure what you can do for me."

The chief considers this. "Probably not a lot, unless the letter was overtly threatening."

"It wasn't."

He shakes his head. "Hard to justify posting one of my officers on your street otherwise."

I jab a thumb in my father's direction. "Well, that's his job anyway. He's been taking nightly walks. Says he's getting exercise, but he's just looking for anything suspicious, I expect."

"That's a good father there. Just make sure he knows not to do anything stupid. He sees anything at all out of place, you call us."

"Yes, of course." I flirt with telling him how I thought I saw someone watching me through my garage window but hold back, still not quite believing it myself. "And my Da's a hell of a bartender. He owns a pub back in Dublin. Can I get you something from the bar?"

The chief shakes his head. "Not at the moment. Can't say I'm feeling a hundred percent tonight."

"Sorry to hear that." This confirms the feeling I got from him when he first walked through the door, that something was off. As I stand near him, I sense it more. For lack of a better way to describe it, it's like some kind of mild...decay about him.

He looks around. "Shame, too, because this house sure does make me want to drink." Chief Sike scans the walls, as if looking for a clue he might have missed before. "This house whose occupants were suddenly *non*-occupants. We couldn't figure out what happened—caught a lot of flak for it, to tell you the truth—and that heaped a lot of stress on me and my department." Now he turns back to me, holds my gaze. "Hit the bottle pretty hard last year, but I've learned to ease up. Didn't want to drink myself out of a job."

"No, I suspect you didn't," I say. I realize the chief isn't looking at me anymore. He's looking through me, his expression as blank as the wall behind me.

"You okay?" I ask.

It takes a moment, but then he focuses back on me. "Sorry, I kinda lost myself there for a second."

"You're a little pale," I say. "You want to sit down?"

He shakes his head. "No, no, I'm okay." Then he laughs, the ironic flavor. "Actually, I'm not okay. I got some distressing news today that I'll spare you the details from. But Syl and I will be headed out soon enough anyway. I'm just glad we came over tonight. Almost didn't make it but happy we did."

Chief Sike puts a hand on my shoulder, which feels so strange. It doesn't feel chummy—more like he's holding me down.

"Glad you're planning on staying in this little town of ours a while," he says. "I expect things will turn around. Maybe these letters stop, you settle in and get a chance to find out what a nice bunch of folks most of us really are." He scans the crowd, sweeping his gaze among all the people he knows so much better than me. "Seriously, Mr. Marlowe. These people here? Wouldn't hurt a fly."

I conduct the same forensic scan, slowly and with all the concentration I can muster, and reach a different conclusion.

"I'd bet all my money at least one of them would."

THIRTY

EVERYONE IS GONE AND the living room buzzes with an afterglow. I sit on the couch, a drink still in my hand and my brain 50 percent numb. Maya sits to my left, my father on a chair opposite us. We replay the night's events, comparing notes.

"The Andersons put quite a few back," Da says. "But it didn't make them any more interesting."

"I got the sense the police chief thinks my house is haunted," I say.

Maya pulls a stray hair off her blouse and lets it drift to the floor. "He may be right. Did you talk to Peter Ainsworth at all?"

"A little at the beginning. I kept meaning to talk to him more, but by the time I came up for air, he'd already left. At least, I didn't see him."

She crosses her legs and leans a few degrees in my direction. "He's a strange one. Seemed completely spooked by being here. I probably didn't talk to him more than a few minutes, but he barely looked at me the entire time. Kept darting his eyes, like something was going to come rushing at him from the shadows."

Similar to the experience I had with him. "What'd you talk about?"

"Well, this was after you bared your soul with your little speech, so when he found out I was your lawyer, he wanted to know if I managed your money. I know he still works for Logan Yates's private equity firm. Maybe he was sizing you up as a potential investor."

"Nothing odd 'bout that," Da says.

She turns her head to him. "No, I agree. But then he started asking more personal questions." Then to me, Maya says, "Like how Holly died."

"Well, I suppose that's not too—"

"And what kind of relationship you had."

This sobers me a pinch. "What?"

"And how you found this specific house."

"He could be your letter writer," Da says. "I thought something was off about him as well. Man looked plastic to me. No emotion, none."

To Maya, I ask, "What did you tell him?"

"I'm your lawyer, what do you think I told him? Three of my best habits are nodding, smiling, and keeping my mouth shut. I told him he'd have to ask you himself."

I make a mental note to pay Peter Ainsworth a visit, sooner rather than later. "But you said something about him thinking the house was haunted as well."

Maya sits up straight and places her hands on her knees. "The last thing he said to me—and mind you, he says this as he's walking away from me—he says, 'Nothing good has ever happened inside these walls.'"

"The hell does that mean?"

But Maya doesn't get a chance to answer, because Bo suddenly appears in the room. Damn it, I totally forgot to check on them, and now I feel like a crappy father. They've probably been on their Xbox for hours. Popcorn dinner.

"Hey, buddy," I say. "Still up? Sorry I didn't check in on you." I reach out my arms, tractor-beaming him in for a hug. "Let's go and get you and your sister to sleep."

He resists coming closer, and then I notice the look in his eyes. It's the same look as when he found the third letter.

"Bo, what is it?"

"Mags," he says, his voice scratchy. "I don't know where she is."

THIRTY-ONE

I'M ON MY FEET before I even realize it, then the booze in my brain nearly topples me. I catch myself, barely.

In other situations, my son's words wouldn't be much cause for alarm. But with the combination of the look on his face and the strangers who were just in my home, my brain goes straight to nuclear.

"What do you mean?" I ask him.

Bo squeezes his little hands together into a ball, holding them against his chest. "Don't be mad."

"I'm not mad."

I'm just fucking panicked.

"When did you last see her?"

"We were upstairs in our room. You were going to come check on us, and when you didn't, we started playing Xbox. I know we weren't supposed to, but—"

"I don't care about the games," I say. "Just tell me when you last saw her."

"Aidan, calm yourself, let the boy talk," Da says.

Bo swallows hard. "She wanted to go spy on you guys. You know, eavesdrop. I wanted to keep playing Xbox. She said she'd be right back. And, and…I dunno. I guess I lost track of time. I've been looking upstairs for her and can't find her anywhere."

"How long ago?" I ask. "Just tell me how long ago it was you saw her."

Now the tears come. Not a torrent, just a flower petal's worth, combined with a sniffle. "Maybe…maybe an hour and a half ago. Maybe more."

So many times, my reaction to a bad situation is to say *it's okay* out loud, even if I'm alone. Because usually I know things *will* be okay. Things are rarely as bad as they seem.

The last time I knew things were as bad as they seemed is when I got the call that Holly had collapsed in my kids' school. I didn't know anything about what had happened to her, but I sensed a foreboding seismic shift in all our lives in that moment.

I say nothing more now. No words of reassurance. No turning to Maya or my father to ask for their help or advice. Because things are not okay, and no one else can make it better.

I tear toward the stairs, scramble up two and three at a time.

As I reach the third floor, I start screaming my baby girl's name. My frantic voice ringing in the cavernous house is nearly the scariest thing of all.

THIRTY-TWO

"MAGGIE! MAGGIE, WHERE ARE you?"

I start with the twins' room. Maybe she walked back in. Check the closet, under the beds. Rip the blanket off her mattress, despite it being clear she's not in bed. "Maggie?"

Out of the room to the guest room adjacent. Fully furnished, never used. Takes less than half a minute to check.

Nothing.

Two bathrooms on the third floor. She's not there.

The more I search and find nothing, the greater my panic grows. Still, I try to reason. She's just wandering around here somewhere. Knows she shouldn't have been spying on the party, and now maybe she's scared I'll yell at her. So I run back to the top of the stairs and call out, "It's okay, Maggie, I'm not mad. We just want to make sure you're okay!"

I listen, listen, listen.

Listen.

Nothing. Piercing nothing.

I run back downstairs. My father and Maya are now standing, staring at me with wide eyes, both looking quite uncertain about what to do.

"You need to be looking," I snap at both of them. "It's a big house."

"Aidan, I'm sure she's fine," Da says, and it's exactly the wrong thing. It takes only two steps to get in his face.

"We don't know anything right now," I tell him. The anger burns like someone put a cigarette out on the surface of my frontal lobe. I drop my voice, lean in. "You should know not to make assumptions like that."

"Dad, I'm scared."

Bo's voice pulls my attention away from my father. The walls close in on me, but I push them away with a deep breath, knowing any panic I show comes across a hundredfold worse to my son.

"Your grandfather is right," I say. "I'm sure she's fine. We just need to find her." I take a knee so I can be eye to eye with him. "You stay with Maya, okay? Grandpa and I will go find her. Maybe she's curled in a ball sleeping somewhere, like a cat."

Bo gives me the look he does when he thinks I'm talking down to him. He doesn't realize I'm mostly trying to convince myself.

I turn to Maya. "Can you?"

"Of course," she replies, then sits on the couch and pats the empty space next to her. "Bo, come sit with me."

He does. Before this, he would have done so with only great reluctance, still seeing Maya as some kind of threat to replace his mother. Now, he scrambles up next to her, so close their legs touch.

"You look upstairs," I tell Da. "Second and third levels. Yell out if you find her."

He almost looks ready to argue, then seems to pull himself from the brink. "Aye. And Aidan, it's fine. Everything's fine. He's fine."

I pause, stare at him. "He?"

This simple confusion, saying *he* instead of *she*, rattles him, and Da's gaze falls to the floor.

He wasn't even thinking about Maggie.

He was thinking about Christopher.

THIRTY-THREE

I HEAD STRAIGHT TO the garage, pulled there by a memory. That night. The face in the window, which was either a distorted reflection of myself or actually someone from the outside looking in.

There are three pedestrian doors in the garage, and I pass through the one leading from my laundry room. Inside the garage, it smells of concrete and the faint musk of old drywall. To my immediate left is a door leading to the driveway. It's locked, both handle and dead bolt secured. I walk along the large motorized doors, peering through the little windows out front. No faces shine through this time. The driveway glows under the haze of a security light. Nothing seems unusual, though my field of vision doesn't extend into the nearby shadows of the night.

"Maggie?"

My voice echoes in the vast garage, occupied only by my car, the heavy bag, and a dozen or so empty cardboard boxes, most of them from my recent furniture and appliance purchases.

The boxes are a perfect place for a kid to hide, I think. If I were playing hide-and-go-seek, that's the place I would choose.

But Maggie and Bo weren't playing, and I'm struck by a horrible thought.

Boxes would make a good place to stash a little body.

I can't think like this. Pretty soon I'll be swept away in a current of irrational fear, and I have to reset the reality of the situation.

She just wandered away because she's a kid. Mags is just hiding from us or maybe crawled into a space somewhere and fell asleep. Don't overreact. Everything's okay.

I don't believe this, but I breathe 10 percent easier by pretending I do. For a few seconds, at least.

One by one, I check the boxes.

"Maggie?"

My guts clench every time I lift a cardboard flap. Exhale a little relief each time a box is empty. I want to find my daughter, but not in here.

Empty. They're all empty.

I take a few paces around the rest of the garage, checking any other place she could be hiding. Nothing.

On the back wall of the garage is the third pedestrian door, which leads to the backyard.

I check it.

A new fear.

This door is unlocked.

THIRTY-FOUR

THERE'S NO REASON FOR it to be. I rarely use this door, and whenever I do, I always lock it afterward.

Maybe the kids left it this way. Most logical answer. Carlos has a shed of tools and equipment in the backyard, so he doesn't need to come into the garage. He doesn't even have a—

Key?

House keys.

Locks.

Were the locks actually changed around the house?

Changing the locks was part of the purchase agreement, and I'm sure I have a copy of the work order somewhere. But do I actually know if it was done?

I don't.

And who would have access to the old locks? Logan Yates could have given keys to anyone.

Peter.

Peter would have a key. He sold me the house, after all.

Carlos could have a key, along with his sister. Maybe some of these neighbors do. Maybe—

Stop, I tell myself. *You're letting your mind run wild, and it's not helping. The locks were changed, and you or the kids left the door unlocked. That's all there is to it. Now get on with it and find your daughter.*

I open the door, step into the backyard. Smells of freshly clipped grass and mulch. The thick night air wraps around my face, mugging me. My pulse pounds in my neck, twice as many beats per minute as normal, I reckon.

"Maggie!" This is a shout, edging on a scream. My voice carries into the dark, over the expanse of lawn, and all the way to the back of the yard, to the—

Oh my god.

To the pond.

THIRTY-FIVE

I FREEZE AS MY body abdicates all function to my brain, which swirls with memories and horror. It takes two seconds for all the symbolism to wash over me. The dread. If someone meant to do harm to me, this would be the perfect way.

My legs find life, and I race back into the garage to find a flashlight. Once I do, it's a sprint into the backyard, over the spongy grass, fumbling to turn on the light as I narrowly avoid running through a pair of shrubs.

The light bounces, scattering like buckshot. Small path, crushed gravel. Gazebo, wrapped in vines. Just past is the pond.

I'm here, panting, but not from exertion.

The pond is small and shallow; an amoeba-shaped plastic membrane maybe ten feet long by six wide but only a foot or so deep. Still, a person could drown in a puddle if someone meant them to.

At the far end of the pond is a small fountain bubbling up and over a series of stacked rocks. As soon as I reach the pond, I hear the water lightly splashing. I've come back here a few times to sit on the nearby bench and clear my mind, and at those times, the sound of the water was comforting.

Now it isn't. In this moment, it sounds like the final death rattle of someone submerged.

And for a second, a moment that lasts no more than an instant but is decades in the making, I'm transported back in time to another body of water. This time, it's the River Tolka, which snakes along the northern side of Dublin and cuts within a hundred meters of the house where I grew up. In this blink of time, it's also summer, the sun well-cloaked behind meaty chunks of clouds. Shadows quiver, hues shift between wicked degrees of gray.

I am fifteen years old.

My brother, Christopher, is fourteen.

I look at his body, which floats faceup in a small pool fed by the slow-moving river. A bird chirps in a tree above me, a steady metronome, announcing the dead. And he *is* dead, of that I'm certain. No need to yank him out in desperation, pound his chest, blow into his mouth. My brother is dead, and a thousand more years of second-guessing what led to this moment won't change a thing.

So he floats, his right arm outstretched, as if reaching for a balloon that started drifting away. I have to decide what to do next, and never has my heart felt like this.

And never had again until Holly died.

And then now. This night, my heart aching as I reach the edge of the pond in my backyard. Whoever wrote the letters knows I had a brother I would tease with that silly Christopher Robin song. Maybe they also know he died. Could be they even know *how* he died. And if that person wanted me to spend the rest of my life trapped in an amber of frozen despair, they would harm my children, and what better way to do such a thing than to recreate what happened to my brother with one of them?

Nausea swells. I struggle to find the resolve to point my flashlight beam toward the water.

But I have to. Because maybe there's still something I can do to help.

Close my eyes. Point my beam. When I open them, I will never be able to unsee the next few seconds again. Not ever.

I lift my eyelids, find the light. It's hitting a spot next to the water fountain, and there's nothing else in that area of the pond except a few leaves, some of them decorative and others from nearby trees.

Not seeing my daughter's body is an instant relief, but that doesn't last long. Now I have to sweep the beam along the rest of the pond, and all I can imagine is the blackness of the water suddenly contrasting with a little white outstretched hand, fingers just breaching the surface.

I grunt in pain, like I'm being stabbed in the stomach. Doing this gives me the momentum to move the beam along the rest of the water's surface. I do this quickly, needing it to be over, one way or another.

Sweet joy nearly buckles my legs. There's nothing in the pond that shouldn't be.

I take a breath, try to slow my heart, but it's paying me no mind. I call out Maggie's name again, this time not as loud, maybe because I've stepped back from the brink of total desperation. And yet, still no answer.

I head back to the house, sweeping the beam crisscross as I go. Nothing unusual, though I'm not focusing all my attention.

Through the garage, back inside, into the living room. Maya and Bo are still on the couch.

The sight of them, sitting together, for a moment shatters my heart. I don't know why. Maybe because it should be Holly sitting there. Or perhaps because I'm deeply comforted that Maya is here, as my friend and not just my lawyer, but I know the twins see her as some kind of threat. A substitute mom being forced on them. I force the feeling away, relapsing to panic. "Anything?" I ask.

Maya shakes her head.

I have a few more rooms to check on the main level, but I first run upstairs and check with Da. I find him in the master closet.

"Anything?"

"No," he says. "And I'm still trying to wrap my head 'round this closet of yours." He points without a commitment to direction. "This space is bigger than the room you grew up in, and yet you've got, what, couple pairs of jeans, handful of T-shirts, and two pairs of shoes in here?"

"I'm a simple dresser."

"I know, son. That's what I'm saying. You're a simple man. Like me. What you goin' about needing a house this size for, then? It's not a Marlowe house. Not by a mile."

"Christ, Da, just keep looking, will ya? I don't need your lecturing when Mags has gone missing."

He grumbles agreement.

"Every last place," I add. "Under sinks, under beds, behind curtains. She could be hiding."

He snaps but it's low volume, making it all the more intense. "I know the difference between finding a child who's hiding and one who's incapable of calling for help."

This slaps me in the face, and twice in a matter of minutes, I'm taken back to that day. The cloudy afternoon when Christopher floated and everyone else cried. When I had to go back to the house and tell my parents what had happened.

I don't even bother to respond. I just leave, because my only other option is to explode.

I leave my father to his search, focusing on mine. The relief I felt back at the pond has been swallowed by a fresh wave of panic.

As I run back down the stairs, I whittle away at the logic, exposing only dark conclusions. She left the bedroom to go spy on the guests at the party. She doesn't seem to be anywhere upstairs and not on the main level or in the backyard. She would never just wander off outside on her own. So, if she's not in the house and she wouldn't willingly leave, that leaves only one conclusion.

Someone took her.

I puke, just a little. Swallow it down, burning, burning.

Taking kids.

That kind of thing happens all the time in this country. Maybe not in Bury, but all it takes is one crazy person. Or a handful of them.

We are watching.

A new memory comes to the forefront of my mind, one I hadn't recalled in years and had no reason to until now. That little girl in Colorado, back in, what, the nineties? JonBenét Ramsey. I remember reading about what happened to her. Rich family in Boulder. Christmastime. The parents hosted a holiday open house, and many neighbors stopped by during the day. All those people, wandering about that large house. Just like my party tonight.

Then that little girl went missing. They searched and searched, and then they finally found her. Dead. In the—

Basement.

The basement.

Fuck.

I haven't checked the basement.

THIRTY-SIX

THE DOOR TO THE basement stands at the end of a long hallway. I check two other rooms along the way, finding nothing. The last room before the basement is the office; I walk in and turn on the light.

"Maggie?"

No answer.

This room has always prickled my skin. This room and the foyer area near the stairs. These are the spaces that have a different feel, like swimming in a warm pool and suddenly hitting a cold spot. I glance at the bookshelves, to the spot Maggie found what she said was blood.

Maybe that explains everything. Maybe I did buy a haunted house.

I turn off the office light and leave before I get carried away with this particular train of thought.

I open the basement door and descend the carpeted stairs. The staircase takes a ninety-degree turn, at which point the carpeted steps turn to unstained wood. The only finished areas of the basement are the steps visible from the upstairs door. The rest of the space is an ugly, sterile void, and I wonder why Logan Yates never bothered making something nice of it. Maybe he thought he had enough living space already.

Or maybe he didn't like the idea of being underground.

The bottom three steps creak like weak bones. The first thing I notice as I step into the room is that the lights are on.

"Maggie?"

Silence.

The basement fills the footprint of the house, no small thing. A series of fluorescent lights hang in arrays from the exposed wood ceiling, the harsh light giving a sheen to the smooth concrete floor. Sheetrock covers the walls; this room is morgue cold.

Not a lot of places to hide in here, but I walk the space. Cobwebs in the corners, dry and wispy, but otherwise, the basement is clean. I run my fingertips along the walls, as if I might sense a pocket of energy, a hiding place. But nothing.

A scattering of carpet scraps covers parts of the concrete floor in no apparent pattern. I don't even recognize this carpet—must be left over from when the house was originally built.

There's only one door down here, and I haven't opened it since we first moved in. It sits at the entrance to the small utility room in the back corner of the basement. I go in.

Furnace, AC, pair of hot water heaters, sprinkler valve, pipes and ducts, cable and internet wiring. Everything in perfect order, or so I was told from the inspection report.

The room hums, the AC blowing through the ducts, delivering cool air to all of the house's lower-floor registers. There's a separate AC system for the upper floors by the laundry room, two floors above. Like the rest of the basement, the utility room is sparse and clean, with only a thin layer of dust coating everything.

I call for my daughter, yielding nothing. When I walk around the mechanical units, I find no opening large enough into which a little girl could crawl through.

As with the pond, I'm happy not to have found her here, because this feels like a space where only tragic things happen.

Outside the utility room, I scan the overhead lights and wonder why they were already on. Would this even be a fun place for kids to play? It's big and open enough, it could be a spot to kick around a ball, I guess. I think, *Would Christopher and I have played down here as seven-year-olds?*

I turn, taking the entirety of it in. *Hell yes, we would have.* I don't know what exactly we would have played, but this is the kind of blank-canvas space just waiting for a world of make-believe.

On my way out, a random thought hits me. I think about this room in all its degrees of empty and cold. And then I think, what's the point of the carpet scraps? There aren't that many of them and they don't provide any comfort or design, so why bother with them at all? It seems a haphazard piece of ornamentation.

I decide to look under each of them. There are maybe two dozen in all, but what I discover is under the seventh. One of the larger scraps, maybe six square feet.

It takes me a moment to absorb what I'm looking at after I remove the carpet scrap. A thick piece of plastic, perfectly square, perhaps a yard wide. Red. The plastic rests flush with the floor, with no visible clearance on any edge. It's unlikely anyone walking over the carpet scrap would've sensed it at all.

There're two small cutouts on opposite sides of the plastic, little more than the width of my fingers. Handles, it seems.

I reach down, inserting my fingers into the holes, and lift. The square piece—heavier than it looks—lifts off the inch-wide shelf of concrete that held it in place.

What lies beneath doesn't make any sense at all.

A lever attached to a circular door. The door: gray, smooth, gleaming metal. Steel, I'd guess.

Then it hits me.

A safe. This is Logan Yates's hidden safe. There was nothing in the paperwork for the house about a safe, yet here it is. Right beneath me. Not a bad hiding spot to store important documents, maybe some gold coins. A bit of cash, just in case. It'll likely be open and empty or locked tight with a mystery inside.

I grab the handle, yank clockwise, then discover it is indeed unlocked. When I open the door, I get the biggest surprise of all.

It's not a safe.

THIRTY-SEVEN

A LIGHT SHINES UP in my face. I blink against the unexpected glare, refocus, and see a metal ladder hooked on the upper ledge, leading at least six feet down.

It's a room.

I'm staring down at a blue floor, linoleum from the looks of it. The room extends to one side, out of view, and now I know with clarity, if not logic, that Maggie is down here. Dead or alive, my little girl is down here. I've never been so certain.

A trickle of drool falls from my lips and plummets to the shiny floor below.

"Maggie?" I yell.

And this time, an answer.

A glorious answer.

"Daddy?"

"Mags!"

I start to scramble down but she appears immediately. Looks up at me, hair back, eyes wide as a rabbit on the run.

"Are you okay?" I'm desperate to hold her.

She nods, unable to hide her fear.

"Can you come up here?"

She does without hesitation, climbing the rungs and nearly flinging herself onto the carpet scrap. She grabs me and wraps her arms around my neck, bursting into sobs the second her face buries into my chest. I reach and stroke her hair, wrap my arm around her back, hold her tight. Her tears catch my forearm, running hot.

I have a thousand questions, but for now I just squeeze her. Questions will come soon, but gratitude and comfort take priority.

She's okay.

She's okay.

We're okay.

After an eternal hug, I gently push her back so I can look into her eyes. Her bloodshot, wet eyes.

"What is that place?" I ask.

"Please don't be mad."

"Sweetie, I'm not mad. I just want to know what that place is and why you were down there."

She sniffles, wipes her nose with her arm. "It's the secret room. I found it last week. I...I didn't want to tell you. I wanted it for myself. Bo doesn't even know."

"But what *is* it?"

"It's a hidden place. I think where you can lock yourself in if you're scared."

Not a safe, I think, but a *safe room*. Logan Yates's safe room.

"What were you doing in there?"

"I...I went downstairs to spy on your party. I'm sorry."

"It's okay, Mags."

"And I got bored, so I came down here. Went down into the secret room. But…"

"But what?"

"Someone closed the lid."

"What?"

"Was it you?"

The panic that has ebbed and flowed through my system for the past fifteen minutes ramps up again.

"No. It wasn't me. I just found it."

Someone closed the lid.

And they placed the plastic cover and carpet back over, concealing the room altogether.

"You couldn't get out?" I ask her. "The cover was unlocked."

She shakes her head, and a fresh wave of sadness washes over her face. "The lid was too heavy. I can open it when I stand over it, but I never had to try to push it open from the steps. I couldn't do it." The sadness turns into new tears. "I yelled and yelled, and no one heard me."

Someone at my party wandered down here and trapped Maggie inside this place. Maybe they even saw her and followed her down to the basement.

"I won't ever go in there again," Mags says.

"You certainly won't." I set aside my urge to see what's in the room so I can get my daughter to a place of comfort. "Come on, let's get out of here."

I carry her upstairs, something she doesn't need but I know she wants.

I call out as I reach the main level. "I found her!" Bo comes rushing down the hallway to meet us, Maya in tow. I set Maggie down, and Bo gives his sister a hug followed by a light smack on the head.

"Why were you hiding?" he said. "We were all scared."

"I *wasn't*."

I calm them down, lead them back to the living room, then shout upstairs for my father to join us. He does, his shoulders sagging in relief as he spots his granddaughter.

Maggie tells them what happened, and I jump in right after.

"Did any of you know about this room?"

A collective *no*.

"And none of you were in the basement tonight?"

More shakes of the head.

"Check the security cameras," Maya says.

"I will," I say. "But first, I want to go back in there."

THIRTY-EIGHT

I DESCEND THE METAL rungs and feel like I'm boarding a submarine. As bizarre as the situation is, now that I know Mags is all right, I admit to myself this is a little exciting. Like I'm discovering pieces to a mystery I'm compelled to solve.

Da's voice from above. "What's down there, then?"

I look up the hole at him. He gazes down, hands on knees.

"I'll let you know."

As my foot touches the floor, I take my first breath down here. The air is stale and unpleasant. I turn ninety degrees to the single side that has an opening.

My first thought: *It's twice as big as I expected.*

My second thought: *Nobody bothered to clear this place out. Maybe no one besides Logan Yates even knew this place existed.*

The room stretches probably fifteen feet long and eight feet wide. This is way more than a safe room. This is a Dublin flat.

To my left: a small bookshelf and a twin bed, the latter of which looks to be freshly slept in. Back left, two small walls form an L, creating a room within the room. Bathroom, maybe. To my right, a seating area with a single leather chair, barely worn. Behind that, two stainless-steel racks stacked with food, the kind of which takes years to expire. And water. Containers and containers of water.

I take a few steps in and see what's on the other side of the racks: a small kitchenette with a very old microwave and electric stove.

The first thing I investigate is the bookshelf, still loaded with volumes. Mostly hardcover, mostly business books. The title fonts have a universal plumpness, suggesting something from thirty years ago, and the titles support that assumption.

Barbarians at the Gate

Liar's Poker

The One Minute Manager

In Search of Excellence

Complementing the business titles are a few survivalist volumes.

SAS Survival Handbook

Live Off the Land

How to Thrive in a Radiated World

Not one piece of fiction, least not that I can see.

Logan Yates must have built this room when he built this house in the eighties and planned it as a bomb shelter. A nuclear bomb shelter.

I glance up. Drunken fluorescents puke garish, blinding light. Way brighter than necessary, already giving me a headache. Next to the lights, air vents. Must run all the way outside, but it would have to be processed air—no use directly breathing in radiation. That's probably chapter one of *How to Thrive in a Radiated World*.

There are no corners in here. Rather, the walls curve before flattening into the ceiling and floor. I rap on the nearest wall—bone white—and hear the sound that only comes from knocking on metal. So my analogy was right. This place is basically the hull of a submarine.

"What do you see?" my father calls out.

I scan the room and say the first thing that comes to mind.

"A time capsule."

A few more steps in and I feel a slow build in my anxiety, like walking deeper into an uncharted cave. My guess about the small subroom was correct: a toilet, sink, and impossibly small shower. So there's plumbing in here as well.

On the other side of the bathroom is the one thing that wasn't readily visible when I first came down here.

An actual safe.

How about that? A safe inside a safe room.

The metal safe is ink black, contrasting sharply against the curved white wall behind it. Not huge, maybe two cubic feet, with a keypad lock on the door. The door is closed, and I try the handle with no luck. I squat and give the safe a push with both hands, but it doesn't give. Likely bolted, or even welded, to the floor.

Well, it's my safe now, and I make a mental note to hire a locksmith to open it. If Logan Yates ran away, the safe is probably empty. But if he was murdered, chances are there are interesting things behind that black steel door.

"Come on, then," my father shouts. "I'm dying to know."

"If your knees can take the ladder, come see for yourself."

"You know they can't."

"Well, then."

I've seen everything, so I head back out. When I reach the steps, I ask Da to close the lid, which he does. There's both a locking mechanism and a handle on the inside of the lid, giving access control to anyone inside the safe room. I lock and unlock the lid with success, then open it. It's surprisingly heavy to open from this angle, and I can see why Mags couldn't do it.

When I emerge, I tell Da what I found down there. He scratches his beard and leans toward me. "Quite the mystery house you have."

"So it seems."

"And now what are you going to do?"

I realize the real question is *what do I want to do?* All this wealth, and what I want to do are the things for which money is meaningless. I want to stare into Holly's face and watch the corners of her eyes bunch as she smiles as me. I want the four of us to be back in our crappy apartment in Baltimore, struggling. I want to relive the birth of my children.

I close the lid and head back upstairs, not answering him.

Maya is reserved with her questions, maybe because the kids are here. But I fill them in on the room Maggie found and what I believe it is. This discussion ends with my strict instructions forbidding any playing in that room, stressing to them we can't be certain there's an active air source supplying it.

Bo asks if he can at least see the room if I go with him. I reply yes, knowing if I don't, his curiosity could overpower my rules. But later, I say, telling them to go to bed.

Maggie asks if they can sleep with me tonight. She hasn't asked this since Holly died, when the kids spent a whole week in my bed.

"Of course," I tell her.

The kids leave, and as I watch them trod up the stairs, I have a momentary stirring of fear. What if someone is still in the house? Maybe a party guest who decided not to leave?

"You checked all rooms upstairs?" I ask my father. "All closets, under beds?"

"I think so. But it doesn't matter. You found her."

"I wasn't thinking about Maggie."

It takes a moment for his thought process to catch up to mine. "Oh, yeah?"

"Someone closed her in there," I say. "It wasn't us, and I don't think Bo was lying about the safe room. Someone from the party wandered off into the basement."

"We were pretty thorough. Not sure where anyone else could be hiding."

I agree with him, but I go around and lock all the doors, then check in on the kids, who are little bumps under the covers of my bed. *Come up soon*, Mags insists. *I will*, I tell her.

Back downstairs, I pour another drink, numbly confident there's no immediate threat. With Maya and Da nearby, I check the security camera footage. The problem is I have one interior camera, which only captures the foyer; there's no way of seeing if anyone left the party to head down to the basement.

The foyer camera does have an angle on the stairs, however, and I see the moment when Maggie descended them two hours ago. She pauses on the last step and cranes her neck, looking for a clear path. She must find one, because she suddenly bolts across the foyer in the direction of the hallway leading to the basement, until she's out of view.

I check for any other motion clips from this camera, finding none until the guests start to leave. I count them all as they pass through the front door. No one is unaccounted for, and no one heads down the hallway toward the basement.

The thing is, the back of the kitchen has an opening that leads to the same hallway, so someone could have gone to the basement from there and escaped the camera's eye.

Maybe I need more cameras. That thought starts me thinking of Owen Brace, and that in turn makes me realize that he—or any of his installation team—knows the exact angle of all my cameras. What if the person writing the letters is someone from his company or Brace himself?

No, it doesn't make sense. How would he possibly know I'd come to him to install the cameras in the first place?

I flip to the motion captures from the camera mounted outside over my garage door. Neighbors walk back to their homes. Others get into their cars and drive away. No one loiters. No one turns around, comes back, peers through the little windows of the garage doors.

Normal.

Everything looks normal.

Of course, I know better.

There's nothing normal about Bury at all.

THIRTY-NINE

Bury, New Hampshire
Day Thirty

IT'S THE LAST WEEK of August, my one-month anniversary in Bury. Time weighs heavy on me, like I've been here for years. I feel older than I should, with none of the wisdom accompanying it.

The day after the party, I didn't seek out and confront any of my guests. I didn't go by the police station and tell Chief Sike about what happened, though I still might.

What I did was buy a gun. A shotgun, along with a box of shells. Didn't have to put my name on a registry. Didn't even have to show my ID. Were I to buy a handgun, I'd have to do a lot more paperwork and spend a few days waiting. But a shotgun that could kill three people at once if they stood close enough together? No problem.

Live free or die.

Now I'm on the couch, trying to make a dent in *Ulysses*. I vowed to commit thirty minutes a day to Joyce, and I'm halfway through today's promise when my father bursts through the front door, red-jowled and moving with the urgency of someone who's just witnessed a horrific crime.

Then I see the piece of paper in his hand. And I know. I know because of the cold that leeches into my stomach and the instant watering of my mouth, signaling a poison in need of a purge.

I don't even give him the chance to tell me what he's found.

"It's another one," I say. "Another letter."

His unruly white hair is especially electric. His beard adds a look of fear rather than wisdom for once.

"You're fecking right, it is."

When he holds the paper out to me, I see how much his hand is shaking. The rule growing up was not to be worried about anything unless Da was worried. That's when you knew something was bad.

"Where was it?" I ask.

"Nearly in the street. Could have been found by anyone."

"No. Not likely." My father takes a couple of walks a day, usually around the same times. They knew he'd find it.

My urge to read it straightaway is supplanted by a need for assurance. Even a crumb. I look into my father's eyes for the millionth time in my life and hope he'll tell me everything will be okay. I don't need to believe it. I just need to hear it.

"Is it bad?" I ask.

He doesn't hesitate.

"Aye, son. It's bad."

FORTY

Mr. Marlowe.

By now you realize how much We know about you and your family. And your house. We know so very much about your house.

There is only one way to get Us to leave. Your money, Mr. Marlowe. The money appeared into your life at random, and now it will disappear. You can go back to being who you were. Just a poor bartender with a dead wife.

Don't try to run, don't try to hide. That will only make things worse.

Instructions will follow.

Sincerely,
WE WHO WATCH

FORTY-ONE

I MAKE IT UNTIL 6:00 p.m.

Hours of boiling rage and stewing paranoia. Time spent making sure my kids were fine and accounted for without trying to raise their suspicions. Telling Da to hell with the police, that they don't seem inclined or able to help and it's high time I did something about this myself.

Time waiting for Peter Ainsworth to get home from work.

At five o'clock, I started drinking, and it was a fiery itch to make it that long.

I kept it to two drinks. For now.

I've googled his address; my drive will be less than three miles.

At six exactly, I leave the house, leaving Da with the kids. He thinks my plan is a bad one. I tell him he could be right.

I leave the shotgun at home.

As I back the Subaru into the cul-de-sac, I wish I'd gone ahead and gotten that new car already. Something big. Something intimidating, along the lines of a black Escalade with windows tinted space black. That's the kind of vehicle I should be arriving in at Ainsworth's house.

The Google Assistant tells me where to go. I obey.

I arrive at 6:10, sunlight still assaulting, leaves glimmering like schools of fish. No car in the driveway. I park on the street.

The house is no small thing. Not bigger than mine, but impressive. I can see Peter trying to be like Logan Yates and coming up a few hairs short.

I have every letter with me, nicely tucked in a large envelope. I grab it from the passenger seat.

Out of the car, up a concrete path that winds for no reason. I knock, thinking, *This door is not as impressive as mine.*

Forever passes, and I do a quick glance for security cameras. Nothing obvious, but that doesn't mean they're not there.

He's not home.

And I think, of *course* he's not. He's in finance. No way he leaves his office by six. I should've known better.

I'm about to leave when I hear footsteps from inside the house. Light but audible.

The dead bolt slides open, followed by the door. Peter Ainsworth is not the person on the other side. It's his daughter.

"Aidan," she says, this wisp of a thing.

"You have a good memory."

"I remember memorable things," she says. A white V-neck top hangs over her long, sinewy frame, little more than a second skin. Green eyes blaze against pale cheeks.

"Is your father home?"

She leans a shoulder against the doorframe and allows half a smile. "You mean you didn't come to see me?"

I thought her first comment was borderline flirty, but there's no mistaking her second. I'm more than twice her age.

"I just want to talk to your dad," I say.

"Do you remember my name?"

"No, I'm sorry. I don't."

She straightens. "Willow."

I sigh. "Willow, is your dad here?"

"Your accent is sexy, you know that?"

I don't want to acknowledge the comment. I don't even want to be here anymore. This kid seems the type to make up a story about how I came on to her, just to watch me squirm.

Then, movement in the foyer and into view comes a man. No, a boy. Older than Willow, I'm guessing, but not much. A black tank top tries to cling to his bony frame but fails. Arms dripping in tattoos. Mossy stubble, and stringy hair poking from beneath a gray wool skullcap. It's a thousand degrees outside and this guy is wearing a wool hat.

"Who's that, then?" I ask.

She bats her eyes. "Are you jealous?" She turns to the guy. "You hear that, Steve? He's jealous of you."

Steve laughs. "He's, like, fifty."

"And I'm guessing you're over eighteen," I say. "And she's not."

He swaggers toward me and it looks ridiculous. "None of your goddamn business."

"No," I say. "It's not." I turn to the girl. "I'm just here to talk to your dad, Willow. Though I assume he's not home, otherwise *Steve* likely wouldn't be here. Right?"

Steve moves into my face, places a hand on my chest. "Maybe you should leave, bitch."

He bares his teeth, and they're disgusting enough, I suspect meth. I cobble together just enough sense to not release all my fury on this strung-out loser. How good it would feel to take the energy I expend on the heavy bag and give it all to Steve. Despite the two drinks in me, the kid wouldn't last ten seconds.

"You'll be wanting to take that hand off me," I say. I hear my accent coming off strong as I transport to the days of the pub, where there were dozens of Steves I had to throw out of the pub. "I've broken lots of wrists in my day, none of them mine."

His eyes flash, anger and drugs. If he's really high, he might do something stupid, in which case I'll have to step up. I'd certainly prefer not to.

Then I hear the purr of an engine behind me, the kind attached to an expensive car. I turn and see a gleaming obsidian Lexus slide into the driveway.

"Fuck," Willow says. "He's home early."

Steve bolts back into the house and, I'm guessing, through the back door, over the fence, and back to the sewer he came from. He's more scared of Peter Ainsworth than of me, apparently. Good riddance.

"Too bad," she says to me. "It was just getting interesting."

I stare down at her. "I knew girls like you growing up. Most exciting things ever at fifteen. Fresh and full of life. Ten years later, they were brittle as bark on a dead tree, worn-out."

I don't say this just because I want to, which I do. I want to see her eyes, how they change. I haven't ruled out this girl as someone involved in what's happening in my life.

Sure enough, those eyes cloud over, the brightness muted in one narrowed squint. In the slightest of facial adjustments, Willow jumps from coy to evil in a single beat.

"How's your freak house?" she says.

"You've got quite a mouth."

She blows me a kiss, frosted. "I guess you'll never know."

I hear the garage door open, but the sedan doesn't pull in. I approach as Peter steps out of the car. He wears a suit so crisp, it could cut diamonds. The man's visible perfection enhances my belief he's guilty of something; the best-looking people are always hiding something.

"Mr. Marlowe," he says. Not Aidan, not Marlowe, but *Mr. Marlowe*. Just like in the letters.

"I need to talk to you," I say.

He sighs, shoulders drop just a touch. "Whatever Willow's done, I'm sorry. I know she rides her bike over to your place from time to time. I told her not to bother you."

I wonder if he even knows his daughter. Wonder if he knows about the company she keeps. "It's not her. It's you."

"What about me?"

I hold up the envelope containing the letters. "I need to know if you're the one responsible for these."

His eyes don't register anything I can detect. I imagine he's good at that all the time.

"Am I supposed to know what those are?"

"Aye."

He reaches back into his car, and for a moment, a vision strikes me. In this vision, he retrieves a gun and shoots me right here in his driveway.

Instead, he comes back out with a black leather satchel, well stuffed.

"I've had a long day," he says. "If you're going to accuse me of something, then I'm at least going to sit on my couch with a drink as you do it. Come inside."

This isn't what I expected, but I do as he says, passing through the garage and into the house.

There's a fully stocked bar next to the living room, and Peter makes quick work of pouring himself a scotch. He offers me one, and I resist temptation and decline, knowing two other drinks already sit inside me. I'm ashamed how hard it was to say no.

There's no sign of Willow, though I'm sure she's around a nearby corner, all ears. I don't care. I've come to say what I need to and can't be bothered with peripheral audiences.

Peter takes off his suit coat, folds it in half, and places it on the arm of a massive sectional. Like his car, this couch is black and gleaming. He sits in what I'm guessing is his usual spot, sips his scotch, then eases back into the cushion. Peter closes his eyes for perhaps two seconds and takes a deep breath, and I consider this is probably the most he allows himself to relax all day.

The moment passes.

"Okay," he says. "Tell me."

FORTY-TWO

I HAND HIM THE first letter, and he reads it.

"You think I wrote this?"

"I think you've got a connection to my house that makes it possible, yes."

Peter reads it again, this time with more care. A guilty man wouldn't read the letter a second time; he'd already be familiar with it enough. Or maybe he's playing me.

"And why on earth would I do something like this?" he asks.

"That's what I'm here to find out," I say.

"Are there more?" he asks.

"Yes."

"Show me."

I do. He reads them in order, then passes through each one a second time.

"The last one," he says. "It's different."

"What do you mean?"

"Here, look." The perfectly manicured fingernail on his left index finger points to the words. "In this one, the word *we* is capitalized. That's not the case in the first letters. Plus, the tone seems…different. Not as coy. And the last one is signed *sincerely*. The first three have more creative sign-offs."

I take the pages from him and read through them again, seeing he's right. How did I miss this?

"Have you talked to Walter?" Peter asks.

"Walter?"

"Sike. Police chief."

"I did, but not recently. I need to give him an update, because something else happened."

He straightens his spine against the cushion. "What?"

Either I'm leaning toward Peter not being the culprit or my need for alcohol outweighs my concern. "I think I'll take that drink after all. Can I help myself?"

A flick of his hand. "Sure."

I pour the same scotch he's drinking, with a little more volume. After a healthy sip—and my, this is the good stuff—I begin talking, pacing the room as I do. I tell Peter about my life from the moment Holly died until this conversation. The timing of the lottery win. The way I discovered Bury, as if predestined to. The energy I feel in the house, and how I know about the disappearances of the previous occupants, which includes his wife. I tell him about receiving the first letter and then my talk with Abril and Carlos. Then the subsequent letters, including the connection to Christopher.

I don't tell him how Christopher died.

Finally, I tell Peter the real reason I held the housewarming party, finishing my speech by describing to him what happened to Maggie in the basement of the house.

This, more than anything, spikes his interest.

"I had no idea about that safe room," he says.

"I figured, because it still has furnishings in it."

He looks up at the ceiling, thinking. "I've probably been in that basement a dozen times over the years. Never knew."

"No one thinks to move a piece of carpet scrap. No reason to."

"When I listed the home," Peter says, "we had all sorts of people in there. Movers to store all of Logan's things. Home inspector. Appraiser. Cleaners. No one said a thing about that room. And if it wasn't on the appraisal report, that means the room was added some time after the house was originally built and Logan never pulled any city permits to do the work."

"And I'm guessing he never even told his daughters. All the time they were growing up there. Never knew."

Peter shifts his gaze to mine. "He must have had it better concealed back then. But I think you're right. Cora never said anything to me. Though how you build something like that without your kids knowing..."

"And someone at my party followed my daughter down into the basement and closed the lid on her."

Peter wears amazement awkwardly, probably because it happens to him rarely.

"And there's a safe in there," I add.

"A safe in the safe room?"

"About as secure as you could get for your important documents. Your secrets. You wouldn't happen to know any combinations he used, would you?"

Peter laughs, white teeth gleaming against his tanned face. "I spent my professional life working with Logan Yates at his company. And I'm not one inch closer to his secrets than I was when I started. All I have are guesses."

I tilt the glass back into my mouth, only to realize I've polished off my drink. How did that happen so fast? Rather than wrestle with good sense, I go over and pour myself another.

"And what are your guesses?" No, that's not really the question I want to ask. I narrow my scope. "What do you think happened to everyone?"

Everyone. Logan Yates. His daughter Cora, Peter's wife. Logan's other daughter Rose, the mystery writer. Rose's son, Max, who was only eleven years old.

Peter leans forward and sets his glass down, rests his forearms on his knees. This is the first time I notice the wedding band on his finger.

"I struggle to envision a scenario where they're all alive," he says.

"What do you know?" I ask. "I mean, do you have any idea at all?"

There's a painting over the fireplace. Modern art, black dots, and red swirls. There's more chaos than comfort in it.

"Cora had been acting...more intense than usual," Peter says. "She was pretty wound up most of the time, but she'd been lashing out more frequently. She had...I don't know. A darkness about her. I'd see glimpses of it, but even with me, she'd keep it tucked away. But ever since her sister, Rose, moved back to town a couple months earlier, Cora seemed more and more unhinged." He presses a palm to his forehead, lets it stay there, as if soothing a sudden ache. "She told me she was going out that night, that was it. No other explanation. Only later did I find out she was over at Logan's house with him and Rose."

"Abril, the housekeeper, saw them," I say.

"That's right."

"But Max wasn't there, right? Abril told me he was at a sleepover."

"That's right." The palm lifts. "He was spending the night with a friend. Micah Wallin. His dad, Alec, had become friends with Rose. She'd called him last minute to see if he could take Max for the night. In fact, Alec Wallin was the last person to see any of them. Cora never came home that night, but Rose showed up at Alec's house the next morning to get Max."

"And the cops talked to Alec?"

"They did. I did as well. Alec said Rose seemed stressed out." He looks to the floor. "No...that's not quite right. He said she seemed scared."

"Scared of what?"

"I don't know. But she mentioned moving back to Milwaukee, where'd she just come from. But she never made it there. The last known trace of Rose and her son was from a security camera at the Boston Logan Airport parking garage. She drove one of Logan's cars there a couple hours after getting Max. The car was found, but no trace of Rose or Max."

"So they flew somewhere."

He shakes his head. "No record of it. And that doesn't even account for Cora or Logan."

Here we are, two men with our only commonality being our departed wives. Mine forever, his still uncertain.

"You really think your wife is dead?" I ask.

He thinks on this a moment and completes the task with a final gulp of his drink. "Were Logan the only one missing, I'd think he was running from something. The law. His enemies. God knows he had plenty of those, and he was the type of person to have an escape plan in place. Like the safe room. A backup plan. But Logan and Cora both went missing, and Rose seemed to be running. That makes me think something happened. Something bad. So when you ask me if I think she's dead, I can't help but say yes. I don't know why and I don't know how, but I don't believe Cora is anymore of this earth."

"That's…that's just awful."

Peter leans back again, this time allowing himself a seemingly rare moment of comfort, head on cushion, eyes to the ceiling.

"It's not awful," he says. "She wasn't a kind person. And her concept of love was distorted at best. But I miss her. Miss her with a ferocity. I guess you know what that's like."

"Aye," I say, thinking *ferocity* is the exact right word. When the hurt of solitude fills you with rage. When you want to hit a wall with your bare knuckles just to have pain somewhere definable, rather than just an uncurable ache of existence. "I felt the same way after losing my brother," I say. "Long time ago. Then my mum. And then, the worst pain of all, Holly." I keep drinking, no longer caring the result, and maybe that's how it's always been. "It's been said loss can either define you, break you, or make you stronger. But that's shite. Because loss…*real* loss. It doesn't do any of those things. What it does is festers. Sits inside you like a cancer. Better some days, worse others. But it never goes away, and you still die in the end."

He looks up at me. "That's about the most depressing thing I've ever heard, Mr. Marlowe."

"Marlowe," I tell him, sipping again. "Just Marlowe."

He clears his throat, I think, just to fill the silence. "So what are you going to do next?"

It's the perpetual question.

"That answer keeps changing every hour." I walk over and place my empty glass on his bar top, which is yet another thing that gleams around Peter Ainsworth. "My last decision was to come over here and confront you. I was convinced you were behind the letters, and lord, did I feel like hurting you. Hell, maybe it *was* you, but I don't think so. I don't feel it in you, but maybe my radar is just jammed up. But *someone* knows everything about me. About my past. My house. About the lottery. And they're trying to scare me into giving them my money. I know there's a reason I won the lottery, but it wasn't to give it away in the face of anonymous threats."

Wine-colored curtains edge the windows, deep and plush. I imagine when they're pulled tight, this room is a tomb. Peter sweeps his empty glass in an arc. "Well, as I think you can see, the last thing I need is your money, Marlowe."

"So what would you do if you were me?" I ask.

He pauses, looks over his shoulder and out the front window. "Hard to imagine me being too upset by it all, considering how little I really care about life anyway. Actually, receiving creepy letters would be a welcome relief—maybe I'd feel something. But I think I'd go online. Find out how much information is really out there about me. What someone could learn if they really set about it. Maybe that'll narrow down your list of suspects." He grins. "It's all rather like a game of Clue, isn't it?"

"Not yet, it isn't." I get up to leave, and as I do, I consider reaching over to him and shaking his hand, then decide against it. "In Clue, the dead body comes at the beginning."

FORTY-THREE

I DRIVE BACK FROM the Ainsworth's, likely past my legal ability to do so. Along the way, my mind reels from the possibility of there being two letter writers, since the letters were indeed different. I feel like I'm inside a snow globe; someone keeps shaking my world then peering in at me.

I pull into the garage, stumble out of the car, almost losing my footing. Proper Irishman can't even hold his drink.

I take one swing at the heavy bag, and it accepts my blow without a wince. It might have laughed at me.

In the house, Da and the kids are eating dinner.

"How'd it go?" he asks. Then he sees the alcohol in my gait and says, "I see. That bad, then?"

I don't answer. His questions make me mad, and I don't know why.

"There's plenty more to eat," Da says. "Sorry we started without you. The littles were nibbling on my ankles."

I wave him off. A shadow passes over his face, one I'd seen many times before.

"Come eat with your family, Aidan."

"I'm not hungry."

Then I look at the faces of my kids. My two beautiful children, each of whom wears a concern heavier than any seven-year-old should. But in this moment, I'm ashamed to say I don't care. I don't want to take care of anyone, including myself. Don't want to be beholden to anyone. Answer to anyone. I just want to be free to put the business end of my new shotgun against my throat, if that's what I fancy to do.

Then Maggie speaks.

"We're going to play in the boat after dinner."

I look down at her, heat flushing my face.

"The what?"

"The boat," she says.

Bo gives me one of his thousand serious looks. "She's talking about the room in the basement. Since it looks like a submarine, we call it the boat."

This is when I lose my mind.

"You are not allowed to go in there!" I'm not talking. I'm not suggesting. I'm shouting. Right here, five feet from their shocked little faces. "We had this conversation. Why do you think it's okay to ignore what I told ya?"

Bo tries to question me. A mistake.

"But I thought we could—"

"*YOU ARE NOT TO GO DOWN THERE!*" And the thing is, as bad as I feel, I also feel good. I want to yell.

"Don't you get it?" I lean over Maggie. No, not lean. Tower. "If you go in there, you could drown. It's dangerous, and you're too young to know any better. Don't you get it? You could *DROWN!*"

This is when it hits me. It hits hard, and I've never experienced anything like it before.

My lungs collapse in on themselves, taking away all my ability to breathe. Sucking in is like trying to drink though a flattened straw. Sudden, searing pain through my chest, and I claw at it with my right hand.

"Good Christ, Aidan, what is it?" Da starts to rise from his chair, and I wave him back.

What is it?

I know what this is.

I'm dying. Heart attack. Has to be.

Yes. Death, please.

Right away, sir.

"Fine," I sputter. "I'm fine." The words barely come out, but maybe they're convincing enough to keep him from calling an ambulance. I remove my hand from my chest, try to appear okay. When I look at the faces of my kids for maybe the last time, I see Holly. Holly telling me to come to her.

I turn and push as hard as I can against what feels like a thousand-pound snake squeezing around me, then leave the room. I want to die. I want to see my wife. But I won't let it happen in front of the kids. They can't watch both their parents take their final breaths.

I make it to the office, close and lock the door, then let this thing take me. It feasts, swallowing me whole. The pain in my chest moves to my ribs, which feel like they're about to shatter. I drop to my knees, then to the floor altogether, soon seizing into a fetal position as I struggle to breathe. Sweat pours, my entire body slick. The heat. Oh god, it's so fucking hot. But don't scream. Just don't let them hear you. They'll find you later when it's over, but don't let them hear it all happen.

A knock at the door. "Aidan, open up."

"Go away," I manage, my voice raspy.

"Either you open the door or I'm calling emergency services."

I'm feet from the door handle. Even reaching over to it would require strength I don't think I have. And I don't want to. I want to be alone, in this office. This place where the current is strong, and now I'll become washed away in it.

I bow my head, manage to suck in the slightest taste of air. What little of it I take in is morphine for my lungs.

"I'm fine," I whisper.

"Eh?"

"I'm *fine*."

"Like hell, Aidan. You're scaring me and the kids to death. Open the fecking door, or I'm making that call."

"Give…just give me a minute," I say.

His silence is acquiescence, and I figure in sixty seconds, I'll know which way this thing is taking me. The clock on the wall is a faux antique bought by the interior designer; real antiques didn't have second hands. I watch it tick the seconds away while I scan my body for things exploding inside. But my heart doesn't hurt the way it did just moments ago.

The minute's up, and there's a rap at the door again. The sound is distinct: the handle of his cane.

Still on my knees, I reach out and manage to unlock the door. He opens it, looks down at me.

"What's going on?"

I tell him the first thing I thought. "It felt like…like a heart attack."

He sweeps this aside with a stroke of his cane-clutching fist. "Marlowes don't have heart issues. Livers? Aye. But our hearts don't give out."

It's not as hot anymore, and I'm slowly catching more of my breath. "Well, thank god for your medical knowledge."

He leans over, looks down.

"Yer fine," he says.

"I'm falling apart."

"You live in a mansion, Aidan. You can take your complaints to someone else."

I rise from my knees, then wobble on my feet, feeling like a boxer who went ten rounds and lost by decision. "You know that's not fair," I say.

"Fair and fairies," he says. "Two things that don't exist." An old line I remember from childhood.

Childhood.

Another twinge in my heart. A gasp for air.

Then I know.

I know what this is. I know because Holly had described episodes like these from people she interacted with in her social work. People with problems, physical and mental. People who'd been abused. People with long-buried secrets destined to burrow their way to the surface one way or another.

Panic attack.

I just had my very first panic attack.

And it was triggered by...

"What was it I told the kids?" I ask Da.

"What?"

I can hear the blood pumping in my head. "Back there. In the kitchen, about not playing in the basement. What did I say?"

He clears his throat, sets both hands atop his cane, and peers so deep into me, I feel judged by god.

"You told them they canna play down there," he says, adding a squint, "because they could *drown*."

Jesus. I did really say that.

Drown.

It's been building for so long, and tonight, it finally broke through my skin. Through my mind, out into the open. Splitting me.

Everything catches up to me here. Now.

All my bank accounts, the money spread across all of them. Generating more in interest every day than I ever dreamed of making as a bartender. And yet, what's the point? None of it does a cent's worth of good to change the past. The skins we carry only shed if we cut them off, and cutting means pain.

I hold my father's gaze, knowing the real judgment hasn't even started. But I can't stop this. It has to come out.

"I need to talk to you."

"That so? 'Bout what?"

It feels like a boulder is making its way from my belly through my mouth, but I manage to reply.

"About Christopher."

FORTY-FOUR

I GO BACK OUT, apologize to the twins, blame everything on stress. It's true and it isn't, and it's the best I can do in this moment. I get limp hugs from each of them, and only after asking. Maggie tells me I scared them, and I can hear Holly sobbing from far away. Bo elects not to say anything, and for once, I'm grateful. To say I feel terrible is an understatement. The hardest part is it's about to get worse.

"I thought I was doing my best," I tell the twins. "But I can do better. I *will* do better. I promise." My forehead is still slick with sweat and my breathing is shallow, but I know I'm on the other side of this thing. For now.

"Grandpa and I need to talk, and I'll come up to your room in a bit. But please, don't go into the basement. Not until I make sure it's completely safe in there, okay?"

More nods, more silence. Maggie's eyes glisten in that post-cry way.

Da comes out of the office, pours himself a drink, then sits down on the living room couch.

"What is it, son?"

He doesn't call me *son* much.

I take a swallow, not even giving myself time to enjoy it. Dim the lights, then sit across from Da in the living room, an ocean of a coffee table between us. The purr of the nearby kitchen refrigerator is momentarily shattered by the tumbling of fresh-made ice into the freezer bin.

"The day he died, I was there," I say. I've rehearsed this so many times in my head, it seems Shakespearean coming out of my mouth. The role of a lifetime, one I'd never wish on anyone.

"I know that, Aidan. You found him."

I initiate an intimate gaze with the carpet, where I suspect it'll stay through most of this. "This is only going to work if you just let me say things straight through. Otherwise, I don't think I can do it."

"Well, then. Okay."

The alcohol has dried my tongue to tree bark.

I continue.

"It was late August, you remember. Christopher and I played some video games in the morning, but then he said he wanted to be alone. Acting weird that whole summer, I remember thinking. But that wasn't unusual. I remembered myself at fourteen. Hormones all-consuming. I figured he was just spending time alone…you know." I put my glass down. "So I didn't see him most of the day, and in the midafternoon, I went down to the banks of the Tolka, half looking for him out of boredom and half just wanting to check on the river. You remember how high it'd been running that year."

"Near record levels," Da says, breaking the oath of silence, but it already feels welcome.

"All those spring rains," I say, keeping my gaze down. "I went to the part of the river Christopher was partial to. Where we had that little fort we'd built, not much more than a collection of tree branches, twine, and old tarp. No one was ever down there but us, like a little hideaway."

"Aye, I recall." I can only imagine the visuals going through Da's head right now as I narrate the horror of that day fresh to him.

"Christopher was in the fort, didn't hear me coming. I shocked him. I remember that so clearly, how surprised he was to see me. I thought... again, you know. Maybe he had some nude magazines there, something like that. The way he turned around, the look of surprise on his face. But then I saw the blood. Blood on his hands."

"What?"

"Let me," I say. "Just let me keep going." Lord, this is as difficult as I'd ever imagined it. "He had...Christopher had, I saw it over his shoulder. He had a rabbit. Dead. All cut open. Right there on a piece of wood, its stomach ripped apart, blood and fur. I thought...at first I thought a dog maybe killed the rabbit and maybe Christopher found it. But then I saw the knife in his right hand. Razor blade knife, like an X-Acto."

My father takes a moment of the ensuing silence to rise from his chair, come over, sit next to me. My cushion leans toward his as he sits.

"Are you meaning to tell me he killed that rabbit?"

I nod, holding back tears.

"Maybe it was already dead."

"No," I tell him. This is when I finally make eye contact and his irises are the color of ghosts, and the bit of skin free from beard as white as a fish's underbelly. "He killed it, because he told me he did. After his initial shock at me finding him, he just spilled his guts. I think he was thankful to tell me, like it'd been a burden."

"That *what* had been a burden?" Alcohol and acrid breath swirl.

"That he'd been doing it for months. Capturing any animal he could with a simple trap he'd built, and then he'd…" That rabbit. The holes in the fur, perfect circles of black. "He'd torture them while they were alive. Spear them with flaming sticks. Or give them poison. Some he'd even just let die of thirst."

"This can't be true."

"I'm telling you it's what he told me," I say. "It's what I saw. This rabbit…it *had* been burned. Then cut open."

"He was having you on."

"No, Da." I shake my head. "He wasn't. Saw it myself."

"But why?"

"I've asked myself that same question for the past twenty years. I think it was who Christopher was becoming. Someone…someone with a darkness. A vast darkness."

My father's voice grows louder. "That's not who my son was. He was a sweet child."

"No," I say. "He wasn't. Not when you look back on him. All those times he was so quick to get into a rage. We fought more than brothers should have."

"But that's the two of you," Da says. "Both quick to anger, not just Christopher."

I know he's right. The slow burn I have inside of me at all times, just needing the smallest amount of fuel to ignite into an inferno. I've learned to control it the best I can over the years, and maybe Christopher would have as well.

"But he was different," I say. "He wasn't angry at all when he tortured and killed that rabbit. He was…*curious.*"

"God Almighty, Aidan. These things you're saying."

I nod. "He was excited to tell me. I think he was hoping I shared the same feelings. But I just stood there, listening as he went on about all the things he'd been doing that summer, wondering who my little brother had become. I barely said a word. I was just trying to process what I was seeing and hearing."

Da reaches over, places a hand on my back, gives a little rub. I don't know if this is affection or him needing support himself. "And then what?"

Heat spreads across my face, down my neck.

"He finally stopped talking. Just stood there, blood on his fingers, staring at me. It just took a few seconds for him to register what must've been horror on my face. The shame I felt for him. But he saw it and told me to say something. Just anything. So I did." I breathe through the words, and it's a struggle. "I told him he was a monster. Said I was going to tell you and Ma everything, because what he did was wrong. The kind of wrong I couldn't even make sense of."

As I take another sip, my hand shakes enough to slosh the gin near to the rim.

"That's when he lunged at me."

FORTY-FIVE

Twenty Years Ago
August 1998
Dublin, Ireland

RIGHT BEFORE CHRISTOPHER LUNGES at me, the breeze shifts and I catch the scent of the Tolka. The damp reeds of the riverbank, the peaty soil, moist and soft under my feet.

He pushes off of his back foot, and I have an impossible amount of thoughts bolting through my mind. I think about how close I'm standing to the water, only feet away. How Christopher doesn't even look like himself, his face twisted in fear and rage, a broken boy sloppily glued together, such a terrible face for someone only fourteen. How lonely this spot truly is, this haphazard fort, which has become a place of death and bones. And how my brother has an X-Acto blade in his bloody right hand, and he might just kill me in the next few seconds.

He lunges, screams as he does. I'm faster, finding time to sidestep, and Christopher stumbles past, nearly losing balance. But he's quick to recover, spinning and slinging the blade hand all at once. I feel the slightest pressure on my shoulder as I scramble away. When I look down, I see the surgical tear in the sleeve of my T-shirt, a concert shirt from the Pogues.

Blood trickles down the skin of my arm. Not a lot, not a little.

"You *cut* me!"

His eyes, both focused and distant, tell me he's heard no words of mine. He pants like a jackal fighting over food scraps.

"Calm down, okay?" I say, hoping I can talk him down. Maybe he's still in there somewhere. "This is crazy."

"You don't understand me," he says. "You don't understand who I am."

I put my hand over the wound, feel the wetness. This is the wound I would pay tribute to for the next four years, cutting my arms with an X-Acto blade on this same day. "Then let me understand."

A cloud passes over the sun, washing us in gray. Christopher doesn't answer. Instead, he comes at me again, faster this time.

In these seconds, I experience the first instance of my life when I consider death a true and likely possibility. Never really thought about it before, not for myself anyway, and not like this. This feels like I'm driving off a cliff, rocks far below, and nothing to do about it.

Details bleed away as he attacks this second time; I just see bits and pieces, freeze-frames from a horror film. At one point he's on top of me, hair glazed in sweat, blade still in his hand, my fingers clutching his wrist. In another moment we've switched positions, and I punch his stomach while trying to wrestle the knife free.

Entangled, spinning, falling, snarling. And somewhere in there, past the adrenaline, past the fear, there's my own rage, having woken up hard and fast. It wraps me up and holds me tight, a comforting blanket of blinding anger. One that tells me everything's going to be okay, and I simply have to do what I have to do. Protect myself at all costs. Kill or be killed.

Suddenly we're in the river, and I don't know how. Black and gray, cold as a corpse. Thrashing, screaming. I don't know if he has the X-Acto blade anymore. I don't know anything, only that he's trying to cut me open and I can't let that happen. For a half second, I visualize all my intestines bursting from my sliced belly like that snake-in-a-peanut-can gag.

Finally I'm more in control than he. I heave myself from the deep water onto a muddy shelf, maybe two feet deep, spit out a mouthful of foulness, still clutching my brother, grabbing his hair and his upper arms. He screams, he screams.

Let me go.

But I don't.

He's weakening, I'm not.

Then there's what happens next.

FORTY-SIX

Present Day

I STAMMER MY WORDS. "It's like I lost time."

"What happened, Aidan?" Da's voice is proper frost.

"I don't remember. I mean, I have zero memory of what happened next. Maybe…maybe I did at the time. Maybe I had that memory for a while before it lodged itself somewhere in my brain and I could no longer find it. To protect myself, I guess. Last thing I saw was the bank of the river. The little shelf of mud where I found some footing. I was holding him. Holding Christopher. He was screaming at me, and I…I don't know. I think I was scared that he still had the knife. Or maybe I was pulling him up to the shore with me. He was always…always a weak swimmer. But I just don't know. How is that possible?"

I look up because I don't want to be alone anymore. But there's no comfort in my father's face.

"Tell me what you have to tell me," he says.

Now my tears come, and when they start, they don't stop, and I taste them. They run into my mouth and I taste them. Pure salt, but I think of the river water that day. How it also ran into my mouth, and I had to spit it out so I didn't gag.

I lean forward, collapse on my thighs, a marionette with cut strings. I sob, my body shaking, but there's no hand on my back this time. My father's chill radiates, clashing with the heat of my shame, swirling and swirling, these opposing forces.

He says nothing else, offers me the silence, which I fill with my sadness. I cried hard after Holly's death, but this is different. This is a regurgitation. A poison leaving my body, maybe killing me on its way out.

I'm tired.

I'm so fucking tired.

And then, when it doesn't kill me, a lifetime later, I say, "All I know is I saw his face, looking up from the water and into the sky. Eyes wide open, probably two or three inches under the surface. Eyes wide open, not a movement to him."

"You killed him. You killed my boy."

I sit up, because there's nothing behind which to hide. Hardest thing I've ever had to do is looking into my father's eyes right now.

"I can't imagine I could have, but he was dead and we'd been fighting. And he'd had a knife, and I was scared. And—"

"But you had the upper hand," he says. "Said so yourself. You were pulling him up to shore."

"I don't know…"

"You were the stronger one, Aidan. You were always the stronger one. He was just a scrawny little thing. *What did you do to him?*"

The human mind is a place of ghosts, things that flitter in and out, appearing and vanishing without ever letting you know if they're real or not. When I think back to that day, which I do with crushing frequency, I have an image of my hands on top of Christopher's head, pushing him down, holding him just a few inches under the water as my feet sink deep into the muddy bank, and he's not even screaming, not even fighting back that hard, as if he knows it's what's supposed to happen, knows that if I don't do it, then he'll still be a monster, creeping ever closer to targets bigger than rabbits.

But that image is a ghost, just as the one I have where I flee Christopher's rage, scamper back onto dry land, and when I turn, he's already floating, a victim of nothing more than an acute inability to keep his own head above the river water before he swallows a lungful of it.

One ghost says I killed him. The other says I didn't. I'll spend the rest of my life not knowing which one is right, all while they both haunt me.

"I was so scared," I say. "I didn't know what happened, but I knew what it looked like."

"Did you *try* to save him?"

The tears come again, releasing themselves with no effort on my part. "He was dead, Da. It was so clear he was dead. His eyes were open. There was just…nothing there. I went numb. Into a kind of shock, I think, where I couldn't even process emotion. I just knew he was dead and I needed to make it look like…"

"Like what?"

"That he drowned. I reached into the water, took hold of his hands. He wasn't holding the knife anymore…must have sunk in the river. I washed the rabbit's blood off his fingers. Then I went to the fort, took the rabbit and some other bones in there, and threw them all in the river as well. Ran home, snuck into the house. Threw my shirt away, cleaned my cut best I could, covered it in a bandage, got a fresh shirt. Went back to the river, and that's when I pretended to find him. That's when I came back to the house, yelling for you."

"You covered up a crime."

"Maybe I did," I say. "I've carried that guilt with me every moment since it happened. Even if he drowned on his own, he was in the river because of me. He attacked me because I called him a monster."

My father leans back against the couch, and his sudden relaxing of his posture unnerves me. I want his anger. I want him to blame me, because the only thing that would feel good right now is any kind of pain.

"I'm not asking for your forgiveness," I say.

Those eyes, I've never seen them with such ice. "And you can go to your own grave knowing I'm not giving it to you."

"But I wanted to let you know how sorry I am. How sorry I am every day since it happened. I thought I'd say something within days after it happened. I didn't expect the police to rule it an accidental drowning so quickly. Thought…there'd be more of an investigation. But there wasn't. Christopher was dead, and not a lot of questions were asked. So I said nothing. Like a fucking coward, I said nothing. I'm so sorry."

His ensuing silence lasts eternal. A thin rivulet of tears streaks from the corner of his left eye, down his cheek, and into the white tangle of his beard.

Finally, he wipes his face. "He coulda become a terrible man," he says.

It's something I tell myself every day. And I counter with the same argument I tell myself each time.

"And he coulda become a great man."

"Aye." He wipes his eyes. "We've both lost our wives, Aidan, and it's a terrible thing. 'Specially with Holly at her age, and I can't imagine that specific kind of pain. But I'll tell you this. There's no suffering in this world as great as when you lose a child." He looks ten years older than when he sat down. "Christopher's death…it broke me. Broke your mom worse, and I do believe it eventually killed her. She never wanted to fight that hard when she got cancer. Didn't really care to prolong her life any longer, I suppose." He locks in on me. "Protect your children, Aidan. That's the only thing you need to do with your life. Just protect them, best you can, because you're broken enough, and it won't take much more to shatter you complete, I expect."

Being shattered sounds lovely.

"Aye," I say, rising. I walk over and pour another drink, craving a numb on top of the numb. I've just told my father the one thing I've hidden my entire adult life, and now I just want to feel nothing at all.

As if sensing my thoughts, he says, "Why now? After all this time, why tell me now?"

"Because I'm supposed to." I drink, and now there's no burn. Silky smooth. "The letters. This house. The money. Everything's happening for a reason, I'm sure of it. And all I know is telling you what happened to Christopher is part of that reason."

"Christ Lord, Aidan," Da says. "The only thing more folly than playing the lottery is looking for reason where none exists."

I'm about to tell him I won the lottery, just in case he'd forgotten. But I don't. I can't.

Because this is when the screaming starts.

FORTY-SEVEN

UPSTAIRS. THE KIDS.

Both of them.

Screaming like they're being torn apart.

And how I run.

Run, despite the wave of alcohol-laced stupor that crashes over me the second I rise from the couch. Out the office, through the foyer, where I take my first of two falls, my feet not talking to my brain. Land bad, hip to hardwood, just at the base of the stairs. As the pain spikes and spreads, I look up and for the first time see the outline of where a picture once hung on the wall, its ghosted trace just discernable. And the energy from this home gives me another jolt, all in milliseconds, and now I'm convinced what hung there was a painting. A scene both beautiful and sad. A field. A cornfield after a rainfall, the black sky moving farther away, taking the storm with it, leaving behind a rainbow that's just an illusion, a jackpot never to be discovered.

What the hell is happening to me?

I shake the image away, get to my feet, and bound up the stairs two and three at a time. Second floor, then third. At the top I fall again, curing my love of drink, knowing if my kids are bleeding, I'll be too drunk to drive them to the hospital but will drive them anyway, unable to bear the interminable wait for an ambulance.

The screams have morphed into calls of *Daddy!* The back of my mind takes this as a good thing, that they at least stopped screaming. The front of my mind pictures pools of blood, vintage-car red, glossy and voluminous, way more than a child's body should hold. On the floor, walls, bedsheets. Random droplets on the faces of stuffed animals, streaked like war paint.

Please god, *no*.

On my feet, bounce off a wall. Bedroom just on the right. I run as hard as I can to something I desperately don't want to see.

Their door is open, but the room is dark. As soon as I reach it, I twist inside and flick on the light switches. Blazing white light.

Instant relief. At least a little.

No blood. No red anywhere.

Bo and Maggie, standing together by the window, facing opposite me. Blinds pulled up, and I see my reflection in the window. In the time we've been here, the window blinds in their room have always been down, and only the slats themselves have been opened. It seems so odd to see this massive window exposed, and in staring at the fuzzy image of myself staring back, I think, drunk on adrenaline, *There he is.* There's the ghost. Right there. He's me.

"What is it?" I say.

Bo, eyes wide. "She was having a bad dream, and I...I went over to her bed. And I looked out the window, and someone was in our backyard."

Someone was in our backyard.

I need ten seconds of information before I do anything else. First things first, I need to assume he's right.

"Did you recognize them?"

"No."

Maggie tucks her arms deep into herself and says nothing.

"Man or woman?" I ask.

"I don't know," he says. "Maybe both."

"What does that mean?"

"There were two people."

A river of ice flows from my gut to my heart.

"Headed which direction?"

"From the pond toward the house."

"Did they see you?"

"No." He swallows. "I don't think so."

I turn my head back to the bedroom door and yell, "Da! Get up here!"

He must've already been on the way, because he's in the room only seconds later.

"They saw people in the backyard," I say. "Wait here with them, will you?"

"And what are you going to do?" he asks.

I shake my head at him, silently telling him he should know better than to ask a question like that in front of my kids.

Maggie squeezes around my hip. "Don't go out there."

"It's okay, sweetie." I hug back before untethering her from me. "I'll be okay."

I don't know this at all.

I'm out of the room, leaving in my wake a trail of protests. To my bedroom and the gun safe, and finally to my shotgun. I load two shells; I think I've done it right. Damn it, why didn't I teach myself proper on this?

Down the stairs, managing my balance this time. Be a bad way to end life, these stairs. Rock-hard, blunt-edged, nasty creatures.

I'm in the garage seconds later, the gun a satisfying weight in my hands.

I slow my pace as I head for the back door.

Two people, Bo said. Two. Maybe a man and a woman.

Makes me think of Carlos and his sister, Abril.

Makes me think of Willow and her boyfriend, Steve.

Or maybe the kids saw vapors of the home's previous occupants. Logan Yates and one of his daughters, floating the grounds.

When I open the door from the garage to the backyard, a wave of cool air hits me. Much cooler than the garage, and it perks me up, washes a thin layer of drunk off of me. I'm keyed in, all senses on high alert. And goddamn, am I spoiling for a fight.

First thing I see is the note on the ground, illuminated by the solitary light bulb responsible for this patch of land. A single page, facedown, a rock holding it in place.

A scan of the landscape—at least as far as I can see in the dark—reveals nothing. No movement. No sound. This doesn't surprise me. We Who Watch are covert operators, foxes not bears, working in the shadows. They've already gone, and the only proof I have is this note and whatever my backyard security camera captured, which I expect will be very little.

I reach for the note and then freeze halfway.

They could be watching right now.

Watching, waiting for me to take the bait. Tensing in joyful anticipation of me reading whatever sinister prose they came up with this time.

I stand straight, take three steps into the backyard, steady the gun in my hands. I'm fully washed in the light from that one bulb, surrounded by darkness. I hear something, but it's not movement. It's an owl, peppering off a call. I haven't heard an owl here before, and it's a little bit beautiful. Enough for me to stand in this light, vulnerable as I've ever been, and wait a good twenty or thirty seconds to hear the owl call again.

There's a satisfaction in its voice. It's calling out to someone, but it's not lonely. I think I'd give away all my fortune to be that owl.

So I call out on my own. Loud, and if there's a drunken slur to my words, I don't hear it.

"*I'm supposed to be here!*" The darkness absorbs my voice. So I turn, giving every direction a piece of my mind.

Back to the dead center of the backyard, I add, "So you can go ahead and fuck off now."

An instant regret, knowing I can do better than that. I wait, hoping for something better to say, but nothing comes to mind.

So I stand here, accepting a heavy silence, pausing for any kind of response.

I get none.

Turn to go back inside, leaving the note on the ground. Then, just as I open the door, I do get a response.

It's from the owl.

He just sounds so fucking satisfied.

FORTY-EIGHT

WHEN I COME BACK from the garage, I make straight for my laptop and fire it up on the kitchen counter, setting the shotgun next to it. Scan all recent activity from my outdoor cameras, both from the front and backyard.

It takes only seconds to discover nothing unusual. I pay particular focus on my backyard cam, but going through the footage…there's nothing. Just silence and an absence of any motion. These are people who know how to avoid the lens of the lone camera back there.

They left a note right at the door. Why be so bold?

To make a point.

"Aidan, what's going on?"

My father's voice echoes from the third floor.

I shout toward the stairs, "It's okay. Didn't see anyone. Just…just stay up there. I'll come up in a bit."

He doesn't answer. I take his silence as acknowledgment.

Back to the laptop, I launch my web browser, my mind going back to my party. To my neighbor, whose name I forget. White slacks and blouse, wrists of gold bangles. She knew I won the lottery, even though that's not public information. What was it she'd said?

You can find out nearly anything on the internet.

Just as Peter Ainsworth said to me earlier today when I asked him what he'd do in my situation. *I'd go online, find out what information is floating around about me.*

I type in the search bar, realizing how drunkenly dizzy I am as I do:

Aidan Marlowe lottery

I half expect to see dozens of articles about me, detailing my life history. As if the world knows everything about me and I was naive to assume any kind of privacy. But there's nothing. At least nothing that seems related to me.

I venture through the first five pages of results. Nothing. Click on Images. None are of me.

To the casual browser, I seem to be anonymous.

But what about a more…dedicated researcher?

Someone who doesn't use Google. Someone who wants a deeper level of data. Are there other areas of the internet that might have information on me? I only think this because of a service that comes with one of my credit cards. An identity theft service with a feature that scans the dark web for any listing of my email address or mobile number. I've gotten a couple of alerts over the past two months, but to be honest, I didn't really understand the implications. Or what to do about it. None of it seemed that urgent.

Now things feel urgent.

Back to Google.

how do I access the dark web

Plenty of information this time, and it doesn't take long for me to realize I can't just hop on the dark web with my web browser. I need a special web browser called *Tor*. I find a link for the download and click on it, figuring it's a fifty-fifty chance my computer's about to be horribly infected.

Download works, I install Tor and launch it. I half expect to be instantly routed to some online black market, but instead, I get nothing. I don't know how to search here. So I flip back to my other web browser and search Google, which tells me the dark web is best accessed with a search engine named Searx. But there is no Searx.com. Every address on the dark web is a series of seemingly random numbers and letters, all ending in .*onion*. So I copy the address for Searx and paste it into my Tor browser.

ulrn6sryqaifefld.onion

Okay, here we go.

I search again.

Aidan Marlowe

The search is maddeningly slow. Finally, some results, but none that makes any sense and most are duplicates of one another. The dark web might be full of criminal activity, but it sure as hell isn't user-friendly.

I type:

how do I find out about someone

A broad question, but one of the first results is for a site named OmegaBitGo, which makes me think of vitamins for dogs. But it isn't that at all.

It's a marketplace. A marketplace of very bad things.

In just a handful of clicks, I find places to buy any number of illegal drugs (meth, the most prevalent), guns, fake passports, forged college degrees, stolen Netflix accounts, poison (ricin showing up the most), identities. There's even an offer from some woman who, for twenty dollars, will write anything you want anywhere on her body and send you a photo.

No, I don't need that.

Identities.

That category catches my eye, and after a few more clicks, I find a submenu of options.

- Social Security numbers (a premium for those with credit scores above 750)
- Bank account numbers and login credentials (I can buy access to an account with $53,000 in it for only $2,000)
- Customer data, including spending amounts at certain stores
- Home security camera footage (particularly creepy)
- Driver's license information

And then.

On this long list of items I can buy to invade the privacy of others is the thing that glows brightest on my laptop screen.

Names of lottery winners

Bam.

Another click, leading to one simple paragraph.

Comprehensive list of state and national lottery jackpot winners for the past three years, including those from states with a nondisclosure policy. List includes full name, current address, date, and amount of winnings. $35.

Thirty-five dollars. Thirty-five fucking dollars, and you can know who I am, where I live, and how much I won.

There's more text just below an animated dollar-sign GIF.

For an additional $100 per name, we can research and attempt to *provide you with Social Security and driver's license numbers. No guarantee! No refunds.*

I can see the plan unfold before me. Someone—or maybe a whole group of people—scours the dark web for names and addresses of lottery winners. Then they split up the list and travel to each of the winners' homes, where they leave creepy notes.

WE WHO WATCH.

Maybe they're successful one time out of fifty, even one out of a hundred. One of those winners gives them money to go away, then the stalkers divvy up the pot. Seems a little far-fetched, but not entirely. I know firsthand that lottery winners are different from the professionally rich. We're not used to wealth. Not used to the pressures of immense and sudden fortune. We're more likely to make mistakes or be vulnerable to outside influences. And much less likely to have a slew of professional advisors guiding us.

I'm going to buy this list, see if I'm indeed on there and if the rest of the information is correct. Hell, I can afford thirty-five bucks, being a lottery winner and all.

But when I get to the shopping basket, I see they only take Bitcoin and a few other cryptocurrencies, none of which I have.

Maya.

The name flashes like a beacon in my mind.

I need help.

I need Maya.

FORTY-NINE

"YOU WOKE ME UP," Maya says, her digital voice muddied with sleep.

"I know. It's getting to be a problem."

"Are you drunk?" she asks.

"Why?"

"Because you're slurring."

"It's been a hell of a day."

A yawn, pause. "Okay, tell me."

I do. Only eight days have passed since she was here, since my party. Since Mags found the secret safe room in the basement. Most of those eight days came and went in relative peace. Until today.

It took me an hour before I called Maya. An hour spent getting the kids back to sleep, telling my father everything was okay. An hour calming myself, inasmuch as that could be done. An hour drinking nothing but water, eating nothing but Advil. It's just before 11:00 p.m. as I tell Maya what's happened tonight. And what I discovered online.

When I finish, she takes a moment to digest my words and says, "So your list of suspects has grown to anyone in the world with access to the dark web and Bitcoin."

"That about sums it up."

"Did you buy the list?"

"I don't own crypto."

"You do, actually. You own a few hundred thousand dollars of Bitcoin as one of your investments."

"I do?"

"Yes," she says. "But it doesn't matter. You shouldn't be buying that list, seeing as it's illegal. The firm can buy the list for you; we have a VPN server that ensures any purchase can't be traced to us or, more importantly, you."

"Okay, great."

"What did the note say?" she asks.

"What?"

"The note. From tonight. You said you left it there. I assume you went back and got it later. What did it say?"

I'd completely forgotten about the note.

"Hang on." I carry her with me as I go back through the garage and into the backyard. The note's still there, exactly where it was before. The night seems even quieter than earlier, and I do a quick survey of the surroundings.

No movement. No eyes flashing from the dark.

I swipe up the note, shut and lock the garage door, head back inside, and settle on the couch.

"*Mr. Marlowe,*" I read to Maya, "*as you can see, We are getting closer all the time.*" I pause, noticing the capitalized W. "*That lets you know We're serious. But all you have to do is follow Our instructions and you can be rid of*

Us forever. You're going to transfer ten thousand dollars to the bank account listed below by the end of tomorrow."

"We knew they wanted your money from the last letter," Maya says. "Though ten thousand isn't very much, considering. Read me the account and routing numbers."

I do. "There's more," I say. "*If you do this, We will come back to you only one more time, requesting a somewhat larger sum. Do as instructed to avoid consequences.*"

"Of course, they signed it *We Who Watch.*" I note the use of the term *sincerely* again. No creative sign-off like in the first handful of letters.

"Go back to the police," she says. "Maybe it's time the FBI got involved."

"Or maybe I do nothing at all."

"I'm not sure that sounds like a good plan."

"Well, apparently anyone can find a list of lottery winners on the dark web and then leave threatening notes at their house. Not that hard to do. Once I give them ten thousand, they'll come back and ask for a million. What if they don't go away?"

"That's a question for the cops," she says. "Will you promise me to go back and tell them what's happened?"

"Fine, though I don't have high hopes Chief Sike will suddenly spring into action."

"Just do it—there're enough notes at this point, they can't just stand by. In the meantime, I can buy the list of lottery winners, see if there's anything unexpected in there. Send me the link to the site."

"You need a special web browser to—"

"You think I haven't been on the dark web?" she says. "I know how to do it. You're not the first client for whom I've had to dig around in some unsavory places." She pauses, then adds, "And maybe you and the family should get out of the house for a little bit. Take a vacation. Get away from there for a few days."

"I've considered that," I say. "But the letters, they specifically warn us against moving away. If we went away for a few days, would that trigger something?"

"Good point," she says.

"I'm so…" I squeeze my eyes shut, hoping to see a lighted pathway to an answer, yet there's only darkness.

"So what?"

"So…*tired* of being scared. Tired of feeling helpless, of just sitting around and waiting to see what arrives next at my doorstep. And it's not just that I'm tired and frightened."

"What is it?"

I open my eyes, and everything looks the same. And that's the problem. I'm just letting everything stay the same.

"I'm angry. And it's not just that I'm scared to move away, worried that they'll hurt my family. That's part of it, of course. But I *want* to be here. Protect and fight for my family from inside the walls of my house. I don't want to run away. And I don't want to just give in to their demands, knowing they'll keep coming back for more."

"So what do you want to do?"

For a sudden moment, I'm transported back decades to the banks of the River Tolka, only this time I'm not myself. I'm Christopher, holding the remains of a rabbit in my hands, looking down at it with the grim satisfaction of being in complete control of another life.

"I want to hurt them," I say, not even knowing who *they* are and not caring. "All of them."

For a moment, I fear I contain some of the awful lust that consumed my brother.

For a moment, I don't care.

FIFTY

Bury, New Hampshire
Day Thirty-One

I WAKE IN A start, my sheets damp with sweat. I'm not prone to
nightmares—or dreams of any kind, really—but this one was movie-
quality horrifying. It probably lasted five minutes but felt like hours.

What I remember most clearly was it happened inside the house. I
was here, in my bedroom, in this bed, and I woke into what I thought
was reality, but it wasn't because Holly was alive. Alive and screaming.

She wasn't in the bed with me. The screams were coming from
outside the room, and I tried to run to her but everything was slippery.
The harder I ran, the less progress I made until finally I went to the
ground and slithered across the room, the only way I could move. The
hardwood floor was wet, slick as if coated in a thick glaze of olive oil, and
I pushed my way out to the hallway and found my wife standing at the
top of the stairs, her back to me, looking down and screaming. She was
standing and yet I still couldn't, so I frantically pushed my way on my

belly, sliding as fast as I could toward her. Then my speed increased and I couldn't stop, and as I reached where she stood, I went sliding past her, out of control.

She looked down at me as I flew over the top of the stairs. For a moment, she stopped screaming and her look was so peaceful, despite the blood oozing out of her ears. She smiled and it was beautiful, but it didn't last because I was falling.

Falling down the stairs, spinning with impossible, disorienting twists, and surely I must have hit steps along the way to the bottom, but there was no sensation of pain. Just falling—endlessly, it seemed—until there was a moment in which things were clear. I saw the bottom landing before I hit it, knowing it would be impossible to survive such a fall yet being somehow at peace with that, but my boy was there, and that's when the real horror set in. Bo, twisted in knots, a tiny little contortionist, faceup at the bottom of the stairs. His neck twisted at an angle that made no sense in the real world, his clothes soaking wet.

I tried to scream but couldn't. All I could do was fall, and then I realized the oil I'd been sliding on was now water, a torrent of it, rushing down the stairs, washing over my dead boy but not carrying him away. The only part of his body untouched by the flowing river was his face, and right before I smashed into the ground, Bo opened his eyes and they weren't his at all.

The face was Bo's. The body and the clothes were Bo's.

But not the eyes.

The eyes belonged to Christopher.

And here, as I wipe the sweat from my face, I know three things for certain. Holly is dead, Bo is alive, and this house is alive. I don't quite know what they mean, but that doesn't make them less true. I think the people watching me didn't just pick me because I'm a lottery winner they found on the dark web. There's more to it than that. I think it's personal.

I need to find out what happened in this house. Peter Ainsworth was little help, as was his creepy daughter. What was her name? Right, Willow.

A series of events unfolds in my mind. I wouldn't quite call it a plan but at least some first steps.

I jump out of bed, head straight to the shower. Scrub away the nightmare, the sweat. Shave, dress, then check on the kids. Still sleeping, good. It's eight in the morning, and I hope they make it to at least nine. They need a peaceful sleep.

Downstairs, Da nurses a coffee and a newspaper on the living room couch. The day coming through the windows behind him is gray with spots of weak sunshine.

"You sleep okay?" I ask him.

"Good enough." His eyes don't leave the paper. "You?"

"Good enough." No more conversation necessary between us, I take my mobile to the privacy of my study. Shut the door.

After three rings, a woman says, "Bury Police Department."

"Yes, Chief Sike, please."

"Can I tell him who's calling and what it's regarding?"

"This is Aidan Marlowe," I say. "And…and you can just tell him this is regarding the Yates case."

"Yates?"

"Yes. Logan Yates. He and his family—"

"Oh, I'm familiar," she says. "Just wasn't sure I heard you correctly. Hang on."

Seconds later, the chief is on the line.

"Marlowe. Was thinking I hadn't heard from you lately." He carries a New England drawl like a heavy weight on his back, slowing him down. "I take that as a good sign?"

"No, Chief. No, just the opposite, in fact."

"Wanna fill me in?"

"The notes are back, and this time they want money. Today, in fact."

"How much?"

"Ten thousand."

"How are you supposed to get the money to them?"

"They left an account number."

He considers this. "Okay."

"I'm not going to do it," I tell him.

"Marlowe, I suggest you bring the note to the station, or I can send a car out to you. We can assist."

"How, exactly? I'm not trying to be confrontational here, Chief, but everyone keeps telling me to go to the police, but so far, the police haven't done anything. So how, exactly, can you assist?"

Sike clears his throat, takes a moment, likely to let his anger settle. "Well, now, that's to be determined. Hate to tell you we have limited resources here, but we have limited resources here. Dealing with tracing account numbers and such…that's something that takes time. But I can send a couple guys out there, watch the house a bit. So that's *something*."

"Do you think that'll do any good?" I know the answer, I just want to hear him say it.

"Hard to say, but I'd be lying to say I suspect it would."

"Look, Chief." I stare out the slats of the window blinds and into the front yard. Quiet as a battlefield before it knows it's a battlefield. "I do

need help, but I don't think from you. Not yet. Whoever is doing this...
it's not random. It's not just about me and the fact I have money. Maybe
I won the lottery, but there's no lack of wealthy people in Bury."

"True enough. So what are you looking for?"

"Last time we spoke, you mentioned another cop. A cop in Milwaukee
who came out here to interview the Yates woman. Rose Yates."

"Detective Pearson. Colin Pearson."

"Pearson, right. I want to talk to him."

"And why is that?"

"You said he was investigating her. I want to know what he knows."

"I don't believe he found out much," Sike says. "And I'm not sure
what good it will do. I expect I know as much as he does."

"You may be right," I tell him. "Still, I'd like to talk to him. Can you
put me in touch?"

"Well, if you're asking me for his phone number, the answer is no.
And he's not even on the force anymore." He pauses, and in the brief
silence, I try to think of options once he kills my request. But he throws
me a lifeline, saying, "Suppose I can call him myself. Still have his number
on my phone, I think. I can give him your info, and if he wants to talk to
you, well, that'll be up to him."

"That's all I need. Thank you."

"Sure thing."

"You can do that today?"

"I'll see to it. Don't get your hopes up, though." He pauses, clears his
throat. "So you say you're not going to wire that money?"

"No," I answer. "You think that's a bad idea?"

"Hard to say."

"Why's that?"

"Because I don't know how much money you really have and what price you're willing to pay for peace. If I had termites in my house, I'd certainly pay a grand to have the exterminator come."

"This is more than a termite problem."

"Yeah, I understand. Guess what I'm really trying to say, Marlowe, is the last thing we need is more problems on Rum Hill Road. In that house."

"I didn't ask for any of this, Chief."

"'Course you didn't," he says. "But you don't know what they'll do if you refuse to give them what they want. Don't know what kind of folks you're dealing with. They might just be fishing and leave you alone once you push back. Or..."

"Or what?"

"Or they might keep coming back, a little more aggressive. Maybe attempt a break-in or follow you when you leave the house. I don't know. If it were me, maybe I'd just go ahead and pay." He lets this sink in for a moment, and it does—and not in a comfortable way. It strikes me a bit daft that the police chief would advocate for giving in to criminal demands. "But most likely they're just testing the waters, seeing what you'll do. Look, I can send a car over there for a few hours in the evening for maybe four or five days. Who knows, maybe we see something."

"I appreciate that," I say.

"Well, stay in touch, and I'll let you know if our guys see anything."

"I will, Chief."

My next call is to the security consultant, Owen Brace, whom I haven't spoken to in some time.

"Marlowe," he says. "Good to hear from you."

I wish I could feel his energy through the mobile. When he was in my house installing the cameras, I didn't detect anything off about him, but that doesn't mean the man can't just be good at cloaking his intentions.

"I need some advice," I say. "I'll pay for it, of course. But I don't want to give you all the personal information you were asking for in your proposal."

A pause. "That's not exactly how I work," he says. "My contract is for a full range of services, not just—"

"Five thousand dollars," I say, with no real reason for choosing that number. "Just for a few minutes with me. Right now. I can wire it to you today."

He falls silent again. "Well, that's a mighty fine offer and I can't say no to it. But I'd hate to disappoint. Tell me what's on your mind, and I'll let you know what I think you should do. Then pay me based on your level of satisfaction with my advice."

"Fair enough," I say.

I keep it as vague as I can, but by the end, he knows there was another letter asking for money at the risk of harm to my family.

"Go to Chief Sike" is the first thing he says.

"Just hung up with him. He's sending a car out to keep watch."

"Okay, good. That's at least a visual deterrent."

"What else?"

Brace sucks in a deep breath. "If they know you won the lottery, it's hard to see a point where they just leave you alone once you give them money. Statistically, most threats are toothless. Now, I know you've been sent several letters, but the chances of them acting on their threats are low. If you give them money, it's like leaving food out for mice."

"The chances are low, but not zero percent," I say.

"No, certainly not zero. There's always a chance they are every bit the nightmare they claim to be."

This takes the wind out of me. "Jesus."

"Here's the truth, Marlowe. The five-thousand-dollar truth. As I've said, the odds suggest you can continue ignoring these threats and they will just stop." His voice is authoritative, like a cop telling me to get out of the car. "But the smaller odds—though much greater than the odds that won you all that money—suggest they are deadly serious. And I can give you tons of advice that can help, as I've told you before. But the truth is, if they're serious and know what they're doing, then you're fucked. They might keep coming back for money, and they also might follow through on their threat of hurting your family if you try to leave Bury."

This is what I wanted to hear. And not what I wanted to hear.

"Email me a bill." I hang up, not feeling in the mood for proper goodbyes.

I steady myself, walk to the kitchen, pour some coffee. No more words pass between Da and me, none needed at the moment. Kids are still fast asleep, I suspect, and I know I'd best start appreciating quiet mornings before school starts.

I stand here a moment, caught by a sudden uncertainty of what happens next. I'm not relaxed, I'm not anxious. I just exist for these moments, staring at nothing, thinking about nothing. I'm vaguely aware of the warm cup of coffee in my hands. Maybe, in the distance, I hear my father ask if I'm okay. Perhaps everything is a thumbprint of imagination, nothing more.

I close my eyes.

When I open them, I'm standing in the foyer at the base of the staircase. Just like that, time has passed. Twenty seconds only takes an eyeblink. Just like when I lost those chunks of time over the past months, those minutes or hours erased from my consciousness.

"Aidan!"

Da's voice jolts me enough to drop my coffee mug, where it falls to the floor, remaining intact but spilling its contents.

"Are you all right?" His expression is a mix of concern and annoyance. "I've been calling your name, and you just zombied over here and went to some other world in your head."

The calm stays with me. I don't know why.

"Yes, I'm fine."

He doesn't know what to do with this answer, so he says, "Well, yer mobile was ringing, which is why I was calling you. You sure you're okay?"

"Yeah, Da. I'm good."

"Well, whoever was calling tried a couple of times, so ya might want to check."

Da hands me my mobile, then hobbles back on his cane to the living room.

I look down at the two missed calls. Same number on each, a 414 area code. No voicemails, and normally I'd never call an unknown number back, certain it'd be a telemarketer. But this time I do.

"Hello?"

The man's voice on the other end is monotone. Maybe fatigued.

"Someone at this number just called me," I say. "Twice."

"Is this Aidan Marlowe?"

"Aye."

"This is Colin Pearson. Walter Sike just rang me up and said you wanted to talk to me."

"Yes, that's right. Thanks for calling me so quickly."

"I don't know how much I can help," he says. I realize it's not fatigue I hear in his voice. It's something deeper, more permanent. Sadness, perhaps. "You want to know about Rose Yates."

"Yes."

"Well, Mr. Marlowe, maybe you don't really want to know."

"And why's that?"

Silence. Then, "Because one time I wanted to know more about Rose Yates. Then I wanted to know more about the entire Yates family."

Sounds like me.

"And what happened?" I ask.

He laughs but nothing's funny. "I could suppose you can say I've been cursed ever since."

FIFTY-ONE

THE WORLD RUSHES BENEATH me, the expanse of America, a patchwork quilt of land spotted by the occasional body of water. I'm thirty thousand feet over the Midwest with a half hour remaining before the plane lands in Milwaukee.

It all happened so fast.

Colin Pearson sounded like a man who hadn't talked to anyone else in a long time. He said I didn't want to know about the Yates family, but he perked up when I told him I bought Logan Yates's house. I guess Chief Sike hadn't mentioned that detail to him.

He was hesitant to say much other than he'd been investigating Rose Yates in connection with her husband's death, but it stopped mattering when the Yates family vanished in the course of one night. Said it didn't matter because he wasn't even a cop anymore.

I knew from his tone that a call wouldn't be enough, so I told the former detective I wanted to meet with him and time was of the essence. He said there wasn't much point in that, but if that was my intention, I'd have to come to him because he was never coming back to Bury. Not ever.

After the call, the rest of the morning was a whirlwind. I found an afternoon flight from Boston to Milwaukee, and then I called Maya, asking her to join me. She agreed. Damn fine lawyer, she is.

I'm fully aware I'm taking a risk by leaving town, but I have decided it's worth it. I don't believe whoever is sending me the letters will really think we're moving away, not so quickly. Still, I wasn't about to have my family remain in the house without me, so Da agreed to take the twins to a hotel for a couple of nights. When they asked why, I just told them I had to leave town for a day or two, and if I got to stay in a nice hotel, then they should, too.

I booked two nights of rooms for them at the Oak Street Inn, the bed-and-breakfast where Maya stayed (and became a fan of their biscuits). Mags was excited. Bo, suspicious.

I said my goodbyes, left for the airport, and have spent this plane ride questioning my decisions. Questioning is an easy thing to do. Finding answers is fraught with difficulties.

Wheels down, I deplane. Maya's flight lands an hour later, so I spend the interim nursing a whiskey sour in the terminal.

When we finally meet in the terminal, we hug, and I have the faint thrill of escaping on an exotic holiday with my girlfriend. The truth couldn't be further away, but still, there it is.

"The partners at my firm are beginning to think you're either crazy or spending a lot of money just to see me again," she says.

They're billing me at double rate because of the work Maya had to shove off onto others to come on this last-minute trip. I told them it was fine. The more I think about my money, the more I want to get rid of it anyway. "Guess they're a little right on both counts," I say.

Late afternoon, we grab our rental car and head to our hotel, a

Marriott in the suburbs. I text Colin, telling him I'm here and confirming a time to meet. He tells me 8:00 p.m., later than I was expecting but okay. Gives me an address in a little town called Whitefish Bay, a twenty-minute ride away.

Dinner at the hotel, I'm not hungry. I pick through a salad, and Maya asks if I want to talk. I tell her *not really*. I don't tell her how I hate the obsession I have with this little world now enveloping me. That I fear once I talk to Colin Pearson, I'll take some final step into an abyss.

I have a drink. Just one, but I itch for more.

Quarter to eight, we take a car into residential Whitefish Bay. The driver tries to make conversation and fails spectacularly.

Darkness creeps.

We get dropped off in front of a two-story house with a pleasant piece of lawn. Big oak tree towering, blocking the hazy light from a streetlamp that's just flickered to life. My stomach tightens into a ball as I knock on the door.

Maya gives my arm a small rub as I hear footsteps approaching.

Colin Pearson opens the door, and his eyes are as sad as the voice I heard on our call.

"Come on in" is the only thing he says.

We step into his house, and I'm immediately struck by a sense of familiarity. I breathe the house in, let it settle in my lungs, and as I breathe it back out, I realize what it is.

It's just like my house.

It's totally different in every way except how it feels on my skin. I can't describe it any better than that.

I wonder what it is about these places that burrow so deep?

FIFTY-TWO

MAYA AND I SIT next to each other on an old couch. Colin splays across from us in a leather chair with brass buttons on its arms. He's drinking a bottle of beer, and there's an empty one on the glass table between us.

"Get you something?" he asks, lifting his bottle. "Got more of these, or something stronger if you want."

We both tell him *no, thank you,* Maya faster than me.

A voice rings from upstairs, old and brittle. "Colin, who is that?"

"I've got company, Mom," he shouts. "Remember, I told you?"

"No," she says. "I hope it's not that Frank Perlmutter."

"No, Mom."

"Better not be. That man is a top-shelf asshole."

Colin closes his eyes, exhales the weight of the world. "Just stay upstairs. I'll be there in a little bit." Then he opens his lids and says to us, "I'm all she has, and her dementia's getting worse. Especially at night. Sundowner's syndrome." He takes a swig. "I moved back in to take care of her."

"I'm sure she appreciates that," Maya says.

Colin shrugs. "Hard to tell most of the time."

"So this is her house?" I ask.

"Our house, really. I grew up here. My wife and I were living up in Madison. I was on the force up there, but we came back down to take care of Mom."

"Is your wife here?"

"No," Colin says. This is when he looks like he just swallowed a thumbtack. "She's not."

If you scraped away the gloom, his face would be boyish. Dark-brown hair, moppy. A light layer of flab around his gut and his neck, which belies the sense he's been hardened by something.

"Colin Pearson," I say. "That's a proper Irish name."

"Cork County, two generations removed."

"Dublin myself. Born and raised."

He nods. "Can't hide the accent."

I take another quick glance around, trying to understand why this place makes me feel the way I feel. There's an air of barely suppressed chaos here, as if opening one closet door might suck us all into another dimension.

"I didn't actually think you'd come," Colin says. "Much less two of you. Who are you again?"

"Maya Falk. I'm his lawyer."

He takes this in. "Okay, then. You should know I'm not on the job anymore, in case you were here in some kind of official capacity."

"No, Colin," I say. "I just want to talk. She's here because I trust her and not many others. This is important to me."

"Must be, flying here at the drop of a hat." He swigs until the beer bottle is empty. "I took a trip like that once, last November. Bought my ticket about three hours before the flight. Cost me an arm and leg, but I didn't care. You know where I went?"

"Where?"

"Bury, New Hampshire." He gets up and walks toward the kitchen. "Bury, fucking New Hampshire." I hear the refrigerator door open and close, and he returns with the six-pack container, four bottles still nestled inside. He sets it on the coffee table, seizes one by the neck, settles back onto the couch. "Went to go see Rose Yates, whom you seem to know a lot about."

"Not as much as you do," I say. "Which is why I'm here. What did you go talk to her about?"

He has a wondrous way of setting that boyish face to stone. "You know, it's mostly a blur. I was in bad shape."

"Bad shape?"

He nods. "Bad shape." And explains no further.

Time ticks by, I say nothing, letting him be the first to speak again. Finally, he does. "I'd been investigating Rose and then starting to poke into her family history. I think the Yates family became my windmill, and I was going to chase it until I went crazy. Or maybe because I was already crazy."

Maya glances at me. I don't hold her gaze long.

"Last November," I say to Pearson. "That's the month the family disappeared, isn't it?"

He looks at me, unblinking. "It is."

"Is that why you went out there? Because they disappeared?"

He takes his time to answer. "No, actually, I arrived the day after they disappeared." He twists the cap off the bottle in his hand and drinks, seeking refuge for a moment behind closed eyes. When he opens them, he says, "Never did get a chance to see Rose."

He's lying.

I'm not a cop. I'm not a body language expert. Maybe it was the little twitch in his right eye as he spoke or his need to go straight back to the bottle after the last word. Whatever it was, if Pearson is trying to do a good job of concealing the truth, he's failing.

"Can we back up a moment?" Maya asks him. "Marlowe bought Logan Yates's home and moved in over the summer. Then strange things started happening, and in the course of…investigating…those things, we learned about the Yateses' history. Then we discovered you were part of some other investigation into Rose Yates. What were you talking to her about?"

Pearson straightens in his chair, as much as the beer in him allows. "Strange things? Like what?"

"I started receiving letters," I say. "From people who say they're watching me and my family. Who know things about me they shouldn't know."

"People? More than one?"

I get up, walk over, reach for a beer. I'm a little ashamed I couldn't stop myself, but not a lot ashamed. "Think I might have one of these after all."

"Help yourself. Plenty more."

As I look down at him, I see a man who probably looks forward to every evening just to numb himself into oblivion. I can relate. And in this moment, this glance, this connection with this man from Whitefish Bay, Wisconsin, I realize that I, too, have the same windmill to chase. The Yates family. Instead of focusing all my efforts on who's writing the letters, I'd rather unravel the mystery of what happened in my home.

Why?

Hell if I know. But I think the two things are related. Maybe if I can solve one, I can solve the other.

Or maybe because I'll never figure out either mystery. Maybe I want to chase the unsolvable. Maybe I'm making this chase because otherwise, I'll end up like Pearson, chasing the numb.

Goddamn, do I miss Holly.

I crack the beer open, suppress a sudden and fierce urge to sob, and say, "Sounds like we both have information to share."

He nods, reaches out his bottle, and I give it a light tap with mine. "You first."

"Okay."

I remain standing as I tell him everything, starting with Holly. About winning the lottery the day she died. He interrupts to ask how she died, and I tell him about her having an aneurysm right in front of my kids.

"I'm sorry, Marlowe," he says. "You can be assured of how genuine that sentiment is."

"Thank you."

"And you won the lottery?"

"Yes."

"Mind if I ask how much?"

Normally, I'd shy away from this question. But normally, I wouldn't have admitted winning at all.

"Tens of millions," I say.

Eyebrows arch. "Good for you."

"I'm not convinced it is."

He considers this. "Well, there's that, then."

I tell him of my inexplicable draw to Bury, my need to start fresh. My connection to the Yates house, how I could tell there was history in that house the moment I set foot inside. Then I describe the letters I began to receive, telling me my family was being watched. How they knew about the lottery, about things from my past, including the Christopher Robin song and the significance of it.

I don't tell Pearson about how Christopher died.

Pearson asks what I did once the letters started coming in, and I describe my conversations with Sike, my dinner party, and my confrontation with Peter Ainsworth. How I heard bits and pieces about the Yateses' history and their disappearance, but none of them pointed me toward who was writing the letters. How I even talked to Carlos, the gardener, and Abril, the former housekeeper, but to no real avail.

Pearson leans forward. "I've been in your house. I know what you mean about how it feels. Like a thousand secrets trapped under the floorboards, radiating."

Wow, he just perfectly described it. "Logan Yates was probably a man of many secrets."

Maya asks Colin, "Did you know there's a safe room in the house?"

"There is?"

"In the basement," she says. "It's like a submarine hull."

"What's in there?"

"Supplies," I say. "A bed, some old books. Oh, and a safe."

Colin's eyebrows arch. "Is it locked?"

"Yeah."

"Be interesting to see what's in there," he says. "Might tell you a little more about Logan Yates. Though, most likely, it's empty."

I take a seat. "Well," I say, "That's what I was hoping you could help with. Anything that could be of help in figuring out who's behind these notes. Maybe...maybe what you know in your investigations could help."

Pearson settles back into the cushion. "I understand you want answers, but why now? What's the rush?"

"The note last night demanded money. Ten thousand dollars via wire transfer, due today."

"That's a lot of cash," he says. "But you have tens of millions."

"That won't be the end of it. The note said there'd be one more large payout, then they'll leave me alone."

"They won't," he says.

"I know. That's why I'm not even paying the ten thousand."

"How did they know about the lottery?"

Maya answers before me. "On the dark web, there's a site where you can buy a list of known lottery winners. Where they live, how much money they won, etcetera. Marlowe won the lottery in Maryland, which is a nondisclosure state. But my firm bought the list, and his name and information were on there."

This is the first time she's telling me this. Maya looks directly at me as she continues.

"Then we paid for more details. The info just came back today. Social Security numbers for you and your kids, your credit history, the fact your wife is deceased..."

"Jesus," I say.

"And with all that information," she adds, "who knows what else they could dig up about you?"

"Aye," I say. "Still, this feels more personal than just blackmail. It feels..." Here I turn to Pearson. "It feels related to the house and not just me, as if the Yates family could somehow have a role in all this. And from what I understand from Chief Sike, you might know more about that family than anyone still around."

"Not more than Peter Ainsworth," he says.

"Ainsworth didn't have much to say."

"And what makes you think I do?"

I sweep my gaze around the room. This house is cluttered and disheveled, as if Pearson's waiting for someone else to deal with it. "Because I think you want to," I tell him. "I think there's something eating at you. Don't know what it is, and it's surely more than the disappearance of Rose Yates. But I'm gettin' the sense that your conversations outside of this house are few and far between, and maybe talking to someone about…well, anything, I suppose…would do you some good. Therapy."

He squeezes his eyes shut for a moment, tilts his head, offers a grin. "You pick up all that from just walking into my house?"

"Guess I'm good about sensing things from floorboards and staircases."

He winces like I just jabbed him with a needle. "Maybe I do have things weighing on me, but I'm not looking for pity. And maybe you're right…could do me some good to talk a little. But there are things I won't tell you. Things I haven't told anyone, because I don't know if I want the mystery solved. What if I solve it and find out there's no more purpose in life afterward?"

"Could be," I say. I've thought the same thing but haven't had the nerve to look that thought directly in the eye.

"So I'll tell you a few things about the Yates family." He downs the rest of the bottle, reaches for another. "But some of it just gets to sit inside me and slowly burn until I die. I hope that's okay with you, because it's the only way this is gonna happen."

"That's fine," I say.

He pops open the next beer and downs at least half, reaching deeper into the numb.

"Okay, then."

FIFTY-THREE

"**SOME OF THIS YOU** probably already know," Pearson says. "Assuming you've poked around online a bit. So stop me if you want." He scratches the back of his neck, then brings that scratch to his stubble-coated jaw. "Rose Yates used to live in Milwaukee. Rose, her husband, Riley, and their son, Max. Max was eleven."

Was.

"Riley McKay died last year. Ingested a lethal combination of sleeping pills and alcohol. Thirty-nine years old."

"Suicide?" Maya asks.

"Coroner ruled it an accidental overdose," Pearson says. "And so said the initial detective who worked the case. But that detective had retirement in mind and in fact left the job before the Yates case was closed out. So it was given to me to finalize things. Dot the i's, etcetera. But when I looked into it, I thought that was an awful lot of pills to take. About ten times the prescribed amount."

"Seems like a big thing to overlook the first time around," I say.

"Yeah, well." He shrugs. "Cops make mistakes all the time. Some of them big ones."

"You went back to thinking suicide?"

"Looked at that, too. But no signs of it aside from all the Ambien and Valium in his system."

"So the wife," Maya says. A statement, not a question.

Pearson points a finger at her and offers a semidrunken smile. "Now where were you when I was trying to convince my superiors of that very thing? Well, I suppose that's not fair. They listened to me, but there wasn't any evidence at all to do anything about it. No evidence pointing to Rose offing her husband. Until I started reading some mystery novels by J. L. Sharp. Heard of her?"

We both shake our heads.

"Well, she's not the most famous author. But she's a sharp writer. Weaves a tight mystery and doesn't mind dabbling in some pretty heady violence. Gets most of the police procedural stuff right, too. So I started reading her books right after the McKay death, and in one of her books, a wife kills her husband by crushing up a bunch of sleep meds and mixing them in his nightcap."

"Okay, wait," I say. "Why did you start reading those books right after Riley McKay died? What's the connection between J. L. Sharp and Rose Yates?"

The semidrunken smile blossoms. "Rose Yates *is* J. L. Sharp. That's her pen name. Rose Yates is…*was*…a mystery writer. I started reading her books when I found that out and was pretty damn intrigued when I came across that scene."

"Did you talk to her?"

"That was the problem," Pearson replies. "By the time I came to work the case, Rose Yates took her boy and moved—"

"To Bury," I finish.

"Exactly. To your house, in fact. Logan Yates's house. Same house Rose and her sister, Cora, grew up in. Rose Yates blazed out of Milwaukee and went back home to Daddy, fast as she could."

Pearson lets that sentence settle on us a bit. Before he continues, his mother's voice rings from upstairs.

"Colin, come up *now*."

He shifts his gaze to the ceiling, mutters something under his breath. "Gimme a minute, will you?"

"Of course," Maya says.

Pearson gets up, lumbers across the room and up the stairs, teetering once before righting himself on the third riser.

Maya whispers to me, "He's drunk."

"That's not drunk," I say. "Not for a man like that. I imagine he needs a fair bit more for *drunk*."

"How is this helping?"

"I don't know. Maybe it isn't. But I'm glad we came."

She squeezes her hands together. "I guess."

I take my mobile from my front jeans pocket, check for messages. None. I shoot a quick text to Da.

Everything good?

I wait a beat, then a few more, no answer. Maybe he's staring at his screen, pondering my stupid question. Everything good? *No, in fact, it's not. I found out my dead son was a blossoming serial killer and you intentionally drowned him. Now I'm hiding out in a bed-and-breakfast with your littles while you're off with some woman, trying to figure out if your house is truly haunted. No, it's not all good. In fact, it's right fucked.*

Moments later, footsteps on the stairs, and I slide the mobile back in my pocket. Pearson comes down the steps—exhibiting an abundance of caution—then plods back to his seat, where he collapses as if someone sliced right through his Achilles.

"We have this ritual," he says. "Mom and me. She needs a last drink before she can sleep, and I'm the one to pour it for her. Gin. Soothes her, or at least knocks her out." He picks up his beer bottle, studies it. "Not the healthiest ritual, but I think we're past that point given her other issues."

"I could see myself doing the same thing with my Da, if it got to that point."

"Maybe you would, or maybe you'd try to help him in other ways." He takes a swallow. "We never really know what we'd do in a situation until it's right there, in our face."

Maya fills the ensuing silence. "So you were saying…about Rose Yates?"

"Right. Back to Bury she went. Her and her son, Max. I wanted to talk to her, interview her more than she'd been by the previous detective working the case. With some wrangling, I got approval for a one-night trip to Bury. I lied to you earlier when I said I never spoke to her. I sure as hell did. Interviewed Ms. Yates in your house. Right in your living room."

"What'd she say?" I asked.

"Not much. You gotta understand, as a mystery writer, she'd interviewed dozens of cops while researching her books. She knew procedure. Cop psychology. Knew when to talk, when to shut up. Once I started asking more direct questions, she shut down pretty fast."

"So you left with nothing?" Maya asks.

"Not exactly nothing." He straightens, or at least slumps less. "I talked to her a second time the next day, right before I left. And I started to think…this is hard to explain, but go with me on this. Started to think there was something more to the Yates family. Maybe it was how I felt in your house. Maybe it was how Ms. Yates answered my questions. Nervous about parts I wouldn't have expected her to be. So I dug around a little more. Spent time with your friend, Chief Sike. Found out what I could on the Yates family. And there wasn't much, except the sister, Cora, had been interviewed back when she was seventeen by the local PD."

"Interviewed about what?" Maya asks.

"Disappearance of a classmate after a party. Kid named Caleb Benner. Cora Yates was one of the last to see him. She wasn't a suspect or anything; they were talking to all the kids who were at the party, just trying to figure out where Caleb went. But when the cops talked to her, Cora was highly evasive and her dad cut the interview short."

"You think she had something to do with Caleb's disappearance?" I ask.

"Maybe. But apparently the Bury PD didn't. No one else followed up with Cora after that one interview."

"Did they find Caleb?"

Another weight lands on top of Pearson; I see it in his face. "No. No body. Nothing. Not ever."

"That's awful." I think of Christopher. What if I had hidden his body or sunk it in the river? What if he was never found, and my parents never knew if he was alive or not? "Why do you think Cora had something to do with Caleb?"

He thinks about this question for a while. Takes his time, drinks more beer, and a stillness falls in the room. Finally, he leans back against the couch and stretches his arms wide along the tops of the cushions. But he doesn't look relaxed. He looks like a man being crucified.

"I went to Bury twice," he says. "First time was last July, when I initially sat down with Rose Yates. Second was last November, which I told you about. Last-minute trip, right after my wife died. During that trip, I sought out the parents of Caleb Benner, who still have a house there. I didn't have much of a plan except to ask them how the hell they kept it going all those years after their son disappeared. I think I was half-crazy then. Maybe more than half.

"I talked to them. It was a morning after a blizzard. Cold as hell. Their house…it was so lonely. They let me in, gave me coffee. I think…I think they were hoping I had information about Caleb." He shakes his head. "*Hope* is the wrong word. I could tell right away their relationship with hope had ended a long time ago. And we didn't end up talking about Caleb much."

Maya jumps in with the same question that just popped into my own brain. "Does that mean you didn't have information about him? Nothing new to report about his case?"

He looks at her, smiles just a touch. "I think I'll let that question just sit there, if you don't mind. But I will tell you this. When I spoke to the Benners, I realized there's no running away from pain. It sticks to you like hot glue. Maybe it cools, maybe it hardens, but the crust of it is always there. Pulling at you. You pick and you pick and you pick, and it never comes off. And that morning after I left their house, I was more uncertain about what to do next than I'd ever been in my life. I thought I had a plan, but I threw that plan out the door."

My voice catches in my throat as I ask, "And what was your plan?"

His gaze drills me. "Earlier, I told you there are some things I'm not going to share with you. That's one of them."

"I want to know what you think happened to them all," I say. "Rose, Max, Cora, Logan—all gone. No one ever heard from them again."

Pearson lowers his head so his chin touches his chest. Almost like he's trying to sleep.

"This is what I think, Marlowe." He lifts his head up, eyes open halfway. "Maybe the letters you've been receiving are more than just random people targeting a lottery winner. Maybe they do have something to do with your house. With Bury." He lets out a long sigh. "And maybe you keep up with your little investigation. I don't know. I can see how it gives you purpose when it's hard to find any otherwise. So you research the Yates family more, find out their secrets. Hell, if you can open that safe you found, who knows what you'll find in there?" He sounds tired. So incredibly tired. "But me? If it were me, I'd go back home, grab my kids, kiss each of them on the head, and then take them and the rest of my life out of Bury forever."

"Don't think I haven't considered it," I say. "But the letters warn us not to move or they'll track us down."

"Every decision carries risk," he replies. "But I'll tell you...that house of yours is a vortex, Marlowe. A fucking vortex, and you still have time to get out before it sucks you down into its belly." He sweeps his arm in front of him. "This house is also a vortex, and I'm gone for good. Sucked down deep. You sitting there, looking at me. I'm guessing you're thinking, *I don't want to end up like that*. And if there's one thing I can help you with, after you spent all that time and effort to come out and see me, is to tell you this: No, you don't want to end up like me."

I decide to ask, because I have to. "What happened to you, Detective? Why aren't you on the police force any longer?"

He doesn't answer. It's not that he's taking his time. He's just not going to answer.

Sounds like me.

I stand, Maya does likewise.

"Thanks for your time, Colin. You've been helpful."

He nods, says nothing. I feel a buzz in my pocket, slide out my mobile. Da has texted back.

All good.

Maya and I make our way to the door, and as we get close, I turn to ask Pearson one more question. After everything we've shared about our lives in our brief time together, there's one last thing I want to know.

"Your mom. You ever consider putting her...you know, like in a retirement home? A place like that?"

From across the room, I see him squint, just for a second. Then, with the hand holding the beer bottle, he points upstairs.

"There's no running from family, Marlowe. Gotta stay with them until the end, for better or for worse. 'Cause that's all you got. Sounds like a goddamn cliché, and maybe it is, but when the shit gets bad, you realize how true it is."

We hold eye contact just a moment longer, then I nod; he does the same. Maya and I show ourselves out with no more words exchanged.

Outside, Maya opens her mobile and summons a car for us.

"Aye," I say to the night as we wait on the sidewalk, the air cool on my neck. "He's absolutely right."

FIFTY-FOUR

BACK AT THE HOTEL, a few minutes before ten. The lobby is quiet, though the bar has a handful of businesspeople who look worn from the day, perhaps from life.

"Join me for a drink?" I ask Maya.

"Sure."

In for a penny and all that.

We sit at the bar, leather stools. The bar top is laminate made to look like wood. Back in Dublin, our pub's bar top is solid cherry that Da resurfaces every other year. A thick and ancient thing of beauty.

I order a whiskey neat, Maya a glass of red. I watch the bartender do his job, thinking about all the drinks I've served over the years. All the conversations, all the spilled beer, the occasional fights. It's what I was still doing not that long ago, back when my life was something I recognized. It's what I'm sure I'd still be doing if Holly existed and my millions of dollars didn't.

"So now what?" Maya asks.

"Pearson knows more than he told us," I say.

"Maybe. But I still don't understand why it matters."

I shake my head. "The Yateses factor into this somehow, I'm sure of it. I think the letter writers knew them, so figuring out what happened to them might be my only way to figure out who We Who Watch is."

What I don't disclose are the even more irrational thoughts churning in my brain. About how I really want to find the boy. Max, the son of Rose. If he's still alive, he's in trouble. I can save him. I took Christopher's life, and this is my chance to save one.

"Marlowe, this doesn't make sense."

"It does. I have to find them, Maya. Or at least find out what happened."

"How?"

"There have to be more clues somewhere."

She sets her glass down, swipes her hands along the bar top as if smoothing out a wrinkled napkin, sighs. "I'm worried about you."

"Thanks," I say, "but I don't need your worry."

"I don't think you know what you need at all. You don't need to find the Yateses. You should be home with your family. As for the letters, you need to rely more on the police."

"You keep saying that and I keep going, and nothing happens. I just get told about the limited resources of the Bury PD."

"Then go again. I'll go with you. Or maybe we need to go higher up the food chain than the Bury PD. You have the resources to fight this, Marlowe, to get more help, yet you seem hell-bent on doing everything yourself, and I don't know why."

"I asked you here, didn't I? That's not doing everything myself."

She turns her body more my direction, leaving her wineglass untouched, as if challenging me to do the same. But I hold my drink even tighter in my hand, as if it's the edge of a cliff, and maybe it is. "You did ask me here," she says, "and I can't figure that out either. I'm not sure how I'm helping."

I choose not to think, instead saying the thing that's been sitting on the tip of my tongue all night.

"I don't want to be alone. I just…" I sip, an easy crutch for a temporary loss of words. "I'm just so fucking alone."

"You're not alone. You're surrounded by your family."

"Not all of them," I say.

Maya now picks up her wine. "I'm not a substitute for Holly."

"That's not what I'm saying." *Or is it?* "All I know is I feel better when you're around. Is that wrong?"

"No, it's not wrong," she says. "But I feel like there's something you're trying to tell me and failing miserably. Is there?"

It's a question that deserves an answer, so I give it thought. Sit here and think in silence, think on these past months. Think long on it, and she drinks her wine, giving me space, allowing me to process. And I have no dots to connect into a perfect picture, but I do—after a spell, I do—glimpse at something I hadn't yet seen. A realization that fades as quickly as it had materialized, but I capture it enough to form a thought around it.

"I have an addiction to hurt," I say. "I'm *compelled* by guilt and pain. So I'll say it: I'm attracted to you, and I don't know if it's a real attraction or just a justification for self-loathing. I canna even tell you how much I value you as a lawyer and a friend, and that's what I need right now. But there's this sublime sting in my gut when I think about you being something more, and something inside me chases the sting. And when I fell down and smashed my head while boxing, I can't say a hundred percent it was an accident. And the letters…the letters. They seem so random, but at the same time, it feels like I earned them. That these people know I deserve to be tortured."

She takes a moment to digest everything. "You aren't responsible for Holly's death."

No, I think. *Not Holly's.*

"I don't know how to explain it."

"Yes, you do," she says. "I think you know exactly how to explain it. Just say what you mean."

The heat comes again, rising from my chest to my face, and how I welcome it. I feed it with more alcohol. "I'm trapped in this house. I can't move for fear of something happening to my family. And I can't figure anything out, the letters, the Yateses—"

"*For fuck's sake*, Marlowe. Stop pussying around and just tell me what you mean."

I slam my drink against the bar top.

"*It should've been me.*"

Silence falls, I catch the stares from others nearby. A pair of businessmen sit side by side at a table, hunched over a single laptop screen. They both look at me, assessing whether or not I'm a problem.

Yeah, I think. *I might just be a problem.*

Maya grabs my wrist, not with anger but to focus me, I think.

"What should've been you? You mean instead of Holly?"

I look down to my left hand, Maya's fingers on my wrist. Then I move my gaze to my right, the one still holding that drink, and I watch, disembodied, as this hand raises the glass to my lips, and I drink the last of the contents.

Shame flows through me as I set the glass back on the bar top, but it's more than that. I feel an anger rising. It prickles my chest, and I begin to feel the first tiny beads of sweat dot my forehead. I think back to the house, to the panic attack I had. This has similar rumblings.

"I gotta go," I tell her, my hands shaking.

"*Marlowe.*"

"I said I gotta go."

She leans in, analyzing.

"Are you okay?"

"I don't know."

I get up too fast, knock the barstool over.

"Marlowe, what's going on? Your face is flushed."

"Too many drinks," I tell her, a half-truth. "I'm fine. Night, Maya."

Her expression tells me she doesn't believe a damn word I'm saying. But she lets me be.

"Good night, Marlowe."

Out the bar, through the lobby, into the elevator.

This is more than an inexplicable burst of anger.

It takes a thousand years to reach my floor, and as the elevator doors finally open, one thought races through my mind.

I'm falling.

FIFTY-FIVE

I THINK I'M ASLEEP, but who can know? Does it matter?

Images. Horrible, eviscerating images.

I want to wake up. Please let me wake up.

Holly's face, dead skin pulpy on skeletal bones. I touch her cheek, it sloughs off, lands on the floor with a sickening splat. Her eyes dissolve into a dark goo, like swatted flies on a counter. Her hair falls out in clumps, each attached to a slice of scalp. Finally, the rest of her crumbles around my feet, and I have to walk through her remains if I want to leave this place.

Suddenly, there's Christopher, sitting on the first step of an impossible stairway, one that stretches completely out of view. He's the same; he isn't the same. His face holds the boyishness I remember, but his eyes are empty holes. My brother wears a suit: ink black, matching bow tie, white cuffed shirt. He could be a waiter; he could be a marionette. He never wore a suit in his life, except the few times at church. And in his casket.

You're dead, I tell him, mostly to convince myself.

We're all dead, Aidan. You're just a dead person waiting to happen.

My house, I think. *This is my house. This is my staircase.*

I look to his left and a boy sits cross-legged in the foyer, hands in lap, watching us. He's completely unfamiliar to me, but I know without pause this is Max McKay, Rose's son. He gives me a little nod, a wry smile, as if he knows everything will be all right. Or it will be horrible, and he's okay with that.

I don't understand, I say.

I look down. Christopher's feet are on the floor, his legs open wide. Between his knees are my children. My beautiful children. They weren't there before, but they are now. Side by side, nestled together, eyes closed; I think they're sleeping. I want to tell them to run away, because my brother turned into something unsavory. But they look so peaceful. They sit in silent comfort with their uncle. This uncle, hardly much older than them.

You took me, my brother says. *And now, I take you.*

With that, he summons the X-Acto from nowhere, a magical flick of the wrist. Same blade from that day, last of his life, surgical steel, so sharp and smooth, you're dead before you feel anything.

I scream.

He doesn't hear me. No one hears me.

It should've been you, he says.

Then he slits my little girl's throat. She doesn't move. The only motion is the skin on her throat peeling back like that of an orange baking to nothingness in the desert sun.

From her gaping wound come butterflies.

A beautiful dozen, colors of the world.

Max starts laughing. Laughing at the wonder of it all, the way only a child can laugh. He gets up and starts chasing the butterflies, which bob and weave just beyond his reach.

Christopher turns his attention to my son.

Bo. He's going to do Bo next.

I'd rather die than watch this, dream or not.

I wake.

I wake, shouting.

Shouting in this foreign room.

Where am I?

Glazed in sweat, boxers clinging.

Hotel room. Hotel room. Hotel room. I keep repeating this, because somewhere it's the truth.

But I'm not in my bed. I swivel my head, see the empty bed, covers pulled back, wrinkled lumps.

I'm sitting at the desk, the kind designed for those businessmen from the bar. Lots of outlets, USB ports, ergonomic chair.

Last thing I knew, I was asleep in the bed. Here I am now, sitting at this desk in the dark, wondering if I was sleepwalking or if I had another bout of missing time. Maybe there's no difference between the two.

Maybe my whole life is actually one long nightmare, and the missing time is just gaps between the dreams.

Maybe nothing is real at all.

And heavens, I think, what a blessing that would be.

PART III

FIFTY-SIX

Bury, New Hampshire
Day Thirty-Five

FOUR DAYS.

Four full days since Milwaukee, since I soaked in the sadness of Colin Pearson. Four days since I ignored the instructions to wire ten thousand dollars to some bank account. Four days since Da and the kids had a nice little adventure at the Oak Street Inn, where, I'm told, the innkeepers cooked up a signature batch of mac and cheese that was the best the twins ever had.

I came home wary of what was surely waiting for me. More notes. Angry demands that I hadn't obeyed. That I had left town.

But there was nothing.

Ninety-six hours later, I walk though my days on permanent edge, knowing THEY are still out there. THEY aren't done with me—just figuring out the next move.

Now, with evening creeping in, I'm on my bed, back propped by hundred-dollar pillows that give only five-dollar comfort, computer warm on my thighs, an electronic pet. And I dive deep, deep as I can into the abyss known as the Yates family.

Despite Maya's skepticism, the Yateses *are* a part of what's happening to me, and in my current state of mind, I might just be an antenna, open to receiving strange transmissions.

Logan is my first subject of research, and what a menacing figure he cuts as his image splashes across the screen. *Business Week. New York Times. Washington Post.* Even the *Atlantic* ran a profile of him, headlined *What Happened to Logan Yates?* I read every article, and the flavors are mostly the same. Private equity magnate, dreaded competitor, shatterer of companies. Then he just vanished, along with members of his immediate family. The police investigate, come up empty. Each story ends with disappointing inconclusion, but the comments are rife with wild and juicy speculation.

Finally pissed off the wrong people.

Must be a cartel connection. They killed the whole family.

He owns a private island. Left the country to avoid the feds.

He killed his daughters, buried them, then fled.

The daughters killed and buried him, then fled.

Fucking one-percenter. Good riddance.

Wouldn't want to be living in that house.

I half expect to see my name pop up in someone's comment, but there's nothing.

On to Cora Yates, about whom I find little. Her internet presence is mostly limited to articles about her father, Bury newsletters celebrating best outdoor holiday decor, and Middleton Prep gala photos. The woman is striking. A double for Grace Kelly. I see Willow in her, though in Cora's face exists no uncertainty. No self-doubt. Just a person with a fierce, piercing gaze whom I suspect was rarely ever told *no*.

Finally, to Rose Yates, the most intriguing and heartbreaking. Rose, the writer who penned mysteries under the name J. L. Sharp. Rose still has a functioning website for her books, and I wonder whose decision it would be to ever take it down.

Four books, the last of which came out just a month or so after she disappeared.

The Child of the Steps

Those words hum. Could be they raise the hairs on my arms a little, or maybe that's just my imagination.

When I look on Amazon, it seems her last book is her most popular. And the reviews, they're notable. *Booklist* called it a "heartbreaking tour de force," and *Publishers Weekly* deemed it "Sharp's best work yet, on par with the masters of the genre."

Makes me want to read it. Perhaps I will.

Her author photo is in black and white, her gaze relaxed but alert, like a grazing deer aware danger always lurks close. She's beautiful but not like her sister. Cora's beauty is genetics enhanced by an unnecessarily heavy hand. Rose is straight-from-sleep gorgeous, the kind of pretty nothing can enhance or diminish.

Just like Holly.

Beautiful dead people.

I'm just about to dig a bit deeper into Rose's life when Gmail alerts me to a new message. I move to click away the notification but am hooked by the subject line.

You want to play?

I switch tabs, click on the email. The sender is rumhillroad@yahoo .com, and the hook yanks harder.

> You think We're making this up? We'll fucking kill you, Irish piece of shit. Then your family. Slice the throats of your dumb kids. Gut your old man. You don't ignore Us. Two days. $10 million. Same wire number as before. Fuck you and fuck your money. We're taking it or your family. Your choice. If it's not in the account by Weds at 5 p.m., We're blowing everything the fuck up.

No signature.

FIFTY-SEVEN

I SHOULD HAVE MOVED.

It's my first thought after reading the email, the words stabbing me like a prison shiv.

Despite the threat against moving away, what are the chances they would have followed me? But I wanted to stay. Deep down, I wanted this threat on some masochistic level. And now? Now it's too late to move. Too late to do anything but follow their instructions.

No, I correct myself. *It's not that we should have moved away from Bury.* We should never have come here at all.

And whatever happens, I'm to blame. I'm to blame.

I scan the words again, looking for clues. It's the first time they sent an email. And the writing style...no playfulness. No casual tone. Just straight-up brutality.

I try to clear my mind, but that's as easy as shooing a swarm of wasps from their sun-baked nest. There are too many things inside my brain, too many loose ends of information leading nowhere. Too many gut instincts and no facts.

And then Holly's voice, deep inside, tickling me, telling me the words she once said when I was trying to understand what to do with my life. The words are truer now than ever.

Figure your shit out, Marlowe.

I almost choke at the thought. "I haven't been further from an accomplishment in my life."

She doesn't say anything else, but that doesn't mean I have to stop talking to her.

"What is it about the Yates family I need to understand?" I can almost picture her sitting in front of me, listening but not leading me in any direction. Letting me figure my shit out on my own.

"It's this place, this house. Has to be. Like…like I'm supposed to figure out all the secrets here."

The word *secrets* feels hot. Glows orange.

What secrets?

I picture her here, guiding me. She nods, looks at the floor, and as I follow her gaze, and as I realize I'm another step into the abyss, and as I seem to see through the floor beneath me and the one below that and all the way into the basement, I see the safe room. And in the safe room is the safe. The safe in the safe room.

Safe. The word glows orange.

That's it.

I'm supposed to open the safe. Whatever answer I'm supposed to find is in there. Everything that's happened since the day Holly died has been leading me to opening that safe.

And I look up and Holly isn't there, but I tell her anyway:

"Thanks, love."

FIFTY-EIGHT

THE WI-FI SIGNAL IS nonexistent from inside the safe room; the steel hull makes sure of that. So when I came down here an hour ago, I had to climb back up the rungs and sit on the edge of the opening, legs dangling down, laptop on my thighs. The basement is noticeably cooler than the rest of the house. The difference between a live person and a dead one, I reckon. Fluorescents blaze from above, reminding me how pale my arms are. Goose bumps dance.

My back is cramped from sitting like this for so long, hunched over my laptop screen.

I continue my online hunt for clues, wanting to be as near the safe as possible while I search. That this place might guide me, tell me what keywords to type. That the spirit of Logan Yates wants me to open his safe, because there's something he wants me to see.

I search and search. Search until my skin chills to the point of unpleasantness. I search until I grow tired, my eyes weakening, as I drown in an LED glaze.

Out of the shadows, a voice.

"Dad?"

I look over.

Bo stands beyond an arm's distance, hands by his sides. Pj's cling to his bony frame, long sleeves on a hot summer night.

"Darling," I say. In my life, I don't believe I've ever called him that.

"What are you doing?"

"Discovering."

He nods. Weight shifts to his back foot.

"Are you okay?" he asks.

"'Course I am. Why wouldn't I be?"

"Because you've been acting weird."

"Weird is all around," I tell my boy. "We swim in it every day."

"Like that. What you just said. That's weird."

He's right. It is weird.

"Tell you what," I say. "Go get me a drink, would you? Just ask Grandpa what I like, he'll know."

His expression changes to a scowl, professionally fast. "I know what you like. Anything we have."

"Hey, now."

"I don't want to get you a drink. I don't like it when you drink." Bo crosses his arms, tight knots.

"That's no way to speak to me."

"Yes, it is."

"Bo."

That look when he crosses the line, which he often does. A look of confidence quietly pressured by the weight of fear, that he knows he'll do as I say if I say it with enough conviction. But not now. Now I think there's no fear. I don't think he cares at all.

"You should be in bed," I say. "First day of school is tomorrow."

"I can't sleep."

"Doesn't matter. You canna be roaming the house."

"I'm not roaming. I'm here, and I want to know what you're doing."

A long breath escapes me. "I'm researching."

"Researching what?"

"The folks who used to live here."

"Why?"

"Because."

"That's not an answer."

"Bo, sometimes I don't understand you."

He absorbs this with curiosity. "Okay."

"I feel like you're different."

"We're all different."

I blink tears away.

"Why are you researching them?" he asks.

So I tell him. Hell, why not? "Because some bit of my brain believes that if I find out enough about them, I could maybe figure out the combination to the safe."

"The safe?"

"Aye."

He points to my legs, which still dangle over the opening of the submarine hull.

"The safe down there?"

"Aye." What other safe would there be?

But his eyes betray him, growing wide with concern. And this time, it's not just his weight shifting. He takes a full step back.

"Did you close it again?"

"What do you mean?"

"Did you *close* it again?" There's a trace of panic there, in that face. Trace of fear.

"Bo, it's closed. I'm trying to get it open. I want to see what's inside."

"But it's already open," he says.

"Wha?"

The boy is lying. A simmer of anger, just a simmer. Heats me enough to melt the goose bumps. "Don't tell tales, Bo."

"I don't understand," he says.

"What's that, now?" I set the laptop to the side, full attention on my boy. "I say, what's that, now?"

"Dad, what's wrong with you?"

Now I stand, but it doesn't feel like standing. It feels like looming.

Bo takes another step back. I take one toward him.

"Bo, I think I've had enough of your—"

Then he shouts. Shouts in this vacant basement of garish light and chilled concrete.

"It's already *open*," Bo says. "You had that guy here..." He pauses, looks up, remembering. "Five days ago. That locksmith. He opened it. Don't you *remember?*"

And there's a truth, one I pluck from my mind, for it sits there right in the front and center, easy for the taking.

No.

I don't tell my son this truth, because I'm scared.

No, I don't remember that at all.

FIFTY-NINE

I DO A HASTY inventory of my mind and am horrified to discover such low stockpiles. Five days ago, Bo said. Five days ago was...damn, it's all so empty. Four days ago, I was in Milwaukee, and thankfully I remember that. But five days ago?

That day. *Think.*

I got a letter, because it drove me to confront Peter Ainsworth. That night, I remember. Came home from Ainsworth's house, borderline drunk. Yelled at the kids, which set off a panic attack. Drank more, then confessed to Da the truth about Christopher.

Yeah, I remember that night.

But that day?

I scan and scan. Pockets of emptiness.

GAP.

"What's going on with you?" Bo asks.

The truth is hard, but it won't do to lie to him.

"The stress...it's been playing tricks on my mind. Sometimes I have these chunks of...lost time. It's okay. I'll be okay."

As expressionless as ever. "That doesn't sound okay."

"Just don't tell your sister, okay? If she asks, I'll tell her. But no need to freak her out."

"So only I get to freak out?"

"We all carry a burden." I close my eyes, give one final push at recollection, fail. "What was in it?"

"In what?"

"The safe, Bo. What was in the safe?"

"You said it was empty."

Empty. Hell, why can't I remember any of this?

I turn from Bo and scamper down the ladder.

"Can I come?"

"Fine," I tell him. He's down here with me in no time.

The safe's door is closed, but when I pull on the handle, it opens with ease. But it was definitely locked the first time I was down here, the night I found Mags. So Bo is telling the truth: I paid someone to open it and just didn't recall anything. I tell myself to remember to check the security video from five days ago to see the locksmith arriving.

And then, another surprise.

If the safe was empty before, it isn't now. There's just a small, white envelope, and funny how the sight of an envelope wreaks such havoc on my nerves.

"What is it?" Bo asks, trying to peer around my body.

"Hang on."

Maybe the safe wasn't empty when it was first opened. Could it be I just overlooked this small envelope?

Doubtful.

According to Bo, five days ago, this safe was empty. Now there's an envelope in it.

I reach out, hands quivering like a junkie in need of a fix. Grab the envelope. My heart leaps, knowing it's *something*. A tantalizing clue. As horrified as I am, I'm equally excited.

And there it is, that realization, in the seconds that pass before I open it. That thrill in my chest, buried under fear and fatigue. But it's there. Now is when I realize my sickness, and it's this:

I don't want this to end.

This addiction to the hurt. It doesn't want to let me go.

It should've been you.

I open the envelope.

A single page, standard computer paper, folded in quarters. No words, just a single image. It's not hand-drawn but just a picture likely downloaded and printed.

It's an ouroboros. Not an exact replica of my tattoo, but damn close.

Ouroboros.

A snake eating its own tail. As I once explained to Holly, it symbolizes that everything has a reason. But here, on this page, deep in the bowels of this house, it doesn't seem so thoughtful, so hopeful. Here, it just looks like a snake eating itself from the inside out. A creature inflicting harm on its own body, because that's all there's left to do when the pain becomes unbearable.

SIXTY

BO'S VOICE. "WHAT IS it?"

"It doesn't make sense," I say.

Bo pokes me. "Dad, what is it?" Fear in his voice, rightly so.

More horrifying than the intimacy of the image is the fact that this piece of paper is *inside* my house.

Then Bo starts to cry, an event as rare as desert rain. The tears come fast, followed by heaving sobs. I drop the letter to the floor and grab him, hold him tight against me, and he pushes back, not hard but enough to tell me my embrace isn't what he needs. But I hold on a few seconds longer, unwilling to relinquish my role. Then I let him go. I let go.

Let go.

After a time, he seems to exhaust himself and sits on the cold floor, wraps his bony arms around bonier knees, and I lower myself to him, put a hand on his back, give a slow rub, which he accepts.

"I miss her so much," he says.

"Aye. So do I."

He wipes his nose, looks up, eyes streaked red. "For a while, I kept expecting her to show up in our room in the morning. Wake us up. That it was all a dream and she was alive. And it hurt every day, because the mornings would come and she wasn't there." Gaze lowered to the floor. "And then one day, I stopped expecting it. Just woke up and knew she wouldn't be there. And that's so much worse."

I'd rightly take on all of his suffering if I could, but all I can do is sit with him.

"Bo..."

"You're not okay," he says, keeping his gaze away.

"What?"

"You're not okay. You're scaring us."

"I'm not trying to."

Along with tears comes anger. Bo stands and makes a kind of eye contact that gives me pause.

"We have all this money, and we're scared." His voice isn't a shout, but it's within shouting distance of it. "Every night, I have to tell Maggie we're safe and I don't believe it."

"Hold on a minute, Bo—"

"You don't know what you're doing," he says, and despite the utter truth of the words, my anger wells.

"I'm trying to figure things out."

"It's not working." My boy, he's leaning forward. Arms back, head forward, an aggressive stance. Rare that I ever see myself in him, but now I do, the angry bits at least, and I can't do a thing about it for either of us.

"I'm doing my best," I say, grinding my teeth.

"Your best sucks, then."

"Hey, watch it. You don't talk to me like—"

"You're drinking too much. Forgetting things. Grandpa is worried, too. We're scared, but you won't listen to us."

"Bo, *stop* it. I am listening to you. I was just going to—"

And then he drops it, the biggest bomb in his arsenal. Kind of surprised it hasn't happened sooner, but that objective reasoning does nothing to shield me from its terrible, blinding force.

"It should've been you."

It's his voice now but it was mine in my head, saying those same words, just moments ago. This ghostly link, it's eerie and beautiful, ethereal. But above all, enraging because my boy wishes me dead.

"Say that again."

He doesn't back away. Rather, he inches a fraction closer.

"It should've been you instead of her."

"Tell me you don't mean that."

He doesn't even offer the courtesy of a blink. "I do. Maggie does, too."

I want to slap him. I can visualize it, from the arc of my hand as I pull back to the open palm connecting across his smooth face. The instant sting would burn through him. The tears would come, but maybe he'd learn to talk to me proper.

And there it is, me barely even realizing it, my right hand in the air, frozen above my head.

Bo moves his gaze from my eyes, to my hand, and then back. His face doesn't tense; it relaxes. He's ready for it. He *wants* it, and that's the worst thing of it. Like his daddy, he welcomes the pain. Craves it, even.

I lower my hand.

"I'm sorry," I say. "Best you go ahead and get upstairs now."

And he turns and runs. Scampers up the metal ladder, disappears out of this tomb. And there's nothing left for me to do but lie down, which I accept. Lie on this cot, which may as well be a casket. Breathe in this stale air, stare up at the curved steel roof above, see beyond it into the everywhere, where all the other colors exist, hues of a rainbow. And perhaps there was a thunderstorm leaving that rainbow behind, the sky dark on one side of a cornfield, light on the other, and in the middle, the rainbow weighs. And I'm so close, I can touch it, and when I do, it feels like taffy, and isn't that something?

And the moment I touch it, everything ends.

The end. I think that's what I want more than anything.

And I close my eyes and fantasize about it, and Holly tells me that's okay. That the end is not so bad after all.

Maybe I fall asleep.

Maybe I don't.

SIXTY-ONE

Bury, New Hampshire
Day Thirty-Six

I WAKE, BACK IN my own room, hearing rain. So subtle, I think it's a remnant of a dream. A dream of dark skies and rainbows and taffy that leads to death. But a quick glance at the six-foot pane near the bed tells me the rain is quite real, and it comes down with intention. I think back to my month in this town and realize this is the first time I've seen it rain.

Morning.

I sit up, swing my legs over the bed, feel the rush of reality swoop through me, nearly toppling me back to the mattress. But I brace myself against it, lean into it, then finally stand firm.

Get a robe, go downstairs, fetch a coffee. In the back porch, I sit and sip, replaying the moments of last night, and I can't be clear how much really happened. Bo, telling me he wished I were dead. Finding that piece of paper in the safe. Being told the safe was opened five days prior, with no memory of it.

That's right. I told myself to check the security video.

I grab my mobile and launch the app, select the camera over the garage door. That'll show me any locksmith vehicle from five days ago.

But.

But it's blank.

There is no footage, because the camera's turned off. It hasn't been deleted from the app, but it's been switched off. I scan the motion sensor's log, finding that the last recording was five days ago. Five days, right in the dead center of the gap time in my mind.

My heart races faster than I can attribute to caffeine. When I check the other cameras, they're all off as well. What the hell?

On impulse I scroll through my contacts, find Owen Brace. He answers on the third ring.

"Marlowe, how are you?"

"I've been better," I say. "Look, I need to understand something. My cameras were turned off five days ago, and I had no idea. Is there any way to turn them off except on my mobile app?"

"The app and the desktop website. That's it. You don't know who turned them off?"

"That's what I'm trying to figure out."

"Well," he says, "both the app and the website are password protected, though if you had your web browser or app remember your password, then I suppose anyone with access to your phone or laptop could've accessed your cameras. Have you had anyone new in your house during the last five days?"

Just a locksmith I don't even remember, I think. But the locksmith would've been in the house at the time he was turning off the cameras, so I'd still have the footage of his van in that case, which I don't.

"No," I say. Then I ask what, to me, is a very obvious question. "Your team installed everything. Could…could any of your guys be able to hack into my system?"

"Look," he says. "I understand your concern and your…circumstances. And I'm not offended by your question. But I guarantee you there's no way any of my employees have the ability to break into your cameras. Can cameras be hacked? Of course they can. They run off your Wi-Fi, and I have no idea how secure you have your router established. But my guys are vetted. I trust them completely."

Frustration wells. "And what about you?" I ask.

Now his tone changes. "What *about* me?"

"Maybe *you* know how to hack. And all that information you wanted from me as part of your contract? That always struck me as odd."

It's out there, and I don't take it back. Brace takes it in for a moment and then responds, "I think you should just go ahead and ask what you're thinking. That'll make hanging up on you easier."

I swallow a stab of nerves. Then, I think, *Fuck it.*

"Are you writing the letters, Owen?"

The call disconnects.

Which, of course, is not a denial.

SIXTY-TWO

I TURN THE CAMERAS back on, one by one, and they respond accordingly. But I have no footage of the past five days, no proof any locksmith was here. Maybe Bo is lying, maybe he isn't. But I can ask Da. I can ask Maggie. They'll know the real answer.

Assuming I even want to know.

I wonder if Bo turned the cameras off. Got into my mobile, found the app, turned them off.

I take another sip and the coffee's grown cold, jarring me. My mobile says it's 9:10 a.m., but what time did I make my coffee?

Movement out the back window. A figure in a gray rain slicker, traipsing across my back lawn. From the gait and the posture, I recognize Carlos immediately, but what is he doing here in the rain?

Carlos.

The kids, they saw two figures in the backyard the other night. Carlos and Abril?

I set the coffee down, wanting no more to do with it. To the back door. I open it and yell, "Carlos!"

He looks up, and my imagination adds a lightning flash, illuminating his face, betraying wide eyes, full of fear. Guilt.

I gesture for him to come to me. He does. I open the door and he steps into the covered porch, but he doesn't look happy to be out of the rain.

"Yes?" he asks.

"What are you doing?"

"Working."

"In the rain?"

He nods. "You pay me to work, I work. Always things to do."

"And what were you going to do today?"

He thinks on this two seconds too long, by my best guess. "I can trim bushes in rain, no problem."

I study his face, his eyes. Carlos struggles to keep eye contact, but that doesn't make him guilty of anything. "What do you do when it snows?" I ask. "In the winter?"

"I no work in the winter. Spring. Summer. Some fall. No winter."

"Okay," I say.

Something looking like relief settles on his face. "You need something else, Mr. Marlowe?"

He turns to leave without waiting for an answer, so I decide to lob a grenade.

"The other night, my kids saw two people in the backyard. Those people left a note for me. One of those letters." Now comes the lie. "I checked the security cameras, Carlos. The backyard camera caught two people leaving the note. It looked a lot like you and your sister."

"No," he says, shaking his head. "Wasn't us."

"It was, Carlos."

"No, no. Not us. Must be someone else." He doesn't look scared or guilty at all. Just adamant in his denial. Maybe I'm wrong. I'm accusing this man of something he didn't do based on zero evidence.

But then.

He says this.

"No camera at the garage door, how you see anything?"

Everything turns on that statement.

I edge a few inches closer to him. "I didn't say the note was left at the garage door."

His eyes widen. The guilt I didn't see before suddenly lights ablaze. "I never say—"

"How did you know that, Carlos?" He takes a step back, and now the man's half outside the porch door, into the pouring rain.

I expect more protesting, maybe he slips fully into Spanish and ends the conversation that way. But he doesn't. He spills it.

"We don't have choice. Please, Mr. Marlowe. We don't have choice." His hands entwine in an honest-to-god plead. "We don't want to be sent home. Not here...legally. I'm sorry. Both of us. Very sorry."

And here it is.

After an excruciating month, a confession. One of the guilty parties, right here in front of me.

I lean in. "Who told you to do this?"

A firm headshake.

"I don't tell you that."

"Yes, Carlos. You have to."

"No, no. I can't."

I feel myself puffing up. I don't want to hurt him, but he needs to think I will.

"All those notes," I say. "You know how sick that is?"

He tenses even more; I see it in his neck. Sweat peppers his forehead. "I'm sorry."

"You...you went into my house. Twice. You locked my daughter in the basement, then you left that picture in the safe."

Worry spreads across his face. "What? No, no, I didn't do that. I don't know what—"

"You *did*. You scared my children."

"I didn't mean to—"

"You didn't care at all," I say. "You're worried about being here illegally? What the fuck do you think I'm going to do? I'm going to call the police, that's what. You won't even be deported. You, your sister. You'll go to prison."

This man is about to throw up.

"No, no, no. We didn't do all those things. Not the family. No police. No police."

"Then tell me who made you do this."

"No."

"Carlos, you have no choice."

"No, I can't."

"Who are you scared of? And how do they know so much about—"

I don't finish my sentence, because with rabbit speed, Carlos smashes my jaw with his right fist.

I've been in lots of fights and lost on more than one occasion. In a scrap, your worst enemy is lack of anticipation. Often, it just takes one punch to start and end a fight, and if you let the other guy hit first, it could be over for you.

He connects square into my jawbone, and my body tells me it has no choice but to collapse right to the floor. That's the second punch: my head against the ground. By the time I can even think to orient myself, Carlos is gone, back out into the backyard and the torrential rain. He's gone, probably forever.

It doesn't matter, I think, finding the concrete of the patio floor suddenly comforting. Blood leaks into my mouth, warm and salty. Fire sears the left side of my face.

Carlos is gone, probably taking his sister with him.

But it's something.

After all this time, one piece of this mystery is revealed.

I smile, imagining my bloody mouth looking just like a clown's.

SIXTY-THREE

A FEW YEARS AGO, I had a physical. Didn't want to, but Holly insisted. Told me I was a parent, and parents have to make sure all their pieces are working because they have a responsibility to others besides themselves. So I went to this doctor, and he asked me a slew of interesting questions, the kind I couldn't imagine an Irish doc asking. He asked me, *Do you feel safe at home?* And I remember thinking, *Now why wouldn't I?*

I know the answer to that now.

The doctor also asked if I drank. *Aye,* I said. *How much?* he asked. *Enough to make my ancestors proud,* I answered. He didn't laugh. Instead, he followed up with this: *Do you ever drink in the morning to steady your nerves?* And I answered truthfully, *No, not ever. I can't imagine such a thing.*

That scene loops in my mind as I sit at my kitchen table, one costing thousands of dollars, if I correctly recall, which I likely don't. I sit here, my face full of ache, the rain spitting like an angry snake against the windowpanes. I sit here, two fingers of bourbon in a square glass in my right hand. Five cubes keep the glass cold, and I press it against my jaw as if that's the real reason for this all. But it's not long before I take my first sip, and as I do, my gaze floats without effort to the digital clock on the microwave. Half past nine in the morning. Hungover from last night, nerves shot to all hell, my face swollen, and I'm drinking bourbon. Guess that doc had a reason to ask after all.

The bourbon bites then soothes, and I hate that it does both those things.

I think about everything. I think about nothing. This takes about three minutes. Then the front door opens, closes, footsteps. Da appears, wearing rain and a scowl. He doesn't notice my face, but he sure as hell sees the glass in my hand.

"You're a right fecking mess, son."

"I've had a morning."

"I'm sure you have," he says. "You couldn't get up to take yer children to their first day at a new school. And look at you now, back to the well, like Charlie at the pub, that old crust. Disgusting is what it is."

Damn it. The kids' first day of school, and I completely forgot. I accept his abuse. I've earned it.

I also think about the twins out there, the first time without either Da or me around. What the hell am I doing? It's not safe to have them out there unprotected.

"What's wrong with you, Aidan?"

A thousand answers, but one floats to the top. "My wife is dead."

"Aye, as is mine. But your behavior deserves a better answer, sorry to say."

"You're cold."

"Cold?" He seems large in this moment, looming as he did when

I was just a child. "After what you've told me, I'm cold? Shouldn't have named you Aidan. Shoulda named you Cain."

It takes me a second, but the reference then hits. "God, Da…"

"Don't *God* me. God isn't anywhere to be found right now. And…" He tilts his head, squints. "What's happened to yer face?"

I tell him about the picture in the safe and how my security cameras had been disabled so I couldn't see Carlos in the act. How he must have a house key and know my security code. I tell Da about our confrontation and how Carlos hit me when it was clear he had no excuses left.

When I'm done, Da says, "Call the police, Aidan. You do or I will. I'm guessing the gardener and his sister have already fled for different pastures, but you still hafta call the police."

The police. Everyone tells me to call the police.

"I will."

"And call Maya."

"What for?"

He scratches at his skunktail sideburns. "Could be she has something smart to say."

"Yeah, maybe."

He sighs, exasperated, followed by silence.

"Listen, Da, I'm sorry…I'm just sorry about everything."

"Aye."

"How was the school?"

This coaxes the barest of grins from him. "Mags was a little nervous, Bo mostly disinterested. But they lit up a touch when they saw how nice that school was. Right fit for royalty, I'd say. And the teacher—Mrs. Braebrun, or some such—seemed pleasant enough."

This eases the pain in my face and moves it to my heart.

"I'll get them from school," I say.

"Damn right you will. Two fifty-five. You can meet the teacher." He scans me up and down. "You can't do much about your face, but you can damn well wash the drink from your breath."

"It's just one drink."

"If I had a euro for every drunk who told me that."

The half-full crystal tumbler in my hand is heavy, and I have a sudden and insatiable urge to see what it looks like in a thousand pieces, so I throw it against the brick of the fireplace mantel. As the glass explodes in a fractal firework show, I'm jealous of its easy destruction, resulting in a thousand scatterings of sharp objects on which to slice one's feet.

"Christ in His name, boy!" Da whirls to the chimney, then back to me. He's right pissed, but I fall inside myself, into a cocoon.

"It's just a glass," I say.

"I don't know what to do about you."

"Maybe you're not supposed to do anything," I say.

"I don't understand you."

I give him no answer because there isn't one. Instead, I walk away. Up the stairs, the hard, cold steps to my bedroom, where I find no peace, no comfort, and only a deafening silence. And that's hell, I believe. Forever solitude, darkness wrapped in a dreamless sleep, twisting, twisting.

Sweat creeps, and not likely from the few sips of drink. Sweat creeps as if running away from my brain, now toxic, boiling and spitting. Bile rises with the same excuse, scorching my throat. And with that, a mass exodus. I make it to the toilet just in time, puke as I haven't since I was an eighteen-year-old, unaccommodated to the amount of poison I now so easily ingest. My ribs threaten to snap like toothpicks with the force of my heaves, and it feels good, feels good, this pain. Bring it on, bring it up, bring it out. Make me over in one massive retch, make this wretch someone decent, someone sane. Someone who knows how to look more forward than back, someone who can breathe in life rather than choke on it.

The toilet is a violent mess. I collapse to the bathroom floor, fold my legs around it, then my arms, cradle it as if it's my own child. Perhaps I scream into this fouled bowl, maybe I just imagine it. But nothing more comes. I'm empty, and that seems about right.

Roll an arm's length of toilet paper, wipe my nose and mouth, flush, and that's that. Don't even bother to wash my hands or rinse my mouth, because, really, why?

On my bed, my laptop and mobile. The light blinks on my mobile, unusual. I've disabled nearly all notifications, and none of my apps allow the flashing LED. For a moment, I'm transported to that day, the one a lifetime ago, as I said goodbye to Holly.

Does this casket make me look fat?

My mobile buzzed that afternoon, and I was so sure it was her, telling me she loved me one last time, telling me she was okay and to move on. But it was a different message altogether.

So this light, what will it tell me? Will it be her this time, telling me I've done fucked everything up? And will I be able to reply, *Don't I know it?*

I collapse on the bed because that's easiest. Grab the mobile, swipe the screen, check the notification. There's a Gmail message from rumhillroad@yahoo.com, the bastard who emailed yesterday.

Today. 5 p.m.

That's all it says.

This time, I write back.

How did you get inside my house?

I send it, wait, swallow thick air as I do.
A minute later.

Today. 5 p.m. And We don't know what the fuck you're
talking about otherwise.

SIXTY-FOUR

I HEAT. BLOOD PUMPS through me fiercely, forcing to break right through my skin. The sweet tang of vomit lingers in my mouth, tempting my stomach to produce more.

All this anger, it pushes me to my limits. I think I need it, as if, were rage not an option, I wouldn't know how to exist. But it's an option, and it's here now. Throwing a whiskey glass against a mantel? That's easy. Effortless. Painless. I need more.

I stand and walk to the full-length mirror in the corner. In the glass, I see the real me, the sweating, huffing, drained, crazy drunk that I am. And I think, *You disgust me, you. You fucking disgust me.*

And the reflection, he laughs. Laughs in agreement, tells me I disgust him, too, and isn't it nice to have something in common? And we are both laughing now, laughing on the edge of tears, on the razor's edge of mania, laughing because it's all such a shame. Shame I can't cope, shame I can't raise my kids proper, shame I don't know how to...

How to punish yourself.

"What?"

You think you're addicted to the hurt? Maybe you need to end it all to get sober. Maybe you need to come to where I am. I call it the Big Dark.

And then the reflection changes. No longer do I see my face but rather one that is shockingly close in appearance but more handsome, more intense. Leaner, hungrier. And the eyes. Those eyes. I know them.

This is not the Christopher from my dream. This is the Christopher from my fractured reality.

I woulda looked like this, he says, this reflection. *I'd still be one year younger than you, and I woulda looked like this.*

"Goddamn," I say.

No god to damn, Christopher replies. *I can tell you that for certain. No god, no devil. No fecking nothin'. I just exist in your unraveling mind. Funny that, innit? I was the deranged one once, and now you are.*

I reach out and touch his face, and he mine.

"Tell me you would've been a bad person," I say. "That you would've hurt people. That you were supposed to die for a reason."

Don't have those answers, big brother. Maybe I'd've become something great. Or maybe I woulda overdosed on heroin at sixteen. Perhaps been a Nobel laureate. Perhaps raped and killed a dozen innocent little ones. We don't get to ever know such things.

"What do you want?"

But, like his life, this reflection is suddenly gone. Maddeningly gone, my brother. He has something to say but prefers to play with me. To taunt and tease me. To hold the secrets of the universe in his pocket rather than reveal them, the selfish bastard.

I can't control my right hand, balling up into a tight, bony fist, knuckles white as fish meat. I watch that fist swing sideways, proper roundhouse. It delivers a devastating blow to this mirror, this piece of glass I never wanted in the first place.

The world explodes.

And as it rains shards and shards, fragments of what used to be my brother and, perhaps, myself, I see it all before me. In all those pieces, I am merely one of them, broken to dust, broken perhaps forever, surely never the same.

Blood streams from my knuckles, dripping on gray carpet, something quite nearly beautiful. Makes me dizzy, but a good kind. Amusement-park dizzy and light in a way I haven't felt in ages. Suddenly, I sense I could float to the moon, should the moon be willing to have me.

It's as if my blood is tainted, both curing and killing me as it leaves my body. I know the cut isn't bad enough to actually end me, but for a moment, I pretend it is. I stare into that void, seeing such darkness, and then, for no reason other than the randomness of firing synapses, a decades-old memory bursts into my mind. From my school days, I'm maybe fourteen and my mate Tim Kilkenny is telling me a joke. We're in the classroom during a very quiet study time, and he leans over and whispers.

A bloke is sitting in a doctor's office. Doctor walks in, says, "Sir, I have some bad news. I'm afraid you're going to have to stop masturbating." Bloke says, "I don't understand, doc. Why?" Doctor tells him, "Because I'm trying to examine you."

I remember the moment he told it. I tried so hard to keep from laughing, but the harder I tried, the more impossible it became. And finally I bursted, and though I knew I'd get into trouble, it was such a liberating sensation. And I laughed and laughed, and it was so contagious that all the other kids—fully unaware of the joke—followed suit.

And this memory brings a smile to me now, and that smile blossoms into its own laugh; and while not as hearty as it was in that long-ago moment, it is genuine and cleansing.

Blood loss and laughter. Maybe that's all I ever needed.

"You know, laughter is the best form of medicine. Unless you're crazy. When a crazy person laughs, anyone near them takes off running."

I freeze, then look over.

Rose Yates is sitting on top of my bed.

SIXTY-FIVE

I DON'T BLINK. DON'T breathe. I think my blood even stops flowing. It's more than just fear. I don't want to scare this ghost away.

Rose turns her head, looks around, her reddish-brown hair spilling over her shoulders. She's wearing a baggy, gray sweatshirt over faded jeans, and she is striking.

"This used to be my dad's room," she tells me. "But I guess you already knew that."

I manage two syllables. "I figured."

"I can't imagine the number of women he's had in here," she says. "Disgusting."

"Where…" My tongue is sand dry. "Where's Max?"

Rose's face flatlines in an instant. "I don't want to talk about my son."

"Is he okay?"

"What did I just say?"

"Am I…are you real?"

Rose rolls over onto her belly, puts her hands under her chin, gazes deep into me.

"What do you think, Marlowe?"

I slowly lower myself to the floor, fearing my legs might just give out otherwise. "If you're not real, then you're the craziest hallucination I've ever had."

"Have you hallucinated before?"

"No. Well, I don't know, actually."

She points at my hand. "You're bleeding."

"Yeah."

"Does that concern you?"

Hell of a question. "I'm more concerned about not being concerned."

"As you should be."

I squint, as if that's the barometer for sanity. "You look like the photos of you online. Which means you're just a projection of what I already know about you."

Rose gives a little shrug. "Or it means I look the same way now as I did in those photos. And that I came back. Walked inside your house. Came up here, found you fighting a mirror, climbed on the bed, and watched to see who would win. I don't think either of you did."

That razor's edge of being just sane enough to realize you're not.

"Tell me something I haven't already read about you," I say.

"What do you want to know?"

"What happened to you? To your family?"

She smiles, and it's genuine and delicious. "We were all hacked up by home invaders and buried beneath the pond in the back. Which would make me a ghost."

"Really?"

In one swift motion, she sits up on her knees. "Or maybe we were being threatened by drug kingpins and we had to run for our lives."

"Okay, I get it—"

She holds a hand up, silencing me. "No, wait, it was a murder-suicide pact, and we paid a third party to dispose of our remains."

"Don't joke. You're talking about your own son."

Her face goes blank once again. "I don't want to talk about Max."

"I just want to know he's okay," I say.

"No, you want to save him. You've got this whole weird hero complex going on. Which is sweet in its own way, but you've got enough problems of your own."

"The notes," I say.

She nods. "Yeah, Marlowe. The notes."

I point at her, blood dripping. "Which officially means you're not real, 'cause otherwise, how would you know about the notes?"

A grin, so easy. "Maybe I'm the one writing them."

This brings a whole wave of bumps along each vertebra. "That means you gave the notes to Carlos and Abril."

"Aren't they sweet? Well, Abril's a little much. But Carlos? He's a doll."

"He hit me."

Rose winks. "You had it coming."

And, I think, *I could touch her.* That's all it would take. I could touch her to find out if she's real. But even if I felt her skin, would I believe it? I don't think I could handle *feeling* a hallucination. Maybe it's like the rainbow in the cornfield after the thunderstorm, feeling like taffy. The end of everything.

"Why are you here?" I ask her.

"Now there's a smart question. I knew you were smart, Marlowe." She scans her gaze along the bloodstained carpet, the shards of glass. "All evidence to the contrary." She takes a sip of her wine. Wait, since when was she holding a glass of wine? But she is now. Red wine, matching my blood. "I'm here to tell you what you won't admit to yourself."

"Which is?"

"Which is you're fucked."

I smile because it seems funny. "In what way?"

"In all ways. Your train has left the station, horses out of the barn, etcetera. You remember that moment at Holly's funeral, the instant you found out you won the lottery?" She waves a dismissive hand. "Of course you remember. Who would forget that?"

"Yeah, I remember every detail."

"So you remember the sound, right? In that moment, that cracking sound. You thought it sounded like—"

"A tree limb breaking," I say. But not exactly like that. It was louder, more...personal, somehow.

"Exactly." She takes a slow sip, relishes the liquid in her mouth for a moment before swallowing. Then her gaze drills me hard. "That was *you* snapping. Funny it makes a sound, isn't it? An actual sound."

"What?"

"That's the moment you crossed the threshold, Marlowe. Really, you didn't have much of a chance after Holly died. But winning the lottery? That was too much for your brain to absorb."

"No," I tell her. "I was okay then. I mean, I was still okay. Could a crazy person have moved his whole family? Bought a house and moved?"

"Exactly," she says. "Think about it. You chose Bury because you *buried* your wife? Does that sound sane?"

"It had meaning."

"And you're seeing faces in your garage door windows? And losing entire chunks of time? And sitting here, talking to someone who doesn't exist?"

It seems silly to argue. "Maybe I've gotten worse over time."

She wags a finger, nail unpainted. "No, it was bad from the start."

"That's not true."

Rose looks so disappointed. "And the notes, Marlowe? Do you really think someone is out to get you?"

This has the effect of swallowing a fist-size piece of ice. "What do you mean?"

She cocks her head. "What do you think I mean?"

"Someone *is* out to get me," I say.

Rose sets her glass down on the side table, gets off the bed, and sits on the floor across from me. Lord, she's imaginary but I can *smell* her. It's Holly's perfume. I know it is.

"You want someone hunting you because you need the agony of it all. You've said it yourself. Addicted to the hurt. Just like all those cuts on your arms. You think pain is an escape, but *there is no escape*. All roads lead to the same place."

"You're not real," I whisper.

"Maybe *you're* not real," she replies. "You ever consider that? Maybe I'm still here in my home, the place where I grew up. And suddenly, sitting on the floor across from me, covered in blood, is this man. This ghost. And he's here to haunt me, and I have no idea why."

"You...are...not...*real.*"

Then she scooches a few inches forward, gives a smile as soft as puppy love, leans forward. Her smell is overpowering; the perfume, it makes me dizzy enough to close my eyes, nearly lose my balance. And in this darkness, I'm with Holly, and she's telling me she misses me and she wants me to join her if only I could, but not that way, not like that, because of the kids. And I tell her I'd die for her. Just tell me to do it and I will, and she believes me, so she says nothing. And then, her lips are on mine, so faint, a desert wind, warm and enveloping. It lasts only a moment, and I don't want to open my eyes and find out it's not her. But I do open them, because at my core, I'm weak and Rose's face is only two inches away, and I'm struck by her loveliness.

She smiles, so gentle, I almost believe it.

"Check your laptop, Marlowe. See what you've been doing."

"What?"

But she doesn't answer. Rose stands, no effort taken. Grabs her wineglass, almost floats toward the bedroom door. As she leaves, she gives me one last look, and now her eyes are blue, a dying glacier, and I don't know why that is. Maybe that's the real color of ghosts.

Now she's gone and, like that, my bleeding seems to start again, more purposeful than before. In a daze, I manage to sleepwalk to my bathroom, find some gauze pads and tape, wrap up my hand in a clumsy way. I make great effort to avoid the mirror.

I fear, should I see myself, my eyes would be blue, too.

SIXTY-SIX

I AM A MESS.

I am wondrous.

I sit cross-legged in my bedroom, aware of my wounds. Hash marks of life they'll be, just like all the others. Everything, everything, self-inflicted, you self-centered son of a bitch.

You still have a chance, I feel myself say. *You're at the brink, but you can come back.*

One breath. Another.

Easy in, easy out.

Slow my heart, still my mind.

Check your laptop, Marlowe.

Such a strange thing for my conjuring of her to say.

Check your laptop.

And so I do.

SIXTY-SEVEN

I LIFT THE SCREEN, scan my fingerprint. The wallpaper picture is of Holly, me, and the twins last year at the Baltimore Aquarium. It hurts every time I see it, but it'd kill me to change it.

I don't know what I'm looking for, but I suspect I actually do. That if I don't overthink it, it'll come to me. Something deep in my brain wants me to look in here.

I let out a long exhale as I launch my email. Poke around the contents a bit, read the emails from rumhillroad@yahoo.com another couple of times but don't find anything new or unusual. So I launch my file explorer, no idea what I'm supposed to look for. Click on a few folders, check my recent downloads. Nothing out of the ordinary.

I launch my word processing app, then stare at the blank screen as if it will inspire an idea of what to look for. Nothing comes, but how easily I get lost in that white screen. Stare at it long enough and it begins to stretch and stretch, deep into the distance. Suppose I've never really considered how hypnotic all those same-colored pixels are, and how comforting. I type a few words—just gibberish, really—then delete them. I gaze on a bit longer, feeling something coming, and when it does, my fingers obey what my brain tells them to type.

Christopher Robin is Saying His Prayers

I lean back, look at the words, knowing them but not knowing why they just came to me. If my subconscious is trying to give me a clue, it's being a bit too coy.

I decide to save the document, thinking I might come back to it later and it may trigger something.

I click *Save As*, and the program opens my last-used folder and suggests the document name *Christopher Robin is Saying His Prayers. docx*. That's good enough, I decide.

And then there's this.

This last-used folder.

A folder named *Scrap*, which sits within my documents directory.

I don't ever recall naming a folder that.

So I launch my file explorer and navigate to it. *Scrap.*

The contents are few. Three files. All word processing documents. All with similar names.

A jolt of electricity rushes through me as I stare at their innocuous, similar names.

Bury1.docx

Bury2.docx

Bury3.docx

Ouroboros.docx

SIXTY-EIGHT

THAT MOMENT OF STEPPING on a nail. You see it, sharpened tip pointing up, as if someone left it on the floor just for you. You see it clearly, even imagine all the specks of rust, the things that will soon poison your blood. You see it as you walk around barefoot, spy it right as your foot is in midair, your momentum unstoppable. See it and know with sublime clarity there's no way it's not piercing into your flesh. That moment between the knowing and the pain. It lasts a split second. It lasts a lifetime.

I open *Bury1.docx*, knowing with icy fear what's going to be inside and it's going to hurt like a motherfucker.

Mr. Marlowe.

Welcome to Bury! Welcome to Rum Hill Road. Welcome to your new house.

We love your home. We've been watching it a long time.

SIXTY-NINE

I DON'T REMEMBER COMING downstairs, but here I am. I suppose I can be forgiven this small lapse, considering.

A vague sense of Da on the couch, reading.

"Come to clear yer mess, then?" he asks.

I sleepwalk past him. The glass shards sit where I left them by the fireplace, a thousand fairies sleeping.

I come into the kitchen, not sure why. I could pour another drink, I suppose, because what's the point of stopping now? But I don't. Not yet.

Da walks in, wearing that look.

"Look, Aidan, this is an incredible amount of stress for you. Maybe... maybe you should be seeing someone."

He looks as old as I feel.

"See someone?"

"Aye. You know. A doctor."

"A psychiatrist, then?"

He nods. "Along those lines, yeah."

"That's what Ma said after Christopher died. And I went, you remember?" My voice is dead.

He looks at the floor halfway between us. "Aye."

"I saw the man maybe four, five times. And you said it was a waste of money."

"I did, yes."

"But not now?"

"We all evolve," Da says. "And yes, I think now is a good time for you to seek help."

How good sleep would feel right now. Real sleep, not the manufactured kind I've had for the past two decades. The sleep of a six-year-old boy, long and uncomplicated, dreams restricted to the horrors of whatever a small child could conjure. Scary dragons and some such. What I would give for two milligrams of youthful ignorance as a nighttime medication.

"I wrote them," I say.

"What's that?"

"I wrote them."

"Wrote who?"

"The letters," I say, still not quite believing it. "I wrote the letters."

It takes a moment, but I see the realization creep up his body and finally take hold in his eyes. "I don't know what you're telling me."

I put a hand on his shoulder, such an odd gesture from me to him.

"I just found them, right now. On my laptop. The first three letters, at least, and a printout of an ouroboros. There they were, on my hard drive."

He peers intensely at me, an MRI machine scanning my brain for anomalies. "You're telling me *you* wrote the letters but don't remember doing it?"

"I don't remember a lot of things. Been happening ever since Holly's death. And now I know what I've been doing in some of that lost time."

He slips away from my hand.

"It don' make sense," he says. "Why would you do such a thing?"

"I don't know," I answer, which, on an absolute level, is the truth.

He's processing, processing. Looks up at me, his beard pure snow.

"But Carlos just hit you to protect the name of the person who forced him to deliver the notes."

I've already thought about that. "And I'll bet you that's another thing I did in my lost time. Made Carlos deliver the notes. Made him swear to secrecy on the threat of me calling the police. He must think I'm a schizophrenic. But he kept a secret because he was afraid of me calling the police."

"And you have zero memory of telling him these things?"

"Zero."

"So that's that, then. This whole thing is a charade, and you've lost your fecking mind."

This makes me smile, despite his intention. "Funny, I'd been thinking that same thing all along."

He isn't listening. "So that means it was *you* who closed the lid of that safe room on Mags," he says. "You couldn't have known about any air supply. So we searched and searched, going out of our minds. And your little girl coulda been suffocating that whole time."

"I don't remember. I promise you I don't."

Now he stands, using his cane to rise. "Lost time? I don't even know what that is, if it's such a thing."

"You think I'm making this up?"

That scowl. "I dunna even know what to believe anymore. All

I know is you have two littles who need you in a desperate way, and you're...skulking about with your mysteries, your conspiracy theories, your...your..." He's working himself in a shaking anger. "Your *obsession* with this family who lived here before. And for what? For what?"

Shame creeps. "I know. I'm done with researching that family...I never should have in the first place. I guess I was just trying to find some meaning in...I don't know. After losing Holly—"

"I lost my wife, too!" Spit flies from his lips, and his face turns an instant crimson. "I lost my wife *and* I lost my son. But never in the years since did I 'lose time' or run about chasing ghosts that I'd invented all along. You know what *I* did? I got the feck on with my life, that's what. I mourned. I cursed God. I turned to the bottle more often than I shoulda. But I moved on, all the while taking care of those I was supposed to be taking care of." He picks up his cane and swings it with such swiftness, I don't even have time to react. The end of it smashes into an empty vase that sits on the coffee table, shattering it on impact. I don't know where that vase even came from, but I'm quite certain it was the only one I've ever owned. "Goddamn it, Aidan! You're thirty-five years old, you've got millions of dollars, and you canna even meet the basic fatherhood requirements."

"Stop it," I say. My head boils, pressure building.

But he doesn't stop. He's pushed past to the other side. "Oh, yeah, or what? You gonna grab that big American gun of yours and tell me how to behave?"

"Please stop talking," I say, my voice a whisper.

He takes a step closer. "You need to be a man."

I have a sudden desire to seize his throat, to grab and squeeze, feel his life vulnerable in my hand.

I don't, but he sees my hidden desire.

"Go on, then," he says. "Give it a try, see what happens. I've dealt with bigger drunks than you."

I stare at the floor. "You should just go home."

"And leave you in charge? I don't think so. You need help, need someone to look after the twins. For now, you go upstairs. No more booze. Go up to yer bed, sleep it all off. I'll get the kids from school, and then tonight we'll figure out what to do with you. But I don't want to see you until later. You understand?"

I'm not sure I understand anything. "Yes."

"Off with you, then."

I rise, stagger a bit, leave the room, and head to the stairs as the world swims around me. When I reach the top of the second-floor landing, I consider it just for a few seconds. Consider the release, a simple fall backward. Consider the simple and wondrous violence possible from the basic ingredients of hardwood risers, human bones, and gravity.

I keep this thought warm and close as I make my way into my bed and collapse in it, just a few hours since I've woken. With my head on the edge, I open a single eye, stare at the unholy mess I've made of the carpet.

These bloodstains, they shine.

SEVENTY

MY MOBILE BUZZES, AND I have a sense it may have done so several times already, a vagueness, memories that could be dreams. I try to reach for it, but my arms are concrete. Legs also. I can blink, that's about it. I see the mobile, shimmering on the nightstand as it vibrates. Yet I can't move. Maybe I'm still asleep, but the afternoon haze streaming through my curtains tells me I'm not. It's laughing at me, saying I'm paralyzed, that I stressed my body to such a degree it's simply given up, leaving only my brain and lungs functioning.

Then my muscles finally listen to my brain, and they explode into motion all at once. I launch out of the bed completely, fall to the floor, and the impact reminds me of my recent pain. The cut to my hand, my bruised jaw.

I crawl back, find several missed calls from Maya. I dial her.

"I've been trying to reach you," she says instead of *hello*.

"I've been sleeping," I say.

"All day?"

"What time is it?"

A pause. "Four thirteen."

I try to do the basic math, but my mind is still full of dry, crumbling leaves. "Yeah, I guess all day."

"Marlowe, your dad called me. Said he was worried about you, and now I'm worried about you."

"I'm okay," I mutter.

"Says the man who drank this morning after getting punched by the gardener, then slept all day."

"Funny," I say. "My father's not usually one for gossip."

"Damn it, what's going on?"

So many things I could say, or I could say nothing at all. But the thought of all the options exhausts me and I don't think I have the energy to spare, so I default to the simplest choice. The truth.

"There's a strong possibility I've crossed to the other side."

"Other side of what?"

"Reality. But I think...I think I'm back now. This morning was pretty wild. I think I hallucinated, but I was finally able to understand it wasn't real. I was starting to feel better, but then I found something out. Something about the notes."

She exhales. "That's why I wanted to talk to you. Your father told me you think you've been writing the notes."

"I don't think it, Maya. I know it. I found them on my computer. I just don't remember any of it."

She doesn't talk for a bit, and neither do I. We're both okay with this. She's the first to finally fill the silence.

"I told you I was a psychology major before law school. I still remember a few things, and what you're describing is called dissociation."

"Meaning?"

"Dissociation is the kind of thing that runs on a spectrum. On one end could be a mild detachment from one's immediate surroundings."

That's not me, I think. "And the other end?"

"Multiple personality disorder." She lets that sit on me for a second, and lord, how it does. "And there's everything else in between. Amnesia. PTSD. Derealization."

"Derealization?"

"A sense that the world is unreal."

It's like swallowing a fishhook, then asking for a second helping.

"Tell me something, Maya."

"What?"

"My wife, Holly. She's dead, right?"

"Yes, Marlowe, she is."

"And I won the lottery?"

"Yes, you did."

"And you're my lawyer?"

"I'm your lawyer."

"So the world sounds pretty real to me."

I hear her breathing, along with the exasperation that swims in it.

"You need to see a therapist," she says.

"I'm not going to—"

"Marlowe, shut the hell up and listen to me, will you?"

I shut up.

"The last time we were together—seems like a hundred years ago—you told me you thought you were *addicted to hurt*. Do you remember that?"

"I do."

"You also said, *It should've been me*. So you're clearly feeling guilt. Maybe over Holly, I don't know. Maybe something else."

I remain silent.

"You're torturing yourself. And the thing is, you like the torture. *Addicted to hurt.* If you did write the letters, that would explain it. A way of bleeding." She pauses. "*Penance.* Does that make sense?"

Bleeding. X-Acto blades. Scars and scars, dry riverbeds on flesh.

"Yes, that makes sense."

"And that guilt," she continues, "it must be powerful enough for you to disassociate long enough to be able to write the letters and place them on your property."

"I think you missed your calling as a therapist."

A chuckle from her, but one that's on life support.

"You know what also happened last time we saw each other?" she asked.

"Yeah, we visited a drunk cop in Wisconsin."

"Also, you admitted you're attracted to me."

"Aye, that too."

A pause. "Is that part of the reason why you feel guilty?"

I hate confronting questions when I'm not ready. But I try to relax my brain, try not to react, and just consider the idea. Let silence fill the room around me.

"You there?"

"Give me a minute to think about that," I say.

She does.

Eventually, some of the fog inside my head clears. "There is an attraction, it's true. But I think the guilt I feel around you isn't about that. It's that...this is hard to describe. You make me feel *safe* in a way she did, I suppose. And that's deeper than attraction. That's something right in my core. And because I feel that way with you, because it feels like how I was with her, there's guilt." I look down at my bed, the one bought after moving here, and realize for the first time Holly will never sleep in it. Never has and never will. "And it's funny. This lost time of mine. I realize it started happening soon after I hired you."

"Are you saying I'm the reason you're crazy?"

This fuels a laugh, one that feels like life itself.

"No," I say. "But you're a part of it. An expensive and glorious part of it."

She accepts this, and I picture her smiling, whether that's true or not. After a spell, she says, "I could never replace her. You know that, right?"

"Aye," I reply. "No one can. Not a soul on this sweet earth."

"No one. And as your lawyer, I'm worried about my future billings, so I want you to seek help, okay? Must be a good therapist in Bury, considering the demographics."

"I will." Maybe I mean it.

"Good. And call me tomorrow. Call me every day. I want us to maintain a dialog at least until…until you're seeing things a bit more clearly."

"*Maintain a dialog.* Quite the sweet talker you are."

"I'm serious, Marlowe."

"Okay," I say. "I'll call you tomorrow."

I think she's disconnected the call because all I hear is silence. But then I hear her breathing.

"You still there?" I ask.

"I just thought of something."

"What?"

"The bank account. The routing numbers."

"What?"

"From the letter demanding money," she says.

"What about them?"

Her words speed up. "I checked them. Remember, I had you read them to me? I checked them just to see if it they would lead to anything. They're numbers for a bank account in the Cayman Islands, but I couldn't get any more information than that."

"But what does—" I stop myself, my brain trying to keep up. Processing, processing. Then I know what she's about to say. "The bank account, it's not mine, is it?"

"No," she says. "Unless you have one I don't know about."

"I don't."

"So how the hell did you write a letter to yourself, demanding money and using a real bank account that's not yours?"

My brain struggles to keep up.

"I...I don't know..."

"And how did you send yourself emails?"

That gnawing in my gut, that bile in my throat. "I suppose I could have set up an account, created a draft email, set it on a time delay."

"And somehow also figured out an accurate offshore account number in a tax-haven country?"

I sit on the bed, fearing my legs will no longer do their job.

"What are you saying?" I ask, knowing exactly what she's saying.

"Maybe you wrote some of the letters yourself." *Tick, tick, tick.* "But what if you didn't write *all* of them?"

SEVENTY-ONE

DUSK.

I make it through the rest of the afternoon, but only because I force myself to think about anything else but the letters. I just couldn't do it anymore. Couldn't twist into knots about their origin, their author (or authors, as Maya suggested), their purpose.

We're all in the kitchen, piecemealing dinner. The twins are tired, but their faces still hold a faint glow from their first day of school. They both have the same teacher—a Mrs. Braebrun—who's apparently as old as a sequoia but much softer in form. They like her immensely, and even Bo admitted his worst fears about starting a new school didn't come true.

"What was your worst fear?" I'd asked him earlier.

"That someone would ask about my mom, and I'd have to tell them she's dead."

"Me too," Mags added.

I swallowed hard, not telling them that day will come soon enough. Soon enough that they'll have to tell someone about their mother, and that someone won't know how to react at all. And that will happen time after time, year upon year, until they're old enough that a dead parent doesn't seem like an exception.

Everyone buzzes around the kitchen, and Da is chipper enough that no one would suspect our fierce argument from this morning. Maybe he's faking his mood. Or maybe he appreciates the fact it's after five o'clock and I haven't poured myself a drink.

And, I think, *tonight*. Tonight's the night I'll go without a drink. Hell, I had enough in the morning to last me all day, right? Tonight I can sip on water, clean me out a little. And maybe this is the one night that becomes two, and two becomes three. That's the path to sobriety. But being *sober*…doesn't that mean I'm a drunk? Am I really willing to admit that?

Don't overthink this, Marlowe. Just drink fucking water for tonight. It's just like fretting over the letters. Let go for now, and tomorrow can be tomorrow.

I grab an empty glass, fill it with water, take a gulp.

"Wash yer hands before handling the veggies, love."

Mags looks up to Da. "Okay."

"And Bo, you can help me cook the steaks if ya want. Show you how to do it perfectly."

"Cool," Bo says, sounding like he means it. They love my father, and I realize, so do I.

It makes me want to say it out loud, and what a rare thing that would be. I want to hug all of them, right here in the kitchen, but I don't. I stay silent, partly because that's such a Marlowe thing to do but also because I don't deserve a moment like that. Maybe soon, but not now.

The doorbell rings.

Been a while since I've heard that. I look over to Da.

"You expecting anyone?" I ask.

He shrugs his shoulders. "I might've made a call or two today. Reached out to folks who might be inclined to offer some advice in yer... situation."

"What situation?" Mags asks, her eyes not particularly full of wonder. Neither of us answers her.

"Maya called me today," I say.

"Yup, she was one of 'em."

I catch his gaze, and I feel both of us soften. "Thank you," I tell him, meaning it fiercely. "So who's at the door?"

Da puts down the potato he's peeling and gives me a look of exasperation. "I honestly could not tell you, son. But you can get to the door faster than me, if you're keen for a quick answer."

So I head over, thinking it's a mistake to open this door because in America, people like to come to your house and sell you things: landscaping services, Girl Scout cookies, a different version of god. But I'm curious because Da said he spoke to one or two people, and I want to know who the second person is. Chances are, that person isn't at my doorstep. But me and chance have a special relationship, so I spin the wheel and answer the door.

The mustache is the first thing I see.

SEVENTY-TWO

"HELLO, MARLOWE."

"Chief," I say, instantly glad to see him. Maybe it's the police uniform, an assurance of authority that comforts me. Maybe it's the handshake, firm. Or maybe he's just one of the few people who know most about what's going on with me, and Da recognized that fact enough to reach out to him.

At least, I'm assuming that's why he's here.

"Did my father call you?"

Chief Sike nods. "He did, he did. But I've been meaning to reach out to you anyway. See how you're doing. I took his call as a sign I need to be following up on the things I tell myself to do."

I open the door wide. "Come in."

As he passes, smelling of sandalwood aftershave, he looks at me and says, "So you're not upset, then?"

"No. I appreciate you stopping by, Chief."

In the kitchen, he shakes Da's hand, and Da gives me a sideward glance I can't quite interpret.

"Sorry, I'm interrupting dinner," the chief says.

"No, no. I'm hoping you can join us," I tell him. "We have enough steaks, then, Da?"

Da nods. "Sure enough. And then some."

"No, I wouldn't want to impose."

"Please, it'd be our pleasure."

The chief looks between us, hooks his thumb into his utility belt as if measuring how much capacity he has to grow his belly, then announces his decision.

"Well, I suppose it'd be my pleasure, too. Thank you kindly."

As I grab him a beer, I notice he doesn't reach for his mobile to call or text his wife. Maybe he was already working late and she wasn't expecting him for dinner anyway.

The chief and I take our drinks onto the back porch for a few moments as Da and the twins remain in the kitchen. He looks me up and down for a few moments and says, "Doesn't take a detective to know you're in bad shape. Bandaged hand, bruised face, and...well, most troubling is you're drinking water."

That makes me laugh, harder than it warranted. Suppose I just needed the release.

"I've had better days." I look down at my water glass. "And yeah, figured it was maybe time for a break."

"Ayuh. Breaks are good, reset your system and whatnot." He immediately sips his beer after saying this. "Your father filled me in on the details."

"What did he tell you?"

The chief relays the conversation he had with Da.

"So this Carlos fella...that explains your face. What happened to your hand?"

"I punched a mirror," I say. "It cut my hand but I shattered it into a million pieces, so I'm considering it a win on my part."

His expression doesn't change. "And why would you want to punch a mirror?"

I tell him the truth. "Because I didn't like the way the guy in it was looking at me."

Another sip. "Ayuh. What'd you tell your kids?"

"I told them I was moving the mirror and lost my footing. The wood corner of it hit my face, I fell, the glass broke, etcetera."

The chief considers this, offers something just shy of a smirk. "God bless the minds of children. They can be so damn smart, but on the other hand, they'll believe just about anything."

I don't like feeling accomplished for lying to my kids.

"Like I said, I've had a day."

"Bet you have," he says. "And many just like them, ever since you moved here."

I'm feeling a growing ache for a drink.

"You know," I say, "I never did hire Owen Brace for anything more than the security cameras, but thanks for referring him to me. I, uh... well, this is almost embarrassing, but I got it into my head at one point that *he* was the one writing the letters. He wanted to do some security consulting for me and asked for all sorts of personal information. It just gave me a bad vibe."

The chief allows a look of surprise, mild as it may be. "Owen? Nah, he's good people. But I see your point. I'm sure in your situation, it was easy to suspect just about anyone."

I'm sure my father already told him, as he'd told Maya. But I feel I need to tell him myself how I was the one who wrote the letters all along.

"Chief, look, I—"

"Not now," he says. Then he gives me the warmest smile, one I haven't seen on him before. "Let's go help out with dinner. We'll have a nice meal, and then we'll talk. Your dad's concerned about you, and now I'm concerned about you. We'll talk. Figure out how maybe I can help."

The next two hours flow like a gentle river; time feels steady and soothing, and there's a sublime synchronicity to everyone's movements. The way Bo sips his milk, how Mags twirls her fork. The chief, clearing the table after dinner. Da and I, washing the dishes; I rinse, he dries, not bothering at all with the dishwasher. Every movement is fluid, beautiful, not chaotic in the least. I slip into my own rhythm, the way I feel when I'm at my heavy bag, and it feels like a million years since that's happened. Dodge, weave, jab. Dodge, hook. Over and over, a boxer's hypnosis. And these are the times I feel a purpose, a reason to *be*, even if I can't say what that reason is. I feel it now, this rhythm, and it gives me joy. Such a different feeling from this morning.

Maybe I don't need help. Don't need a psychiatrist. Maybe all I need is this synchronicity, and if I can find it at a dinner table, I can likely find it anywhere. All I need to do is stop thinking, observe the world around me, and just let it all go.

"Mind if I grab another beer?"

The chief is already at the refrigerator.

"Of course," I tell him.

He grabs one, pops the cap, makes its acquaintance.

"You know what I want to see?" he asks. "That safe room of yours. In the basement, I think you said. Can you show it to me?"

For a moment, there's a break in the flow of this river, as if someone just tossed in a large rock from the banks. It doesn't last long, but it's there, ripples and all.

"Sure."

SEVENTY-THREE

I GO DOWN FIRST. He follows. I take a glance at my mobile before he gets fully inside my secret submarine. Nearly eight o'clock, and one bar of service. Slide it in the front pocket of my jeans.

The chief plants his feet on the ground, gives a turn, whistles.

"Well, this is something," he says. "Can't say I'm surprised Logan Yates woulda built something like this, but from the way you described it, I didn't think it would be this big." He walks past me, a tight fit, and the handcuffs secured in his utility belt brush against my waist as he scoots past. He'd taken the belt off during dinner. I didn't notice him slipping it back on.

He scans the jars on the storage rack. "This food still fresh?"

"According to the dates. So I guess he kept replacing it."

"So it wasn't just the Cold War in the eighties that had him scared," the chief says. "He kept this place ready to go up until the day he disappeared."

"I suppose the man had worries."

"Suppose he did at that." The chief removes the baton from his belt, sits on the edge of the cot. I try to remember if he had that belt on the first time I ran into him at the station. I don't think he did. Do police chiefs even need utility belts?

"Did you know Logan Yates?" I ask him.

"Knew as much as anyone could know him," he says. "Which means no, not really. 'Course, he'd been here years before me but never was even a blip on my radar. No reason to. Just one of many wealthy folks in this town."

The way he says this, there's a bitterness.

"Until he disappeared."

"Ayuh." He polishes off the contents of his beer bottle, and I count in my head. Five? Six? I think six. Six beers since he's been here, and though he appears stone sober, he's probably not fit to drive. Not for a while, at least. "Well, no, I guess that's not 'scatly true," he says. "Was on my radar before that. When that Colin Pearson came out and told me he had suspicions about Logan's daughter, Rose."

"And what did you think?"

He lets the question hang for a few beats. "Well, I thought Pearson came an awful long way just to do a little fishing."

"But then they all…they all disappeared."

"That they did." He flicks the fingers of his left hand. "Poof."

Maybe I should tell him Rose Yates was just in my bedroom today, according to my delusions.

"You led the investigation," I say instead.

"I was *part* of the investigation. Some federal boys took the lead."

"And what did you conclude?"

The chief folds his arms, then reaches up and scratches the side of his face. No, he doesn't scratch. He digs, leaving behind flushed grooves.

"Well, I concluded it was the damn hardest investigation I'd ever been through, causing me more than one sleepless night. And nothing became of it. Not one thing."

"But surely you must have had a theory."

As soon as my words float to his ears, his face changes. He doesn't wear his usual calm but serious expression. He bunches up his eyes as if receiving a tetanus shot, then turns his head a few degrees to the left. A meaty vein pulses in the side of his neck.

"You know what my theory is?" he says. "That the Yates family has a lot of fucking money and they could afford to disappear, and that's what they did. They vanished because they needed to, leaving blue-collar chumps like me to have to figure all that shit out." As he speaks, his foot knocks over the empty beer bottle, and it's unnaturally loud as it rolls on the metal floor a few feet away.

"But do you think—"

"Fuck them," he jabs. "Off the record, speaking not as the police chief, I say *fuck them* and good riddance. You think it makes me look good not solving the case? I can assure you, it does not."

This is when I feel the wave. It emanates from him, and I picture his energy like a growing tsunami, only a foot high when it leaves his body but the size of a building when it crashes into me. In these last few seconds, the chief has become someone else, and though he looks not all that different, I feel it.

Something is wrong here.

Very wrong.

SEVENTY-FOUR

A THOUGHT COMES TO me, sudden and fierce. More than a thought. A realization.

And this realization, real or not, is followed by a shortness of breath and a spider-webbing of heat through my body.

Think, Marlowe.

Think about the letters. I know you're supposed to be letting all that go for one night, but we're done with that now. Time to think, and think hard.

Maya was right, I didn't find *all* the letters on my laptop, did I? No, just *some* of them. The first three and the picture of the ouroboros.

A name flashes in my brain.

Carlos.

Carlos hit me because he was afraid. Afraid of the person who told him to deliver the notes. I thought that person was me.

But if you were in this country without documentation, wouldn't you be afraid of the police more than anyone else?

My left knee buckles, almost bringing my body to the floor.

"You okay?" the chief says.

I don't know what to say. I don't know how to act. Because here's the thing: How the hell do I know any longer what's a logical thought or a crazy one? Odds are I'm wrong about everything.

But still. This fire in my chest.

"I...I get a little claustrophobic down here. I'm sure it'll pass."

He nods, looks at me like a cashier eyeing a would-be shoplifter in a 7-Eleven.

"You're more than just claustrophobic, according to your dad. Which is why I'm here. I'm worried about you."

"I'm okay."

He nods at my bandaged hand. "Oh, yeah?"

"Being okay doesn't mean I'm perfect. Just okay."

The heat rises to my face, and I'm sure I'm glowing red. Too many thoughts compete for my attention. The thought that I'm wrong. The thought that I'm right. That I should get the hell out of this submarine. That maybe I was right to be curious about a police chief wearing a utility belt. That maybe I should just...

Ask him.

Just ask him.

Now, wouldn't that be something?

Find out, Marlowe. At least probe a little bit.

"You look like hell," he says. "Maybe we should get out of here."

Go with your instinct.

And what's my instinct?

The money. It has something to do with money.

"You called yourself a blue-collar chump," I say. "But you're the police chief."

He mulls this. "Suppose that was a bit harsh. It's not like they pay me nothing."

"Still, it has to be difficult. So many rich people here, and you're not one of them." I study him. There, that twinge in the sides of his eyes. A micropain. "You, dealing with all their bullshit. DUIs of millionaires, and I bet they think they can get out of anything."

He's holding his breath, it's obvious. "That's sometimes true."

"Probably entitled kids telling you how their dads will get them out of any trouble they got in."

"Also true."

I take a tiny step toward him. "And then, finally, a real case. Not some petty misdemeanor. A whole family goes missing. Could be murder, even. But in the end, it's probably just like you said. Money. They could all afford to disappear."

The man's coiled. So still. So much contained force.

"Could be."

"And also like you said, not solving their vanishing makes you look like an idiot."

His words are coated in crushed glass. "That's not what I said."

"But it's the truth, right? A real case to solve, and you come up empty. Some people would call you a damn idiot."

He stands, and the simple act of him doing so is unnerving. I'm likely stronger than him, but he *knows*. Knows how to apply force, knows how to read people. Especially people who pose a threat.

"Watch it, Marlowe."

"I'm just saying."

He thumbs his belt, his hand close to his gun. The gun has a strap snapped in place over it, but I'll bet that doesn't slow him down at all.

"Saying what, exactly?" he asks. "Because now I'm really curious."

This is the moment when you see your foot stepping on the nail and can't avoid it. The moment between the knowing and the pain. I have to do this, even though, logically, it could be a terrible decision. Perhaps a devastating one. But it could also be the thing that saves all of us.

"And then someone like me moves in," I say. God help me, I can smell him. The musk, the testosterone. "Probably richer than most of the people here, and I didn't do a single thing to deserve it. I picked some numbers at random, and *bam*, millions. No special skills. I was a *bartender* before this, for Chrissake. You must be thinking, why him? What has he done to deserve this money? And then, to make it that much worse, I moved into the house of the very same people who made you look like an idiot."

His thumb moves no closer to the strap covering his gun. But he does turn and pick up his baton, then holds it loosely in his right hand.

"You've got a question in that brain of yours, Mr. Marlowe? I'd suggest now is the time to ask it."

"Just Marlowe, at least to my friends. And I think you know my question."

"Maybe I want to hear you ask it."

I step to the edge of the cliff, then let gravity do its thing.

"Did you write the letters, Chief?"

SEVENTY-FIVE

THE CHIEF SMILES, AND I suspect that grin has been on the business side of hundreds of suspects in the Bury PD's interrogation room.

"And there it is," he says. "Good for you, Marlowe. *Goddamn it*, good for you, son."

"It's a serious question."

"It sure as hell is." He's close enough that if he swung the baton, it could easily connect with my skull. "But the thing is, your father told me *you* wrote the letters. That it was you all along." Now he laughs. "What a crazy bastard. You wrote them and didn't realize it."

"I did write some of them," I say. "But not all of them. So maybe I am crazy. But not completely."

"Okay, okay. Well, let's do this. If you're accusing your town's police chief of a serious crime, let's hear what ya got. Tell me your theory around these letters."

"Maybe you put down the baton," I tell him.

"I will not, Mr. Marlowe. And I've got a steel-trap memory, so you better be careful what exactly you tell me because I'll remember every bit. That could be useful, because I sure as hell see a court date coming out of this conversation."

The sides to people, like a Dungeons & Dragons die. The one with twenty faces, and so rare you'd roll that singular result you were hoping to see. This side of Chief Sike, whatever exactly it is, I don't expect it comes out often. Maybe others have seen it, but not many.

"I regret not pouring myself a real drink," I say.

"Yeah, that doesn't surprise me. I'd let you go get one, but I'd have to go with you. I'm guessing you're happier having this conversation here, where no one else can hear us. Not your dad. Not your kids."

One deep breath. One, just to get this all rolling.

"I think I've got issues," I start. "Real problems. Ever since Holly died. Since I won the money. I think…maybe something broke in me. And the result is I lose time. I don't remember what it is I do in that lost time. It's just gone. My lawyer—who's also dabbled in psychology—says I'm disassociating."

"Fascinating," the chief says, his voice as flat as cardboard.

"Yes, I did write some of the notes. The first three, and then a printout of an image. I don't remember writing any of them. I don't know why I would have."

"Because you wanted attention," the chief says. "Deep down, you needed the world's pity. Poor little man, lost his wife and won the lottery. Luck of the Irish." That baton, it's loose in his grip. Maybe I'll have a chance to take it from him, if it comes to that. "And you had me fooled," he continues. "Until your dad called me today, I was convinced those letters were real. Spent more time looking into it than I ever told you. It just didn't make any sense. Hell, thought maybe it had to do with the Yateses, but that didn't pencil out either. All I knew for sure was someone was out to get you." He chuckles. "And all this time, that person was you. Self-sabotage of the highest order."

As sweat builds and tension thickens, my mind slows, as does time. All my days in Bury play in sequence, and things begin to click into place. Things I never saw before, things I couldn't see because I'd blocked them out.

"It was the party," I say. "When you were here for the party."

"Oh, yeah? Well, then, tell me about that."

It's so clear. It's so clear. "The woman, I don't remember her name, she said you could find anything on the internet. Maybe that, I don't know…got you thinking."

"Thinking about what, exactly?"

"About me. About my family. You knew more than anyone else because you knew about my letters. You knew I was scared, vulnerable."

"You were indeed vulnerable." I catch faint vapors of stale beer from either his breath or the bottle on the floor. "And then what?"

Then I see it almost as clearly as watching it on my security cameras. "You followed my daughter into the basement."

His mustache gives a mighty twitch. "And why might I have done that?"

"I don't know," I answer. "Maybe you saw an opportunity."

Now he slaps the baton gently into his other palm, over and over. But he doesn't say a word.

Fuck it, I decide. *I'm all in.*

I take a step closer to the chief, trying not to show the fear I feel.

"Tell me you didn't write the other letters," I say. "The ones with the capital *W*s, which didn't appear in the others. You capitalized *We*, and I hadn't." There's enough shift in his facial expression for me to know I

landed some kind of punch. "Tell me you didn't write the only letters…
and both emails…that demanded money. Specific amounts of money,
with wire instructions."

"I don't have to tell you shit."

"No, you don't. But I think you want to, Chief."

"Yeah? And why's that?"

"Because you want my money. What're you gonna do, leave here
and go write more threatening notes? I've already ignored the demands.
How're you going to get my money if I keep ignoring you?"

It feels like we've used all the air down here, even though the hatch
is open. I've never suffered from claustrophobia, but it claws at me now.

"So you think I'm just going to stand here and confess to what you
want to hear?"

A thirty-year-old sentence reads in my head, back from my days as
a lad in Dublin when church was a constant, the words coming from
Father Doughtery's own voice.

"Confession is the path to absolution."

The chief takes this in, offers something close to a smirk.

"Sit down," he says. He takes a step to the side, though there isn't
much room. "Here, on the cot."

"I don't think I want to."

"Maybe not," the chief says. "But you will."

I assess, inasmuch as I even can anymore. I decide the choice of
whether to sit down or not isn't the hill I want to die on. That hill is
likely in the near distance.

I sit. He remains standing. Then, with the casual elegance of a stage
actor who's rehearsed to perfection, the chief unsheathes his service
pistol and gently holds it against my head. I flinch at first, pull back.

"Now, now," he says. "Come on, son. You need to feel it. Feel the closeness. Feel the cool of it all."

Odd thing is, it's not that hard to lean my head forward, toward death, until my forehead rests against the tip of the gun. And he's right, the gun is cool, feeling almost welcome against my feverish skin. I lean in, because at this point, there's nowhere else to go.

"You want me to tell you stories, is that it, Mr. Marlowe?"

"I told you," I say. "It's just Marlowe."

The gun digs in a little deeper. The silence lingers, not unwelcome.

"It's just that I'm tired, Marlowe," he says. "I've been tired for a while. You're on the job long enough, that ache carries with you, eats at you, nibbles the life out of you. It's common among cops, but I figured I'd keep going, because hell, in Bury, it's not that stressful to keep the peace. I can make it to retirement, no problem. A full pension is a mighty incentive."

I look up, catch his eyes over the barrel. "But something happened."

He nods. "Something always happens. In this case, the Yates family happened. These rich fucks, disappearing. Not being able to figure that out took a toll, I don't mind telling you."

Suddenly, I feel calm. As if I'm finally listening to the advice I've been giving myself all along.

Let go.

"Lots of unsolved cases out there," I say. "It's not like this is the only one."

"It's the only one for me," he says.

"If it means anything, I think they're okay," I say.

The gun presses harder. "I don't give a shit if they're okay," he says. "I just want to be able to explain what happened to them. And I can't."

I study this man, and there's more to what he's telling me. He's not just tired. He's not just frustrated he couldn't solve the mystery of the Yateses. I look at him and see Christopher, on that day decades ago. Bloody knife in hand the moment I caught him with that rabbit. He was a boy who wanted to make an excuse for what he was doing, shield me from who he really was. And now, decades later, Chief Sike is trying to do the same thing.

"You can tell me the truth," I say.

"That would make things easy now, wouldn't it?"

I don't know if he's talking to me or to himself.

He stands there, a man looking quite more lost than found. And as seconds pass, his energy fades, just a little. Becomes muted, bold colors washed in gray. Then he removes the gun from my head and sits down on the cot. He told me he was tired and now I see it, a river run dry.

"Yeah, well. Fuck it all," he says. Then the chief looks up at me. "So you want the truth?"

"Yes. I do."

"You know we're in this deep, right?"

"Meaning what, exactly?"

He takes a deep breath, like it's his last. "You're a broken man, Marlowe. And so am I. Which means just about anything could happen in the next few minutes. There's risk here. To me, to you. To your family." He takes a few beats. "You understand me?"

Of course I do.

"Death surrounds us," I say.

He nods, grinning. "Well, ain't that the fucking truth."

SEVENTY-SIX

HIS GUN MIGHT BE holstered but the strap covering it is open, easy to snatch. I'm sitting less than two feet from him, and the weapon is close to me but closer to him.

"Tell me about your wife," he says, his gaze straight ahead.

"Why?"

"Because I want to understand how much you loved her."

I don't even have to think long on this request. "I loved her so much, I'm not going to tell you a goddamn thing about her. You don't deserve to know her."

He nods, and I think I hear him swallow back a heaping of sorrow. "Ayuh, Marlowe. You get it."

"Get what?"

"Get the reason for being. Or maybe for not being anymore."

"I don't follow," I say.

"Death eats at all of us, just some faster than others. Your wife? Death gobbled her up fast, like a saltine. Mindless bingeing."

"Jesus."

"It's true," he says. "Others, it takes its time with. Savoring."

"What does this have to do with—"

"I'm dying, Marlowe." There's little emotion in these words, the most devastating words a person can say. "Found out around the time you moved here, then was told it was terminal on the day of your party. Can't say I haven't at times thought you brought bad luck with you to Bury."

I want to be surprised, but I'm not. In fact, I can't believe I hadn't picked up on it before.

"How are you dying?" I ask.

"Pancreatic cancer." He says this slowly, giving attention to every syllable, naming his enemy with respect. "Though around the house, I call it Big Daddy Long Shot. Truth is, I don't even have hope for a long shot. Doc told me that straight up, so I'm not treating it. I'm just…"

"Waiting," I say.

He rubs his knee. "*Waiting* is a funny word, Marlowe. It implies time needed before an action. No, I'm not waiting. I'm actively dying."

The air is getting thinner in here. "How long?"

"Not likely going to be handing out candy at Halloween this year."

I want to tell him I'm sorry, but I don't. I know what's coming next will overpower any sympathy I have for him.

"It's about the money," I say. "That's it, right?"

The chief rises, walks a few steps away, leaves me sitting alone on the cot. I picture him turning around, gun in hand, leveled at my skull. Would they even hear a gunshot upstairs?

He does turn, but his hands are empty. He keeps his gaze to the floor. "That's a part, in more ways than one. I've been on the job a long time. Dealt with more than my fair share of other people's miseries. Put in my years, made a moderate salary, have a pension to look forward to.

All stuff I signed up for and never complained about. Least not for the most part, even when I came here, a place where the average citizen is worth at least ten times what I am. Some of them more. Lots more. But that's the job, and I'm good at my job."

He pauses. I fill the silence with the first word that undoubtedly comes next.

"But…"

He shakes his head, as if considering what a goddamn shame something is. "Then I get the news, and it shakes me to my core. Doesn't make me scared. Makes me *angry*. Angry. Not at God, but at all the fine folks in Bury. The people whose kids get caught with heroin, and think they can pay me to make the problem go away. Or people who call the station to report a neighbor with dead patches in their lawn. Or claim they saw a suspicious person on their street—and oh, by the way, that person is Black one hundred percent of the time. I became angry at these people who don't appear to work at all, and yet their bank accounts have more digits than their Social Security numbers."

"You're talking about me," I say.

"I'm talking about everyone. The Yateses, and how much that family put me through without even knowing or caring. But eventually, yes, you became a source of my anger."

"The party."

He shrugs. "I don't know, maybe. Maybe it was before. But the party…that's where I got the idea."

A sadness weighs on him, slumping his shoulders. I need to remind myself that just minutes ago, he had a gun to my head. He's dangerous and unpredictable.

I need to be the same.

"The idea to write your own letters."

"That's right," he says. "Of course, I knew about the letters you were getting and even felt a little sorry for you. But the night of your party, it just came to me. I realized *I* could be writing you letters as well and using it to squeeze some money out of you. Even counsel you to do so."

"All you wanted was money?"

He spits, as if getting rid of a little cancer and buying himself an extra ten minutes of life. "Fucking money. Few months ago, you probably had next to none, and now look at how surprised you are that money can mean something to a person like me."

"It's not—"

"I don't give a shit about spending your money on myself." The anger is here now, in this little room, growing larger by the second. His. And mine. "But what I'm leaving my wife with is not a lot, even with the pension. Her family genes suggest she's got thirty more years to go, and I will not let her spend those worrying about how she's gonna get by."

"So you wanted mine."

"I know how much you won. You think I didn't research you? Explore the part of the internet most people never see, find out everything I could about you? Damn straight I did. No reason you couldn't part with several million dollars and never miss it."

I almost tell him he's out of his mind, that he could never hide millions of dollars, even if I'd agreed to pay him. But of course he could. He would have figured out exactly how to launder the money through a shell corporation, because he's likely been on the investigating end of such things over the years.

I stand because I want to hurt him. Not because he tried to steal my money but because of what he put my family through. My kids. Because of the threat he still represents, I stand.

Now he takes out his weapon, lets it hang by his side.

"Sit down, Marlowe."

"Don't call me Marlowe anymore. We're not anywhere close to being friends."

"Fine, *Aidan*. Sit."

"I don't want to sit."

"I'm not asking."

His sincerity is apparent in his gaze, coming from eyes that now appear gray, the color of dried-out river stone, untouched for millennia.

I sit because I have no real plan. Not yet.

"So what do you want?" I ask.

"For you to give me ten million dollars."

I laugh. "So what, then, I transfer ten million dollars to that account of yours and you'll go on your way? We'll see each other out and about on the street, give each other a little nod and wink?"

He shifts his footing. "You won't be seeing much more of me."

"And your wife? She won't wonder where *ten million fucking dollars* came from?"

"That side of the business is my concern only."

I stare at him a moment longer and note how he looks made of wax, a dull sheen and a frozen expression. Then I sweep my gaze along the inside of this bizarre room, wondering how it came to be that I'm here. It all seems so improbable, even for a man with the kind of odds I carry around.

I stand again, just to see what he'll do. He tells me to sit back down, and I tell him no. Up comes his gun, pointing right at my gut.

"You going to really test me?" he asks.

"I don't know. Maybe."

The chief is granite hard to read, at least to the level of nuance I need. There's no question the energy I feel from him is negative, but I can't tell if it's malevolent or desperate. Or just tired from his body attacking itself.

"Bad idea," he says.

I don't move an inch, and I try not to think about what getting shot in the gut would feel like. But I need to see what kind of a person really lives inside that skin. A lot of people do desperate things in the situation he's in, but that doesn't mean they lose all sense of morality. Maybe that's the chief. Maybe this is all a wild bluff, and he couldn't really bring himself to harm us.

The other end of the spectrum is horrifying to contemplate. Maybe the chief is the adult that Christopher would've become and I'm just a scared rabbit to him, waiting to be burned and sliced open.

"I just need to ask you," I say. "What will you do if I don't give you the money?"

He slumps a little, shoulders heavy, but the aim of the gun stays true. "Well, of course I'd kill you down here. Too tricky to get you back upstairs. One tap to the head and you'd be down for good. The shot would be loud, no doubt, so I'd scramble upstairs right quick and kill your father as fast as I could." His eyes aren't even looking at me anymore. I don't know what he's seeing, but it's far beyond this room. "Your kiddos would be hysterical, and rightly so, seeing their dead granddad. But that wouldn't even compare to their fear when I rounded them up and gave them the choice of who got to watch the other die. I'd kill 'em both, of course, but one of them would be spared that final horrific sight. Just imagine. The last thing you see on this earth is your twin sibling's head exploding." He coughs, spits on the ground, a frothy glob. "Helluva decision a kiddo that age has to make. My guess? Your girl would volunteer to watch me put a bullet through your son's eye socket. In my opinion, girls are tougher than boys but, moreover, they're more compassionate. She'd do it because she loves her brother too much to make him watch such a thing. 'Course, she'd probably black out soon as his skull shattered, which would be for the best anyway. Then she wouldn't feel anything at all when it came her turn."

I've never been collapsed by words before but his take me to my knees, at which point I vomit, a singular, violent heave, bringing Da's cooking up in seconds.

"Christ Almighty, you got my shoes!" he says.

I pant, looking into the mess on the floor as if I could read it like tea leaves, searching for answers. I absolutely believe every word the chief just said, which means yes, he is Christopher. And a person like that doesn't just take the money and leave. They take the money, kill everyone, and then leave.

I need to act. I'll likely die doing so, but I have to do something.

"You believe me?" the chief asks.

My throat is scorched. "Yes."

"So you'll do as I ask?"

Needing to say something, I reply, "I will."

I look up, he beams, even as he moves the gun in the path of my head. "You know," he says, "gotta say, it would feel satisfying to shoot you here and now. Not worth risking ten mil, but boy oh boy, could I create a beautiful mess in here with you. Who knows, maybe you want me to do it. Put you out of whatever delusional sense of misery you have."

I figure my best chance is to attack in the next thirty seconds. Can't wait too long. I try to summon all my knowledge of fighting, of balance and stance, of destructive punch combinations, of pressure points and soft-tissue vulnerabilities. Nothing comes. My mind dulls, not sharpens. When I most need the razor focus from adrenaline, I feel only heady resignation.

I'm going to fail.

I'm going to die.

Holly, I'll try. But I'm not feeling good about this. But I swear I'll try. Hard as I can.

And then, sudden movement behind the chief.

I see legs, then a torso. Coming down the ladder into our little room. Sike's back is to this person, so he doesn't see. But I do.

My god.

It's Bo.

And he has my shotgun.

SEVENTY-SEVEN

I KNOW IT'S BO, but my brain struggles to comprehend the sight of my seven-year-old boy silently climbing down into this metal tube while holding my gun. Then watching as he levels the gun at the chief's back.

How can any of this be real?

But it is, and this is our only hope. Maybe we'll get out of this. Maybe we'll die.

I close my eyes. I have to, otherwise the chief will see my gaze flick over to Bo.

I close my eyes and have to trust, to believe in the moment.

And in this darkness, this place where I hear only my own heavy breathing, I imagine it's not Bo down here holding the gun but rather Christopher. Christopher here to save me, after all that happened between us.

I miss you, I tell my brother.

Aye, he says. *Same.*

And I'm sorry, I say. *You don't know how sorry I am about everything. I wish everything could be different.*

In my mind, Christopher raises the shotgun a few degrees, holds it steadily, aimed at the back of the chief's head. The chief doesn't suspect a thing.

I'm sorry, too, Christopher says. *And I never did blame you. For all you knew, I just drowned.*

I don't reply to this. I don't have to.

Besides, Christopher adds, *you were right about what I was going to become. Because of that day in the river, I never got the chance to do all the damage I was bound to do.*

In this imaginary world behind my eyelids, I nod and smile. *Well,* I say, *you could do a little damage right now, if you're so inclined.*

My brother returns the smile.

Oh, I have inclinations all right, he says. *No trouble at all to shoot this man in the back of the head. Problem is, some of the shot might hit you. Hopefully it won't kill you, but you have to be prepared for that possibility.*

I'm okay with that, I say, meaning it.

No, he says. *I need to hear you say it. Not to this illusion but to your boy, to the one who's really holding the gun. Need you to say it proper, out loud and all. Clear as a bell. You need to tell him to do it, otherwise he mightn't.*

This is when I open my eyes, hold the chief's gaze so tight, there's no chance of me looking over his shoulder to my son, who is just a blurred figure in the background. I stare right into the barrel of the chief's gun, that dark void, which I imagine as a tunnel to Neverland, a place where my brother never did grow up.

"Go ahead," I say. My voice, it's so calm. "Do it. Pull the trigger. *Now.*"

SEVENTY-EIGHT

"I *WILL* PULL THE trigger, you crazy fuck. You tell me again and I just might do it, money or not." The quiver is back in the chief's hand, but my attention only stays with him for a second more. I lose the battle of focus and can't help but taking a split-second look at Bo, who has indeed raised the gun to aim at the back of the chief's head.

A split second, that's all, but that turned out to be too long. Maybe Bo didn't realize I was talking to him, telling him to pull the trigger. Or maybe he just lost his nerve. Whatever the reason, it's too late.

The chief's eyes widen, just a hair.

And then he turns.

SEVENTY-NINE

THE CHIEF SHOOTS FIRST.

Shoots my boy.

Bo flies, as if snatched by a giant hawk.

Then the blood.

Then comes the blood.

EIGHTY

THE FIRST TIME I ever kissed Holly was after I'd spent the day giving her and her family a proper Dublin tour. She and I went to dinner alone that night, and as I walked her back to her hotel, she took my hand, turned my face to her, reached up, and kissed me. It left me dizzy in a way I'd never known.

What if she hadn't done that? What if she'd instead scurried back inside her hotel and then disappeared from my life? She'd be only a vague memory to the thirty-five-year-old version of me, a wisp of a pleasant dream I once had. But she *did* kiss me, and lives changed forever. Lives were created. Bo and Mags would never have existed if Holly hadn't plucked into my pub that day and remarked about my ouroboros tattoo, the snake eating its own tail.

What does it mean to you? she'd asked.

That everything's a circle, I answered. *A circle and a cycle. And behind it all, a reason.*

I catch a glimpse of that tattoo now as I leap to my bleeding son. As I lunge, horror wracking my entire system, I catch the tattoo out of the corner of my eye. How it's faded but how it's still today what it has always been: hope. And that day comes back to me. So strange it does, in these seconds of terror, but there it is. I can smell the head of the Guinness Holly'd ordered, see the gleam in the eyes I'd soon come to memorize. I gave that answer about the tattoo with such hope, such belief. That everything *does* exist for a reason.

I got that tattoo two years to the day after Christopher drowned in the river.

And now, here, in this foreign land, in this safe room in the subterranean dwelling spot of a house I should never have rightly owned, I think, if this is all happening for a reason, I surely can't understand it.

"Bo!" I scream, hardly aware. I push past the chief, not even thinking of trying to overpower him. I just want to reach my little boy. Here he is, a little heaving sack on the ground, a fresh stream of red off his right shoulder. Of all the anger and all the fear, the confusion and the panic, something settles in my broken brain, a thought that's either right or wrong, but damn if I don't think it's right.

He'll be okay, this thought tells me.

He's shot in the shoulder. It's bad, yes. Any wound is bad. But he's gonna be okay. I know it.

I promise you, Holly. He's gonna be okay.

I hold his face, my palms sweatier than his cheeks. He's breathing hard, on the edge of hyperventilating, but he doesn't scream. Could be he's going into shock, which would be worse than the wound itself.

"I got you," I tell him. It's a whisper of a thing, but he seems to hear. I say it again. A third time. Finally, he nods.

"It hurts," he whispers back.

My mind flashes without me asking it to, flashes back to the afternoon Bo found one of the letters. How I promised nothing bad would happen to him or Mags. How I told him not to question but to simply trust what I was telling him.

Now that promise is one of the many broken things in this house.

"I know it does," I say. "I'm gonna get you help."

Bo gulps, his eyes wide. I read his expression as easy as a book. *How're you going to do that?* it says.

I look over and there's the shotgun, just a couple of feet away. Maybe the chief is in his own kind of shock by what he's done, but he hasn't run up and taken the weapon away, so I make my move.

I can't save Bo by holding on to his face and telling him stories of promise. I need to get rid of the threat.

I grab for the shotgun and roll away from Bo as soon as my fingers seize onto it. I'm expecting a bullet at any moment, and I can only hope it hits somewhere benign enough, I can still get a shot off.

I swing around, my back on the ground and my knees bent, hold the gun between my legs, and level it at the chief. He's not even looking at me. The horror of the reason why becomes immediately apparent.

"Don't," he says. The chief has his gun pointed directly at Bo, who suffers on the ground maybe six feet away. Bo pushes away with his legs but he's at the nose of this metal tube, with no room to put any more distance between him and the man who's already shot him once.

"Don't," I say.

"Lower your weapon. You know I'll do it."

I swallow a breath full of razor wire. But I don't lower my gun.

I try to calculate, but math was never my thing. If I pull the shotgun trigger, would there be enough time for him to take his own shot before hundreds of tiny shotgun pellets tore him apart?

Shoot him.

I can't.

You can do it.

Yes, I can. But at what cost?

What other choice do you have?

But I can't. I can't risk it. And by lowering my gun, I'm maybe risking my whole family. But how do I take the chance of watching Bo's skull explode, knowing I could have prevented it?

I can't.

So I lower the barrel of my gun, slowly, until it's at an angle to the ground between the chief and me.

"Smart man," he says. "You can take direction, a good sign. So let's focus on getting that money transferred."

"He needs help. Right now."

The chief shakes his head. "I've seen worse gunshot wounds."

"*He's fucking seven years old!*" As my scream echoes in the safe room, I wonder how far sound is traveling up the open hatch above us. The gunshot, my yelling. Can Da hear us? Did Bo tell Da he was coming down here?

Of course Bo didn't tell him. Da wouldn't have allowed him to sneak down here on his own, carrying a loaded weapon.

Loaded.

Hell. Is it even loaded?

I dunno. I suppose it doesn't even matter at this point. I don't risk taking a closer look to find out. Instead, I remain locked directly into the man pointing his gun at my boy.

"We're going to figure out a way to get that money transferred," the chief says, his weapon still aimed at Bo. "And we're going to do it before your kid gets so much as a Band-Aid."

There's no time to waste, and yet I can't help but ask the question. It comes out of me, pure curiosity and wonder.

"How can you do this?"

I want to know. I really want to know.

But the chief saves me the precious seconds it would take to explain how a man dedicated to protecting his community became the threat itself. And I know the answer is more than his wife needing money. Of course it's more than that. And it's more than spending his career protecting citizens richer than him.

"You don't understand who I am," he answers.

EIGHTY-ONE

AND THE WORDS. THOSE words. They come to me like a scent from decades ago, a foul and unmistakable stench. A particular kind of decay.

Those were the exact same words Christopher told me on the banks of the River Tolka. After I saw what he did to that rabbit. After I confronted him, and after he used the same blade he'd eviscerated that poor animal with to cut my arm. A scar that hasn't faded.

You don't understand who I am.

And so I realize there's the same decay in the chief's brain, one that's likely been there his whole life. Who knows what he's done over all his years? Perhaps this is the worst of it, but I suspect not. I think this man is who my brother may have become, had he a chance. I always wondered that, always fretted that I took away a life that was precious. And now my answer is here, feet in front of me. There may be good things about the chief, as there were about Christopher, but they are far outweighed by his footprint of evil.

I glance down. The metal floor gleams, caught by the overhead fluorescents, and glows in a way I hadn't noticed before. My brain inadvertently processes this place, its construction, against my will. I want to spend all my mental energy on what to do next, but my brain knows better, telling me I should think about the floor.

The floor.

What about the floor?

Cold, hard, steel. Impenetrable.

So what? I'm not expecting a nuclear blast in the next minute.

No, of course not. But you know what buckshot does in a place like this?

My brain asks itself these questions in the time it takes a bee to move from one flower to the next. Even less time for the realization to come to me, and when it does, I almost laugh. I can feel it. A maniacal laugh, finely coated in craze. But I suppress it.

Because I could very well be wrong.

"We need a computer to transfer the money," I tell the chief. Bo starts to sob, and it's all I can do to keep my gaze from his. I have to focus. I have to calculate. "My computer is upstairs."

"So we go upstairs," the chief says. "You'd better have ten million in a liquid account."

"I do." I have no idea if that's true.

"Well, then, it's a lucky day for both of us. No doubt your dad and daughter are gonna see me holding a gun on you. You'll be quick to tell them to stay in eyesight and away from any phone, otherwise there'll be a god-awful massacre waiting for the Bury PD on Rum Hill Road."

He's an actor, and not a good one. He's going to kill every last person in this house, no matter what. He won't leave things to chance. Furthermore, and more importantly, he wants to.

I turn an inch or two to my right, subtle as I can, and chance a split-second look at the angle of the shotgun. It's at about thirty degrees, the barrel pointed to a spot about halfway between the chief and me. I look back to the man, knowing the angle of my gun is closer to vertical than I need it to be, so with the greatest of care, I raise it to about forty-five degrees.

"Okay," I say. "We'll do that. But then you have to be out of our lives forever."

For the first time, I see his grip loosen just a touch on his gun, and though it's still aiming at Bo, the urgency is gone. He knows he's won. Then comes the grin, a snake's smile, and it's not happiness. It's a deeply satisfied malevolence.

"I promise you after tonight, we won't ever cross paths again."

This, I believe.

"I just wanna tell my boy something," I say. "Just a word of comfort, and then we'll go up. Okay?"

The chief tenses once again, his hand newly snug around the pistol, a display of dominance. He's not worried. He's just exerting his control.

"Sure, Aidan. Give him comfort. But make it fucking fast."

I turn my attention to my son, and I think, *What a brave kid.* Coming down here to protect his own da. Protect his family. And what can I say that sums up everything I feel about him, this kid who stood in the church courtyard before his mother's funeral and considered the tree he was looking at had outlived her? He's so complicated, so flawed, so perfect. What can I tell him that conveys the love I have that is unique to him? There are no words to say such a thing. There's only advice.

"Cover your face, Bo."

EIGHTY-TWO

BO DOESN'T HESITATE; IT'S as if he was expecting such an instruction. His hands immediately fly to his face, and he makes the additional wondrous decision to turn his body to the wall.

The chief starts to turn to me, that fucking grin just on the edge of evaporation. But it's too late. It's too late.

I pull the trigger of the shotgun, not knowing if it even has a shell in it.

It does, and god almighty, the blast.

The first thing I'm aware of is the kick sending the gun flying from my hand; a shotgun is never meant to be fired with only one hand on it. It makes me think what a terrible idea this was. That the math was fuzzy, the execution flawed. That there's no way the buckshot hit the correct angle on the steel floor and ricocheted into the chief's body. And, at first, I don't even look.

I look at my son, who didn't scream.

Bo!

"I'm okay." His voice is muffled, but I think it's because I'm half-deaf.

And then I look.

Look at the chief.

He no longer holds a weapon on my boy. He no longer stands.

And, seeing him slumped on the floor, I soon realize he doesn't even have much of a face any longer.

Shreds of skin, nose gone, eyes filled with blood, teeth exposed behind tattered lips.

The man is down, a weird hiss coming from him, like the last steam expelling from an arriving train. Then comes a groan, and it may be his final one.

I rush to my son.

You okay?

He nods, eyes wide, then ventures a glimpse at the dying man.

Don't look at him. Don't look. Look at me.

He does.

Put your arms around my neck. I'm taking you up.

Bo reaches up and clings to me, and I can tell it pains him to do so. I still have to figure out how I'm going to climb the vertical metal rungs while holding him, but if it means getting Bo help, I'll make it happen.

I lift him up, scoop my arms under his legs, kiss him on the cheek.

It'll be okay. You know that, right?

I look him in the face and can tell he's looking behind me.

I'm telling you, don' look. You don' want that in your head the rest of your life, son.

Once again, he looks away.

I love you, Bo.

He stares at me and he seems poised to echo my words, but there's suddenly a struggle behind the eyes. They grow wide, and his breathing quickens. Then he starts gulping, a fish caught in a net on the deck of boat. Gulping and struggling.

I do believe he's going into shock.

Hang on, Bo. Hang on. We're getting you out of here.

I carry him to the ladder, look up, still not knowing how to get him up. Then, music to my ears.

"Aidan?"

Da.

Da's here.

Down here! I need help! Bo is hurt.

Moments later, his face appears in the circle above me. I don't think I've ever been so happy to see my father.

"What the hell happened?"

Not now, Da. Bo needs help. I'm gonna hoist him up to you, okay? But he's been shot in the shoulder and he might be going into shock, so be gentle as you can.

"Shot? I thought I heard something down here. Oh, my sweet Jesus—"

Not now, Da. Just help.

He closes his mouth, steels his eyes, then reaches out as I lift Bo high above my head. He's going limp, I can feel it.

Stay with me, Bo. Stay with me.

The weight lessens as Da grabs him, and suddenly it's gone. Bo rises like a ghost out of this hell and into the light above.

Thank god.

Thank God.

He'll be okay.

Maybe, someday, I will be, too.

I want to laugh and cry, I think together. But more than that, I want out of this room. After all this mess is sorted out, I suspect I'll be sealing this room up forever.

I want to take one last look at the man I killed. I want to tell the corpse I'm sorry, and truthfully, I am. Doesn't mean I wouldn't do it all over again. But I am sorry.

So I turn and look at Sike.

He's a character from a horror movie, bloody and grinning. And he's got his gun pointed right at me.

He says something. Maybe it's his last words, and maybe they're full of wit and revenge. But I don't understand them. It's just a gurgled mix of muddy syllables, because the man barely has a mouth to speak with.

His fingers work just fine, though. Because then he shoots me.

EIGHTY-THREE

RELIEF.

"All I feel is relief. Is that what you feel?"

I look down at Holly, and she gleams in heady sunlight. She's naked, as am I. A breeze wafts through creamy linen drapes, ghosting them, the air heavy with salt. Somehow it makes me think of wine, but I can't say why.

"I'd say satisfaction more than relief," she says. "I love how you make me come." She reaches up and cups my face, pulls me toward her, and her kiss, it's like the first one we ever had. Dizzying.

I steady myself then roll over, absorbed by puffy, white bed linens. She reaches out, touches my right arm, tracing her fingertip along the path of the scar given to me by Christopher, then continues down my forearm until she reaches the scars given to me by myself.

"You're always chasing the release, aren't you?" she asks.

"What do you mean?"

"The pressure builds and builds in you. Lust. Anger. Joy. Everything just builds until you do something to release it all at once. Like popping a balloon."

Her words are vague, yet I know exactly what she means. She's never said this to me before.

"I love you," I tell her, knowing it's not an answer to her question.

She accepts it anyway. "I love you."

I manage to get off the bed and stand, my legs as wobbly as a newborn foal's. Bare feet on cool Spanish tiles. I stare through the rustic windows of this room and out upon an expanse of blue, and not only do I know we're on the edge of a sea, but I know exactly which one. The Caribbean.

I turn and look back at her. She's younger, by a factor of about a decade. Then I walk into the bathroom—same pebbled walls I remember—and look in the mirror. I'm ten years younger as well, though it may as well be twenty. I'm leaner, no hints of gray, and sport a goatee that lasted only a couple of years. Moreover, I look happy. I don't wear the weight of the world in my face.

This is Belize. The trip we took a few years before the twins. Holly had a travel agent friend who got us a deal on a resort we never could've afforded on our own. Even with the discount, it was still out of our price range, but we did it anyway. We did it and never regretted a thing. It was the best vacation we'd ever had alone.

No, I realize. *This isn't Belize.*

This is heaven.

I'm in heaven with my wife, and isn't that a thing?

I walk back into the room, dive onto the bed. Holly doesn't say a thing. She knows I know, so we don't have to pretend this is a dream anymore.

"It's just an overwhelming relief to be here," I say.

She touches my arm, and I nearly cry. "I know."

"I fucked up," I tell my wife. "After you…I fucked up. Went soft in the head. Bo…Bo is hurt."

She nods, neither blaming nor absolving me. "He'll be okay."

"You know that?"

"I know that."

Then, I think, if I'm dead as well, why don't *I* know that? I have no sense of Bo or Mags, or what happened to Da. I just smell the sea air mixed with the smell of Holly's skin, and it's like the biggest shot of morphine a person could handle without passing out. Intoxicating and relaxing, and I want to sleep a thousand years but also never miss a moment.

"I'm so sorry," I say.

"For what?"

"For not being the father I was supposed to be."

She smiles, those crinkles on the edges of her eyes bunching just so. "There's still time, you know."

The breeze stops, the drapes still.

"What do you mean?"

"You were *always* a good father," Holly says. "But there's still time to be an even better one."

And the feeling starts again, so ripe and sudden. That feeling of panic, the compression of my chest. The shallow breath, the sudden sweats. I don't want to feel like this at all.

"I…I…"

She shushes me, so gentle. "It's okay, baby. I know."

"Know what?"

She knows everything, I think. And I know nothing, which is what this is all about.

Now real pain in my chest. I might be having a heart attack. Imagine that, dying twice.

"It hurts," I say.

She's concerned, but she isn't. "I know. It's okay." She strokes my arm and I don't want her to stop, but I know she will.

And then I realize my time here is short, that this is just a preview of something to come later.

So I ask.

"Are you okay?"

She smiles then laughs. And that laugh might hurt more than anything else, because it's Holly's laugh, and I hadn't heard it in an eternity, and I might have to wait an eternity more.

"Yeah, Marlowe. I'm okay. Just promise me something, okay?"

"Anything."

"Figure your shit out."

I nod.

"I will."

And she kisses me, just like on that very first night outside the hotel. I could live forever in this spin, twisting, twisting.

It doesn't last, and when it's over, I touch her face, which feels so real. But it's not.

But still.

It was damn good to see her.

My chest explodes.

EIGHTY-FOUR

THERE'S A DOCTOR, TELLING me something. Something about my chest.

Says something about distance. About two more millimeters to the left and I'd be dead.

The weight of the world is back, heavier than ever. Can't move a muscle. Want to sleep, but the pain gnaws fierce.

He tells me I'm lucky.

Machines beep.

People in blue gowns, waltzing all around.

Lucky.

I'd laugh if I could.

Doc, I'd say. I was just in the Caribbean with my wife. We were poor and ecstatic. And now I'm here, human again. A human full of pain and loneliness and worth millions. You don't know anything about luck.

But I can't talk.

But then I can, because there's one thing I need to know, and it's so important, I make my mouth work, despite the Herculean struggle to do so.

"Bo," I say, my voice a razor-wire rasp.

And then he answers, but it's not his voice I hear. It's Holly's. But the answer is the truth, all the same.

He'll be okay.

I shut my eyes because she's here, and maybe I'll catch her ghost for a fraction of time, or at least long enough for one question.

"What...what was it all for?"

I don't see her, but still, she comes to me. She is nowhere and everywhere, all at once.

You needed to break before you could heal, she says.

"Am I still broken?"

Yes, but you're healing. And not just from me but from Christopher. It wasn't your fault, Marlowe. It wasn't your fault.

In a dream, I'm crying. Chest-deep sobs wrack and shatter walls of toxic plaque that've been building for decades. In the hospital room, not a single tear escapes, but it doesn't matter. All that matters is the place I share with her for this moment.

"I'm not going to be with you again, am I?"

Not like this. But someday, yes. And then it'll be forever.

"I like that."

Me too.

And with that, she leaves because I feel it all change inside my head. I smile. Smile because she always used to make fun of the way I'd leave a party quietly, without fanfare, not wanting people to realize I was gone. I never like to formalize an exit, because that way, I don't have to acknowledge a good thing ending.

There's a name for such a thing.

It's called an Irish goodbye.

EIGHTY-FIVE

Bury, New Hampshire
Day Ninety-Seven

THERE WERE TWO PEOPLE in Bury out to get me. One of them saw an opportunity in my wealth, viewing me as an unstable but worthy target. The other saw me as just the opposite: worthless. Neither of them thought I deserved all I had.

The chief—one of these two villains—didn't know I had written the initial letters…how could he? But he knew I had millions and leapt into the fray to clean me out before the cancer did the same to him. That ended with a blood-soaked safe room, a dead police chief, and a tremendous collective headache for the New Hampshire State Police and FBI. It'll be several more months before it'll all be sorted out, but my team of lawyers assures me my name will be in the clear. After all, I was simply trying to protect my family in my own house.

But this other villain…he's much more cunning, more insidious, and dangerously unpredictable. Where the chief wanted money, this other person wanted nothing to do with my material wealth. He wanted to shatter my soul, deeming me unworthy to possess one.

Aidan Marlowe, at your service.

I've been seeing a psychiatrist, and she's given me a fancy term for my actions: non-suicidal self-injury. It describes the cuts I've been giving myself since Christopher's death. My alcoholism. The writing of the notes, tormenting myself and my family. The obsessive and illogical pursuit of the missing Yates family. All the acts of harm I've thrown my own way, cognizant or not. Most likely, I subconsciously chose to fall on the concrete floor of the garage, splitting my head open.

Addicted to the hurt.

The word my psychiatrist keeps circling back to is *deserve*. That I felt I didn't deserve to live after Christopher died. That Holly didn't deserve to pass at so early an age and it should have been me. That I certainly didn't deserve to win the lottery, much less feel any degree of attraction to the lawyer I hired to sort my life out in the wake of winning.

It was all too much. My brain just couldn't take it anymore, so it started losing time and the villain in me took over. I decided I didn't deserve what I had, so I began to *de-serve* myself.

Self-sabotage as self-medication.

How about that.

In addition to prescribing some temporary meds, my doctor said it would be good to "journal." Write everything down as a method of healing. So here, two months since the chief shot both my boy and me, with both of us mostly healed but forever scarred, I open my laptop and launch an empty screen on my word processor. It looks like a snowstorm from which I'll never emerge.

But I start, committed to pushing forward, typing those very first words, knowing all stories have to have an opening sentence before they can have a closing one.

Thus, the journal—and journey—begins.

I thought I couldn't handle another minute in the funeral home, but this church is worse.

EIGHTY-SIX

December 20, 2018
Baltimore, Maryland
Day One

I STEP THROUGH THE courtyard of the church, all my senses tingling with unpleasant familiarity. I haven't been here in seven months. It was a thousand years ago. It was yesterday.

There's the oak tree Bo stared at that day. He told me it was older than his mother, and he was likely right. I don't go through the church, no reason to, don't want to. I walk around the building and head for the graveyard.

The frigid wind bites, telling me winter comes tomorrow. Winter on a Friday seems right, giving us the weekend to adjust. My feet leave the sidewalk and crunch along clipped and frosted grass, the shade of which has turned from the violent green of summer to an anemic yellow. Everything turns, everything fades. Some things never come back.

Then.

Holly's grave.

The ground blends perfectly with the surroundings, the sutures of her burial seamless, as if she's been here forever.

I look around, beautifully alone. Then, back to her.

"Hello, love."

If Holly's energy still exists, then perhaps she's been with me the whole time and my coming here was unnecessary—no reason to think her spirit would just be hanging around this place. But I suspect this visit is really for me. A step toward healing.

"Got some things I want to talk to you about," I say. "The first being, I miss you fiercely."

I pause—already pausing, barely yet begun—and listen. The only sound is that winter breeze, rippling over tips of tombstones and sweeping the dormant grass. Last time I was here, I heard the sound of a large tree limb snapping off a trunk, though now I know that was something inside of me breaking.

I take a breath, watch the frosty exhale ghost away, then begin. I start with the easy stuff.

I tell Holly how Bo and I are okay, no permanent damage, at least not physically. That I continue to see a psychiatrist, and am working on Bo to do the same but won't force him. I explain how the kids will be starting school after winter break, back at the same place they were last year. Here in Baltimore, the place where she died. And I asked them if that was too much, and they'd both said no, that it was a way to be close to their mother somehow and that maybe I wouldn't understand, but I did. In coming back to Baltimore, the kids are back with their friends now, and that's a mighty salve.

I tell her how Da went back to Ireland but is returning for Christmas, arriving tomorrow. How we're renting a home for a year or two while I look to build something in the suburbs. Not a mansion, nothing like the beast on Rum Hill Road, something simple and warm, with a regular-size front door. How the kids asked for a full-size arcade room and I told them no. That's not how simple works.

I explain how I've been journaling and that journal took on the size of a book. How I wrote down everything I'd remembered from the funeral until the day we left Bury, and I'd left that journal in the safe inside the safe room of my former house. "Figured the next occupants of the house should know a little history of what happened, in case they start feeling strange energy or seeing ghosts. They have a right to know. And in a way, I'm carrying on the tradition. Leaving a message for the new occupants of 1734 Rum Hill Road."

Finally, of the easy stuff, I tell my wife how I'm no longer losing time and I quiz myself often just to be certain. It's a good thing, I say to Holly, because I've learned that time can end with the blink of an eye or the rupture of a blood vessel, so it's a damn waste to lose any of it while I'm alive.

Now comes the harder stuff.

I take a breath, look directly into where her eyes should be, then tell my wife about Maya, admitting I'd been attracted to another woman.

"I don't even know if it was a real attraction or something my brain needed at the time, but I can say I don't feel it as much now. But that doesn't matter. Point is, I've realized my emotions are not a zero-sum game, and whatever I spend on Maya doesn't take from my deep sum invested in you. And I'll always credit her with saving my life, maybe the lives of Da and the kids, too. She was the one who first realized I wasn't the only author of the letters. That gave me enough sense to fear the chief when he came over that night, along with the confidence to confront him in the safe room. Had I said nothing to bring everything to a head then and there, who knows what could've happened? What later violence could have unfolded when we were least prepared for it?"

Holly says nothing, of course. I don't try to convince myself she's okay with all of this. I do know she'd be more okay than I would be, were I in her position.

Next, I tell Holly how I've been hurting myself, have been for a long time. I think she knew this all along, but it's a relief to say it out loud. I admit I truly don't know who locked our little girl in the safe room that night, but that it could have been me and there's no greater shame I could feel. And I don't skirt around my drinking, telling her I'm easing to a full stop. "I can't go cold turkey, it's not safe," I say, "but now I'm down to two a night or less, some days none at all. I'll get there. I'll get there." Now I crouch, rest my wrists on my kneecaps, breathe in the musk of her earth. Tears well, one falls, soaking up the winter wind as it does, streaking a chill on my cheek. "I don't want to hurt myself anymore."

I stay like this for a moment, long as I can, in truth, until my legs demand I either sit or stand. I sit, right next to Holly, her bedside, feel the cool through the seat of my jeans. I stroke the grass as if it were the back of her hand, the top of her forearm. She always liked that.

"There's one other thing I have to say."

The hardest part.

"It's about Christopher."

THE DAY I STARTED TO HEAL

TIME IS UNKNOWABLE AS I talk about that heady summer day on the banks of the River Tolka, telling Holly the one thing I kept from her, the one thing I was going to say when we were alone at the funeral, the one thing interrupted by the buzzing in my pocket. That text message, the one I was sure would be from her, talking to me from the otherworld, but instead how I found a few pixels informing me I'd just won thirty million dollars.

Before taxes, the universe says.

And how I broke in that moment.

I remain on the ground, as close to her as I could be, and minutes have passed since I finished telling her what happened that day between my brother and me. The silence between us feels good, a thick comforter pulled over us on those winter nights we kept the thermostat low to save money. I don't feel relief about telling Holly the truth about Christopher, which surprises me. Rather, I have a sense of something else more meaningful than relief. Restoration. A delicate paintbrush dabbing a fresh coat over my scratched and scarred surface.

I'll never be good as new, and that's okay because I haven't been good as new since the day before Christopher died, back when I didn't realize how guilt could make physical and mental pain feel so damn good. Like a fine steak and Guinness, both served fresh.

I'll never be good as new, but I'll be better than I was, and I have a whole lifetime ahead to keep improving. To become a better father to the twins and a better friend to myself. Can't have one of those without the other.

The best may not be yet to come, but lord willing, the worst is over.

Did you finally figure your shit out, Marlowe?

I smile down at her, knowing the voice in my head is mine and not Holly's, but that doesn't mean I'm delusional. It just means she's forever in me, that's all.

"Not quite yet, love. But I'm getting there."

The cold from the ground rises through my hips, up my gut, settling in my chest. The temperature of a thousand ghosts.

Before I stand, I tell her one last thing, the one thing we always said to each other no matter the time of day, no matter how rushed we were, no matter our moods, no matter how much we even meant it in that very moment. The thing we said because it was our one truth, without which everything else would have been a lie.

"I love you."

I stand, blow her a kiss, which sinks into the brittle grass and maybe, someday, finds its way down to her.

As I turn to leave, my mobile buzzes in my pocket. Text message, I know. My only notification that vibrates twice.

I smile, almost laugh. Knowing it's her and knowing it can't possibly be. Last time this happened, I began my journey to being lost. This time, instead of seizing on the possibility, I do what I should have done all along. *Let go.*

I remove the mobile from my front pocket, turn back to my wife, and place the device facedown at the base of her tombstone.

And so I leave her, knowing I'll be back, but not for a few days. Long enough for the battery to drain, and maybe for a rain or snowstorm to forever damage the sensitive electronics.

Long enough for it to die.

But it won't matter; all the unimportant things in this world are easily replaced.

It's those precious ones that, once gone, are gone forever.

I suppose that's what makes them precious.

TO DISCOVER MORE ABOUT THE YATES
FAMILY, CONTINUE READING FOR THE
FIRST PAGES OF *THE DEAD HUSBAND*.

ONE

Bury, New Hampshire
August 11

THE NAME OF THE town is Bury, but it hasn't always been. The local government renamed the town from Chester after a local Union soldier named William Bury did some heroic thing or another a hundred and whatever years ago.

Poor Chester. They took the name of a whole town right away from him.

Bury, New Hampshire.

Most locals pronounce it *berry*, though there's a small faction of lifers who insist it rhymes with *fury*. Doesn't matter how it sounds out loud, in my head this town always makes me think of underground things, burrowed by worms, hidden from light. Secrets.

I grew up here. Part of me has always been buried here.

Thunderheads jostle for space in the summer sky. The air is heavy enough to create a drag on my steps, or maybe it's just my natural hesitation to walk up the long stone path to my father's front door. The house in which I grew up looms, as it always has, grand but not beautiful. Rum Hill Road is filled with mansions, but none of them feel like homes.

Max grabs my right hand as we approach the door. He does this when he's scared, feeling shy, or simply wants to be somewhere else. In other words, a lot of the time. Not atypical for any eleven-year-old, much less one who's going through what Max is. What we both are.

I look down and the diffused light from the gunmetal sky makes his blue eyes glow, as if all his energy is stored right behind those irises. Max has his dad's eyes. Looking at my son, this fact haunts me, as if I'm seeing the ghost of Riley. I don't want to see any part of my dead husband in Max.

It hits me again. I'm only thirty-seven and a widow. It's both depressing and freeing.

"It's okay," I tell him. I think I've said those two words as much as I've said *I love you* to him over the past month. One phrase is the truth. The other is a hope.

"I don't like Bury," he says.

"We just got here."

He gives my arm a tug of protest. "It's not Milwaukee. It's not *home*."

I tousle his hair, which probably assures me more than him. "No, it sure isn't."

We reach the front door, a curved and heavy slab of maple reinforced with iron hinges and bands. My father told me when I was a little girl that a door like ours conveyed wealth and strength. That we needed a thick door, like a castle, because it sent a sign to all who tried to enter. I asked him who we needed to protect ourselves from, and I'll never forget his answer.

Everyone.

For a moment, I have the impulse to ring the bell of the house where I spent my childhood. I try the door. It's locked, so I press the doorbell and hear the muffled ring of the familiar chime inside.

I'm surprised when my father himself opens it. He stares at me, then offers a smirk that never blossoms into a smile.

The air of the house leaks out and crawls over me. Smells of the past. The aroma of time, of long-ago fear. My father is one of the reasons I left this town and never looked back. He's also one of the reasons I'm back. Now, in this moment, a time when I need to be here but am dying to be anywhere else, my past threatens to scoop me up and wash me out to sea.

Perhaps this is how it all ends.

Maybe I was always meant to drown in Bury.

READING GROUP GUIDE

1. What would you do if you won the lottery? Would that change if your win came after terrible news like Marlowe's?

2. Like his father, Marlowe always plays the same lotto numbers, but Marlowe's numbers each represent something significant to him. If you were to use significant numbers from your own life, what would they be and why?

3. In choosing Bury, Marlowe leaves behind everything he knows. Why did he do that, and what are the unintended consequences for himself, Bo, and Maggie?

4. Threatening notes would be disturbing no matter what, but how did you feel about the signature: WE WHO WATCH? How does the suggestion of a group change the way Marlowe investigates?

5. Despite the threats and the house's unsettling history, Marlowe refuses to consider selling. Why? Would you cut your losses in his position?

6. Describe Marlowe's parenting style. How does his concern for Bo and Maggie manifest itself?

7. The security advisor triggers Marlowe's paranoia. Would you be willing to fill out the invasive questionnaire? Did you see an alternative?

8. List Marlowe's coping mechanisms. How many of them are self-destructive?

9. How did you feel when you found out how Christopher died? If he'd lived, what kind of man do you think he would have become?

10. Marlowe believes in fate and superstitions. Do you? If everything happens for a reason, how would you explain the end of the book?

11. Characterize Chief Sike. How did your first impression of him compare to your feelings at the end of the book?

A CONVERSATION WITH THE AUTHOR

Marlowe and his dad hail from Ireland. Do you have ties to that part of the world?

Not currently, though I recently did some genetic tracing and learned I'm 72 percent British and Irish, so maybe my long-dead ancestors were summoning my characters to be Irish. My only time in Ireland consisted of a 48-hour whirlwind trip from Colorado to Dublin to see my favorite band. Some dude tried to mug me in the street, so there's that.

Marlowe is a very unreliable narrator. How did you keep track of what you knew as a writer versus what he knew as a narrator?

Marlowe becomes more and more unhinged as the story progresses, which was quite intentional (and fun as hell to write). But when you're writing from the perspective of someone like that, it's easy to conflate things imagined and real. So I needed to literally write those things out to keep it all straight. There's a list of "what Marlowe believes" and "what really happened." The tricky part is I don't outline, so both those lists continue to grow as the story progresses. Then, of course, there's endless amounts of editing after I get hopelessly confused with it all.

The New Neighbor shares a setting with your previous book, The Dead Husband. What kept you coming back to Bury, New Hampshire?

Man, I loved creating Bury. It was the first time I set a story in a fictional location, and I was a gleeful little kid with Legos in regard to all the world-building I got to do. I don't have any desire to write an endless series of books set in Bury, but I knew that after writing The Dead Husband, I wasn't yet done with that town. I wanted to return to Bury and, most importantly, back to the Yates house. That mansion was its own character, and I wanted it to loom with a purposeful menace over the two books. I think it does.

In need of support, Marlowe summons his father. Who would you call in his position?

Let's hope I'm never in his position (well, except maybe the lottery part). But I'm pretty sure I'd call my buddy Drew, who's a cop in California with the coolest and most easygoing demeanor you can imagine. He's the person you want around to keep things calm when everything is spiraling out of control. I'm not sure he'd know what to do either, but he'd keep me from freaking the hell out.

Where do your characters come from? Are there any you can point to that resemble people in your life?

Well, as most authors would probably say, my characters are a tapestry of both people I know or have observed, either in life or fiction. I rarely set out thinking of specific traits from specific people that I want a character to exhibit; rather, I think of traits I find interesting for someone to have, then see how real that feels when I'm writing it out. Looking at Marlowe, for example, I see bits of myself, bits of some of my friends, and a smidge of Jack Torrance from *The Shining*. That character needed to be, at his core, a good person but one who was so broken from life events that he had to fight against a slow untethering from reality, often failing.

What do you read when you need a break from thrillers?

Currently, my TBR pile consists almost completely of nonfiction. I particularly gravitate toward memoirs and biographies, because I love a good origin story. I think reading true-life accounts of extraordinary people provides me with key insights as I'm crafting my own characters, who I want to also be extraordinary yet relatable. Right now, I'm reading the biography of stage and film director Mike Nichols (*The Graduate*), and it's fascinating.

ACKNOWLEDGMENTS

I dedicated my second novel, *The Boy in the Woods*, to both my kids. Looking back now, I realize how messed up that is. That book is easily the most dark and disturbing story I've written, with the opening scene featuring a kid getting pummeled with a rock. Mea culpa. So now it's time each of my kids has their own dedication, and this one is for my boy, Sawyer, who's just an all-around amazing guy and fun as hell to hang out with. One thing he isn't, though, is a big reader. Hey buddy, your name is in the dedication...now you have to read it. There'll be a quiz later.

To my tireless agent, Pam Ahearn, thank you again for all your advice and magic. To my editor, Anna Michels, and the entire Sourcebooks/ Poisoned Pen Press team, I owe you my constant appreciation. Thank you all for continuing to believe in my stories and making them better.

Coming out of a pandemic, I've learned how deep my gratitude is for my inner circle. Jessica, we make a good quarantine couple. Mom, it's good to be together again after too many missed holidays. Ili, how the hell did you finish high school without a single B? I'm endlessly proud of you and all you've achieved (Go Green!). Henry, I can't wait to see where your creativity takes you. Sole and Craig, I'm happy we could all be maskless together during 2020. And of course, a huge thank-you to my Old Possum critique-group friends: Dirk, Linda, Sean, Abe, Sam, and Lloyd—I'm so glad we're destroying each other in person now and not on Zoom.

Dad, I think you would have liked this one.

To all readers, thank you for picking up (or downloading) this book. None of this works without you.

Carter Wilson

Erie, Colorado

June 2021

ABOUT THE AUTHOR

USA Today and #1 *Denver Post* bestselling author Carter Wilson has written seven psychological thrillers as well as numerous short stories. He is a four-time winner of the Colorado Book Award and an ITW Thriller Award finalist, and his critically acclaimed novels have received multiple starred reviews from *Publishers Weekly*, *Booklist*, and *Library Journal*. Carter lives in Erie, Colorado, in a Victorian house that is spooky but isn't haunted...yet.

To check Carter's appearance calendar, subscribe to his irreverent monthly newsletter, or to inquire about his availability for speaking events, book clubs, or media requests, please visit carterwilson.com.